"I'm not made of glass, Hunter. I can handle the truth."

Before those punishing meetings at the bank and funeral parlor, he might have disagreed, based solely on what her brother-in-law had told him. But he knew better now.

"All I meant," he said in his defense, "is that I'll make sure Connor gets to know his dad."

"*You'll* make sure?"

"I'll help, I mean. If it's okay with you."

Brooke looked up at him through her thick lashes. "Why wouldn't that be okay with me?"

Oh, I don't know…maybe because you believe I killed your mother?

She avoided his gaze. "Beggars can't be choosers. I'm in no position to turn down any help that's offered."

She'd easily convinced both bank managers that Connor would soon become her son, legally. If Hunter didn't have that DVD from her brother-in-law to suggest otherwise, she might have convinced him, too.

Dear Reader,

Tragedy. Sooner or later, we collide with it, head-on. It tests our mettle, and whether we pass or fail that test depends on what we do when the dust settles. Dust ourselves off and plow forward…or let it hover over our lives like a dark cloud?

Secrets. We all have a few. Some (kept to surprise a bride- or mom-to-be, or the child who finds a cuddly puppy under the Christmas tree) are good. Others are harmless, like our little trick for housebreaking that puppy, or the secret ingredient in our spaghetti sauce. Still others (that exam we cheated on in college, the time we fudged on our taxes, finding out that our best friend is cheating on her husband), not so good.

Though we go to extreme measures to guard those not-so-good secrets, life goes on. We find innovative ways of coping, so we can pretend, for a few moments at a time, anyway, that the dark cloud doesn't exist. And we'll do just about anything to take those ugly secrets to the grave.

But imagine how it might feel if the person you most admire *already knows* your darkest secret, like Hunter Stone, who thinks he's responsible for a young mother's death, or Brooke Wright, who agrees with him?

That question is the cornerstone of *Raising Connor*.

The dilemma reminds me of a line from an old song that goes something like "…into each life a little rain must fall." When tragedy blows into Hunter's and Brooke's lives, they're forced to choose: set aside more than a decade of resentment to care for an innocent, orphaned baby boy? Or allow misunderstandings to brew into a fierce storm that will destroy them all?

It's my hope, dear reader, that you'll never face a life storm like that, but if you do, I pray you'll look for the rainbow overhead that will lead you from the darkness and into the soft, warm light of enduring love.

All my very best to you,

Loree

HARLEQUIN HEARTWARMING

Loree Lough

Raising Connor

✎ A Child to Love ✐

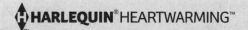

Recycling programs
for this product may
not exist in your area.

ISBN-13: 978-0-373-36643-9

RAISING CONNOR

Copyright © 2013 by Loree Lough

HHARLEQUIN®

Printed in U.S.A.

www.Harlequin.com

LOREE LOUGH

With more than four million books in circulation, bestselling author Loree Lough's titles have earned five movie options, hundreds of four- and five-star reviews, and industry awards. She splits her time between her home in Baltimore and a cabin in the Allegheny Mountains, where she loves to show off her "Identify the Critter Tracks" skills. Loree has one hundred books in print, including reader-favorite series such as the First Responders, Lone Star Legends, Accidental, Suddenly and Turning Points. She loves to hear from readers and answers every letter, personally. Visit her at Facebook, Twitter, Pinterest and www.loreelough.com!

Raising Connor is dedicated to Larry, the real-life hero who makes it easy to write about men who make their women feel loved and respected. To my beautiful daughters, who grew up and became my dearest friends, *and* blessed me with loveable "gran-dorables." To my dedicated agent Steve Laube, and my astute editor, Victoria Curran; their guidance is priceless. Last (but certainly not least), I dedicate this story to my readers, whose letters and emails inspire me to continue writing...no matter what.

Acknowledgments

Heartfelt thanks to all the helpful individuals and agency personnel who helped make *Raising Connor* a more realistic and believable story: Howard County Department of Social Services, attorney Harry B. Siegel, the courageous crew of the Key West Coast Guard Station and dear friend Pam Jansen, author of *How I Became a Fearless Woman.*

CHAPTER ONE

JACK STEERED THE squad car into the convenience store parking lot. "Okay, probie, fess up. How long without sleep now? A week?"

"More like three days." Hunter frowned, wishing he hadn't taken that extra shift so his buddy could be with his wife in the delivery room. "And I slept. Some."

"Uh-huh." Jack shifted into Park. "If you say so." He turned off the motor. "I have a hankering for one of those any-way-you-want-it sandwiches."

Hunter groaned. "You stood in line fifteen minutes last time you ordered one of those artery cloggers."

Jack sang a verse of "If You've Got the Money I've Got the Time" as he got out of the cruiser, then leaned back in long enough to say, "You coming?"

"Better not. I have some stuff to enter into the computer." They sure loaded down the new guys on the force with the grunt work. He only hoped he could find enough hours in the day to do everything he had to, plus sleep and survive probation.

"Coffee?"

"Nah. I'm good, thanks."

"Okay, later," the older man said as he ambled away.

The store's ceiling-to-floor windows allowed Hunter to track Jack up and down the aisles, stacking junk food and Mountain Dew in his arms. If his partner wasn't more health conscious, he'd die of a heart attack long before he reached retirement. When Jack stood under the Order Here sign, Hunter swiveled the keyboard closer and fired up the reports software. How much junk had his own grandfather and father—not to mention his uncles and brothers—choked down during their years in uniform, he wondered.

Yawning, he made note of the time…two minutes after three…then leaned against the headrest and closed his eyes. Jack didn't know it yet, he thought, grinning, but when he returned, *he'd* be on the receiving end of some ribbing for a change.

Frantic shouting and gunfire startled Hunter awake. The dashboard clock was the last thing he saw as he bolted out of the car: four minutes after three. He'd fallen dead asleep in just two minutes?

He grabbed his shoulder radio, talking as he crouch-walked toward the store's entrance. "C-four-two-one. We have a 10-10 at the farm store, 9164 Baltimore National Pike. Shots fired. Robbery in progress." Then he drew his weapon, took a deep breath and abruptly shouldered his way inside.

Big convex mirrors, hung in all four corners of the store, helped him take quick inventory: a male clerk cowering at the register, two women—a bleach-blonde in her early sixties and a brunette of forty or so—huddled beside the ice-cream freezer, an overweight guy hunkered down near the coffeepots.

What was so important that they couldn't wait for the safety of daylight to shop?

A skinny wild-eyed male in a baggy ski mask leaped onto the counter, shouting and waving a 9 mm Glock. Hunter, who had managed to get inside and behind an endcap display of candy bars without being seen by the guy, recognized the weapon instantly because he was holding one just like it. Unless he'd miscounted, the guy had already fired four rounds....

"Empty the cash drawer!" the masked man snarled. "Do it now."

The terrified clerk didn't move fast enough, and the robber shot him. Hunter had to resist the urge to charge directly into the action. *Just stick to the rule book,* he told himself as the clerk collapsed to the floor, writhing in pain. The robber jumped down on the other side of the counter. While he was busy stuffing money, cigarettes and methamphetamine-based cold remedies into a ratty backpack, Hunter ducked behind a rotating rack of batteries. *By the book,* he reminded himself. *Do it by the book...*

"Jack," he whispered, creeping down the bread aisle. "Psst...Jack..."

The dark-haired woman caught his eye, gave a barely discernible nod toward the dairy case. He could see a man's leg on the floor protruding out from behind it. Instantly, he recognized Jack's spit-shined department-issue black shoes, unmoving and pointing at the glaring overhead lights. Hunter's brain had barely had time to register *he's dead* when the brunette made a run for the door...and another eardrum-splitting shot spun her around. Her gaze locked with Hunter's as she crumpled like a marionette whose strings had been cut. Her lips parted, formed the word *help,* but even before she hit the gray tiles, the vacant stare in her big unblinking eyes told him she was dead.

Hunter, who'd turned twenty-three on his last birthday, had just completed the sixth month of his eighteen-month probation. Did he have the experience—was he man enough—to take out the gunman before he killed again? He saw Jack's motionless foot poking into the main aisle.

"This is for you," he muttered, steeling himself down on one knee. One of his partner's favorite expressions came to him: *If I have to shoot somebody, I want them to* stay *shot.* Hunter took aim at the robber, held his breath and squeezed off two rounds.

HALF AN HOUR LATER, amidst the crackle and hiss of radios and the rapid-fire questions of a gap-toothed detective, his heart was still hammering against his ribs.

"Three dead," said the grizzled sergeant, "counting the perp." Eyes on Hunter, he added, "Great shots, rookie. Bet he fell over like a tree, huh." He faced the suit. "You got somebody lined up to do notifications?"

Hunter didn't hear the answer, because his brain had seized on *three dead.* The woman, the perp… He hung his head. And Jack.

The detective blew his breath out through his teeth and studied Hunter. "If we do things right, maybe it won't have a negative impact on your probation."

If he could find his voice, Hunter would have told him that his police career had ended the minute he closed his eyes in the car. Cops—his brothers among them—would never let him forget he'd fallen asleep on the job. He would never let himself forget.

If he'd gone into the convenience store with Jack, the holdup probably wouldn't have gone down. Surely not even a strung-out thief was idiot enough to take on two armed cops.

His little nap cost his partner and a civilian their lives.

CHAPTER TWO

Fifteen Years Later

Brooke watched her father fall to his knees, sobbing. Heard her sister, Beth, wail as the surgeon said, "We did everything we could, but..." Mom had only gone to the 24/7 store because they ran out of ice cream halfway through their straight-A girls' movie marathon. The young uniformed officer in the waiting room kept repeating, "Sorry. Sorry. Oh, my God, I'm sorry...."

IT WASN'T THE young cop, she realized, groggily coming to, but the phone ringing.

Grabbing it, Brooke glanced at the bedside clock. Who but that idiot Donald would call at ten past three?

Still reeling from the haunting images of her recurring nightmare, she hauled herself out of bed and clicked Talk as she headed downstairs.

"Are you aware what time it is?" she whispered into the handset, determined not to wake her sleeping nephew.

There was a pause, and then an unfamiliar voice said, "I, uh... Sorry to disturb you, ma'am."

So it wasn't Donald after all. Now she wished she'd taken a second to put on her slippers, because the tiles felt like ice beneath her bare feet. Wished it *had* been Donald, because no one called at this hour with good news. Her thoughts went to her grandmother. Day before yesterday Deidre had been down on all fours giving Connor a piggyback ride, but at seventy-five—

"I'm trying to reach Brooke O'Toole?"

"That's...me."

"Right." He cleared his throat and then identified himself as a deputy sheriff of Monroc County. Before she had a chance to visualize the dot that marked Monroe County on a map of Florida, he explained how a Miami-bound charter flight had gone down in the Atlantic, just off Key West. There had been no survivors, he was sorry to say, and, as next of kin, she needed to give him her okay before he could release the bodies.

Brooke didn't hear much after *no survivors*. Her sister and brother-in-law had decided to end their island-hopping trip with visits to Ernest Hemingway's favorite haunts, including Sloppy Joe's saloon.

On Key West.

Heart pounding, Brooke squeezed her eyes shut. Before turning in for the night, she'd been online, checking her email. Wouldn't a story like that have popped up on her search engine's opening page?

Any minute now the deputy would realize his error and apologize for contacting the wrong Brooke O'Toole. Or she'd wake from this ghastly dream and eighteen-month-old Connor would still have his mom and dad, and she would still have her little sister, and Beth and Kent would come home tomorrow, exactly as planned.

"Ma'am? You still there?"

"Yes. Still here."

The deputy listed all the agencies that had participated in the search—FAA, Florida Fish and Wildlife, the sheriff's department—and had cooperated to keep their findings from the media until after next-of-kin notifications had been made.

During her years as a nurse in Virginia Commonwealth University's shock-trauma unit, Brooke had learned that state troopers were normally assigned the sensitive task of informing relatives about tragedies. She was about to ask why the deputy had made this call instead of passing the information to the Maryland State Police when he told her that a Coast Guard diver had pulled a Ziploc bag out of the water. In it, he said, the authorities found passports, boarding passes and baggage claim tickets, a computer-generated itinerary that confirmed the Sheridans' names on the passenger manifest...and the photograph of a young boy.

In the silence that followed, Brooke realized she'd been holding her breath. She exhaled. Swallowed, hard.

"It says 'Connor, 14 months' on the back of the picture," the deputy added. "And it was paper-clipped to a list of people to contact in the event that…"

"In the event that something awful happened to Beth and Kent."

"I, uh… Well, yes, ma'am. In that event."

Brooke blinked back tears. She hadn't realized she'd said that out loud.

"I know it isn't much comfort," the man said, "but we can be reasonably certain no one suffered."

She shut her eyes. In other words, the impact had been such that they'd died instantly. Brooke leaned on a kitchen chair for support.

His voice cracked slightly as he asked for her email address. Was that because he was new at this "inform the families" job, or because of the grim nature of the task itself? "Is there anyone I can call for you, ma'am?"

"There's only my grandmother. But I'd like to break the news to her myself."

"Well…then…do you have a pen handy?"

Of course she had a pen handy, because her oh-so-organized sister—who'd gone to all the trouble of tucking important documents into a waterproof bag—had tied a dry-erase marker to a string and taped it to the whiteboard beside the phone. Hands trembling, Brooke uncapped it.

He rattled off his home, office and cell phone numbers. "If you have any questions…"

It seemed ludicrous to keep him on the line, but she couldn't hang up. Not yet. *Things just can't end this way.*

Brooke thought back to when she had helped Beth and Kent unload their suitcases at the terminal. Kent had reminded her where she could find Connor's pediatrician's number…in the polka-dot address book beside the phone. Their favorite plumber and electrician were there, as well as… Hunter's number.

Hunter Stone was one of their emergency contacts. She would never understand how that man had become close to Beth and Kent. For years it had been a wedge between the two sisters, and now Beth was gone, along with any chance to apologize.

"If you have any questions," the deputy repeated, "call me. Anytime."

And though it seemed ridiculous to thank him for calling, that was exactly what she did.

Connor's sleepy sigh whispered over the baby monitor as she hung up. The kitchen clock counted the seconds, and the muted chimes of the family room mantel clock signaled the quarter hour.

She noticed the notes she'd taken on the white-board as the deputy had explained everything she needed to do to bring Beth and Kent home. The black scrawl didn't look anything like her hand-writing. Brooke turned off the overhead light.

A shaft of moonlight slanted through the windows, painting a silvery stripe across the room and illuminating the whiteboard.

Eyes burning, she slumped to the hardwood floor and drew her knees to her chest. She hid her face in the crook of one arm and let the tears fall.

When a stiff neck roused her, the kitchen clock read 4:05. Brooke stood at the kitchen sink and splashed cold water on her face. As she reached for a paper towel, she glanced out the window, where, in a tidy brick-lined flowerbed, the blue-gray light of dawn picked up the purple shoots of Beth's roses.

Farther out in the yard, she could just make out the yellow bucket swing Kent had hung for Connor.

Beyond that, the trio of birch trees Brooke had bought the couple as a housewarming gift had already begun to bud. She couldn't see them now, but she'd noticed yesterday.

Yesterday.

She swallowed past the lump in her throat, remembering that when her mother was killed during a convenience store holdup, staying busy had helped.

Brooke started a pot of coffee. Threw a load of towels into the washing machine. Made her bed.

"Gram is right," she muttered, emptying the wastebaskets. "A trained monkey could perform monotonous household chores." It was still dark when she backed out the front door, fumbling with the garbage bag's red drawstrings.

"You're up and at 'em early...."

The voice—deep and vaguely familiar—startled her. She turned to find herself face-to-face with Hunter Stone.

Hunter Stone, who'd been asleep in his squad car when he should have been in the store, stopping the gunman who killed her mother. Hunter Stone, who'd spent a good part of the fifteen years since then trying to atone by playing big brother to Beth and best friend to Kent.

He held her gaze for a blink or two—long enough for her to read remorse on his face.

Hunter took the trash bag and jogged down the driveway, adding it to one of two metal cans with SHERIDAN on their sides.

He was wiping his hands on a white handkerchief when he returned to the porch. "Look," he said, tucking it in his back pocket, "I realize I'm the last person you want to see today of all days, but I wanted to ask if there's anything I can do."

Today of all days? So he'd heard about the crash? When she'd only just found out an hour ago? It meant his name wasn't just on her sister's emergency contacts list by the phone; it had also been with them while they'd traveled. He was just that important to them. In disbelief, she reached for the doorknob.

"Have you told Connor yet?"

She stopped but didn't look at him. "It's four-thirty in the morning."

He checked his wristwatch and did a double take. Seemed embarrassed. "Guess you have some tough decisions to make in the next few hours, huh?"

Starting with how to get you off this porch.

"I can take Connor off your hands while you make arrangements. He's used to me, so..." Hunter shrugged. "But if you're more comfortable leaving him with Deidre, I could drive you...wherever."

I'd sooner crawl.

But he was right. She needed to set up appointments with the bank, the funeral parlor, a lawyer who'd help her protect Connor's future. The nightmare had just begun.

"Do I smell coffee?"

Brooke couldn't believe her ears.

Hunter pinched the bridge of his nose. "I hope you won't take what I'm about to say the wrong way...."

Everything about him rubbed her the wrong way.

"I know you and Beth haven't exactly been on the best of terms lately—"

She pressed her lips together.

"—so I thought maybe I could bring you up to speed over a cup of coffee."

Fists balled at her sides, she willed herself not to react.

Obviously, he'd mistaken her silence for an invitation; Hunter made a beeline past her into the house and directly for the kitchen, to the cupboard where Beth kept the mugs. She slowly followed him. "You drink yours black, as I recall."

On the few occasions when they'd attended barbecues or birthday parties at Deidre's or at Beth and Kent's, she'd stayed as far away from Hunter as space would allow. And yet he knew how she liked her coffee. Was he aware she liked to cool it with ice? she wondered, opening the freezer.

If she dialed 911 and reported him as an intruder, would he leave quietly?

One of her grandfather's favorite maxims came to mind: keep your friends close and your enemies closer. Maybe during one of her sister's friendly sharing sessions with him, Beth had divulged something that would help Brooke find the will, so she'd know what sort of funeral to plan.

Funeral.

Beth was gone.

Brooke's heart beat double time as the dizzying truth struck her. If she didn't get hold of herself quickly, she'd break down. She took a deep breath, grabbing a handful of ice.

"Beth loved this time of year," he said sadly, "because she could throw open all the windows." Then he turned on the TV like he'd been doing it for years. Hunter tuned to Channel 13 and adjusted the antennas...

...and brought Beth and Kent's wedding portrait into focus.

"A local church is mourning the loss of two well-loved congregants this morning," said the anchorman.

Brooke gasped.

Hunter fumbled with the remote, and when it failed to turn off the set, he yanked the plug from the wall. "Sorry," he said. "I just thought...background noise would help...."

Brooke couldn't move. Couldn't speak. Seeing Beth and Kent's smiling faces—in living color on the morning news—hit her like a roundhouse punch to the gut. One by one, the ice cubes clattered to the floor.

She took a step toward the paper-towel holder, but Hunter blocked her path. "Leave it," he said, his fingers closing around her wrists. "It isn't going anywhere."

She looked up into his face, seeing for the first time how haggard he looked.

Dizzying, disjointed thoughts spun in her brain. Call her new boss, ask for an extension on her start date; call the new landlord to plead for a refund of her deposit. Find Beth and Kent's will and their checkbook; call Deidre to tell her about Beth. How would she tell *Connor?*

Never in her wildest dreams could Brooke have foreseen herself leaning into Hunter, sobbing.

CHAPTER THREE

GROWING UP THE youngest of four boys, Hunter hadn't had much experience with touchy-feely stuff, but when Brooke melted against him, his arms automatically held her.

Unexpected? To be sure. Uncomfortable? Most definitely. Because the DVD in his inside jacket pocket was the only reason he'd come here today. When her brother-in-law handed it to him the week before their islands vacation, he'd sworn Hunter to secrecy. No one could know about his living-color will, not even Beth.

Listening to Kent's vindictive portrayal of Brooke almost made him sorry he'd agreed to carry out its terms…and made him feel likc a voyeur. "A woman like that," Kent had said, "should not be allowed to raise my kid just because she's connected by blood."

Kent had left nothing to chance. In the note tucked into the DVD case, he had written:

In the event that something should happen to Beth and me on our trip, you, Hunter Stone, are to deliver one copy of this disc to a family court lawyer of your choice and another to my sister-in-law. You are then to immediately and permanently *remove my son from her care.*

Frankly, Hunter didn't understand that level of hostility, because it seemed to him that Brooke was crazy about Connor, and the feeling was mutual. If she was guilty of anything, it was stubbornness and grudge-holding…against him.

So no, he didn't understand Kent's attitude, but after fifteen years of dodging Brooke at every O'Toole function, it would probably feel good to have the upper hand for a change.

At least, that was what he'd thought until he saw her on the porch, damp-eyed and rumpled, and couldn't bring himself to deliver it. Finding out that her sister was dead, seeing the video, losing Connor all in the same morning? Only a heartless heel would do that to her.

So he'd left the DVD in his jacket pocket, told himself there would be plenty of time after the funeral to hand it over. Plenty of time to get a handle on his own grief at losing the friends who, for eight of the past fifteen years, had been more like family than neighbors. Time to find ways to support Brooke any way he could, because it was what Beth would have wanted.

He searched his mind for a word, a phrase that might comfort her, that wouldn't sound phony or trite. Ironic, he thought, that his contractor's toolbox was full of gadgets and gizmos, yet he didn't know how to fix the brokenness in Brooke.

She spared him by stepping back. Way back.

"Sorry for soaking your shirt," she said, plucking a napkin from the basket on the table.

Those eyes, sad and scared, looked so much like her mother's that he could scarcely breathe.

"Nothing to be sorry for," he said, meaning it.

"Next time you come over, bring it with you—"

Even her hair, illuminated by the fluorescent ceiling fixture, reminded him of that night.

"—so I can wash and iron it. It's the least I can do after blubbering all over it."

Brooke blew her nose, hard, then tossed the napkin into the trash can and got busy cleaning up the floor. "I'll bet imitating Canada geese wasn't on Beth's 'My Sister Isn't *All* Bad' list."

No, but plenty of other things were. For starters, Beth had assured him that despite the way Brooke had always treated him, she was a good and loving person; her bitterness, Beth insisted, was proof that her sister's loyalty ran deep. "Give it time," she'd said. "Brooke will come around, just like I did."

He hadn't believed it then. He didn't believe it

now. Still, he got onto his knees to help her sop up the melting ice cubes.

When they finished, Brooke stood at the sink and lathered her hands. "I have to email my electronic signature to Florida before Connor wakes up."

A hint that he should leave? He could hardly blame her for sounding less than enthusiastic about spending time in his company. Besides, he'd been in her shoes when his dad died a year ago and knew that after emailing her signature to the deputy, she'd have her hands full making appointments and searching Beth's office for documentation to bring to the meetings.

The DVD was out of sight, but hardly out of mind. It didn't seem fair that with it, he had a virtual arsenal of ammunition to shoot down her attempts to keep Connor, yet she had to make all the final arrangements.

"Guess I ought to go. Call me if you need any—"

He didn't understand the anger in her eyes. Especially since, not five minutes ago, she'd soaked his shirt with tears.

If she thought he'd gotten off easy after her mother's death in the convenience store shootings, she was wrong: he couldn't remember the last time he'd slept more than two hours at a stretch or a night when his dreams weren't filled with the sounds and images of the shooting. Beth had been wrong, too: Brooke would punish him with her dying breath.

As she'd stood crying in his arms, a weird thought had crossed his mind: *Give her the disc. Don't fight her for Connor. Tell her you'll help her raise him...to prove how rotten you feel about that night.* But in this moment of lucidity, he realized how wrong that would be, because Connor deserved better from life than to spend it under the thumb of a woman so consumed with hatred and bitterness.

He took a few steps closer. "You might not believe this, but I don't blame you for hating me. *I* hate me for what happened that night," he said, meaning every word. "But, Brooke, can't you set it aside, even at a time like this?"

He prepared himself for a scathing retort.

"A time like this," she grumbled, putting her back to him. "Connor hates eggs," she said, grabbing oatmeal from the cabinet. "He'll be up soon, so I need to get his breakfast ready."

He stood, gap-jawed, wondering what any of that had to do with what he'd just said.

"I'm not the least bit hungry," she continued, "but I'll eat...to stay sharp. For Connor."

She riveted him with an unblinking stare, and he felt like a bug, caught in a spider's web. He'd been a fool to come over here; should've taken the disk to a lawyer, like Kent told him to, and let the chips fall where they may.

"Eat. Don't eat," he said. "It's none of my business." And he meant that, too.

"Your coffee's getting cold. Have a seat, will you?" she said. "Because *I* need to get something off my chest, and I prefer to do it eye to eye, without you towering over me like Goliath."

Oh. Great. Hunter exhaled a ragged sigh. He had a good idea that what she needed to get off her chest was about her mother and his incompetence, and he'd take it on the chin. After the funeral, he'd take off the gloves and do everything in his power to get Connor as far from her spiteful influence as possible. Unlike her sister, Brooke apparently had no understanding of forgiveness and generosity.

He sat, then looked up at her and met her steady gaze blink for blink. "Okay. I'm sitting," he said. "Hit me."

She leveled him with a look that made him think she might just do it.

"I thought you said you wanted to be eye to eye?"

For the second time in as many seconds, it seemed as if she might clean his clock. Then she shook her head, sat across from him and folded her hands on the table. Eyes blazing, she opened her mouth to speak…

…and the phone rang, startling her so badly

that she nearly overturned her coffee mug. Too early for a social call, he thought as she got up to answer it.

"Yes, this is Brooke O'Toole…." Shading her eyes with one hand, she walked toward the sink. "So that's it, then. You're absolutely sure."

He heard the catch in her voice and resisted the urge to go into the living room and pick up the extension to find out what had caused it.

After she hung up, Brooke continued facing the wall, cupping her elbows, shaking her head. Finally, she returned to the table.

"I asked for fingerprint identification," she explained, though he hadn't asked who had called or why. "More proof it really was them. Since Beth is a teacher, I knew hers would be on record. But it seems Kent had a record of his own." She stared at some unknown spot on the wall behind him. Then, rubbing her eyes, she added, "The deputy thought it might be a good idea to speak with a lawyer in case Kent's former burglary victims have a mind to sue the estate for restitution." She held her head in her hands. "Estate. What a joke. I haven't even had a chance to look for a will, if there *is* a will."

His heart pounded out an extra beat as he thought of the disc.

"I wouldn't worry," he said. "That trouble Kent got into…it happened a long, long time ago, and he paid for it with months in juvie and years in the Marines. I didn't know him back then, but I'd bet my entire business that time served is what turned him around. The military has a way of turning boys into men."

She aimed a guarded look his way. "And you know this because…?"

"Because fifteen years ago I enlisted in the army."

He watched as she did the math, realized what he'd just admitted.

"And Kent was in the Marines." She harrumphed. "Well, that explains a lot."

"Such as…"

"Such as why Kent couldn't tolerate a mess of any kind and went ballistic when the news reported stories about kids who broke the law." She frowned. "And why he was so tough on me when my stupid choices came to roost at his door. I was never his favorite person."

That, Hunter already knew. But he'd only heard things from Kent's point of view. "Why?"

"Because I tried to talk Beth out of marrying him. And more than once, after he got drunk and threatened her, tried to talk her into leaving him. That's why he looked for ways to discredit me in Beth's eyes."

Admittedly, life had dealt Brooke a pretty bad hand; hopefully, whatever she was about to tell him wouldn't force him to lay down the card that would make her fold, here and now.

She ran a finger around the rim of her mug. "Wish I'd known he had such a rough childhood."

"Why? It wasn't any harder than yours and Beth's. Different kind of hard, but no harder."

Focusing on the spot behind him again, she winced.

Her actions and attitude told him she hadn't yet fully absorbed the reality of her loss. He'd felt the same way after his dad died. Helping his mom make the grim plans and cope with financial concerns in addition to the shock of losing her mate had allowed Hunter to sideline his grief. If he hadn't stepped up, any one of his brothers would have. But Deidre and Connor...they were the extent of Brooke's family now. She couldn't lean on a seventy-five-year-old or a toddler. And his presence wasn't making things easier for her.

Hunter turned toward the door but her quiet words stopped him.

"Guess it's true what they say."

Two feet of tabletop—and fifteen years' worth of bitter memories—separated them. He had to remind himself that Brooke wasn't some untested teenager but a full-grown woman who'd survived disappointments and losses. She didn't need him to protect her. So how did he explain his odd desire to do just that?

"'Be careful what you ask for.'"

"What did you ask for?"

"Proof."

Remembering the whole fingerprints explanation, Hunter nodded.

"Well, I got it, and then some, didn't I?"

She seemed on the verge of tears. He could walk around to her side of the table, take her in his arms, and this time, he could take a little comfort while giving it.

It was a stupid, crazy, dangerous thought, and he squelched it by reminding himself how much she loathed him…and why. Listening to his heart instead of his head had led to his downfall more times than he cared to admit. This time, it could cost him in ways he couldn't predict. Worse, it could cost Connor.

As if on cue, the baby's voice crackled through the monitor.

Brooke was on her feet in an instant.

"Oh no. He's up early…." Halfway to the hall, she stopped, leaned on the doorjamb and hid behind her hands.

And I have no idea what to tell him, he finished for her.

If Connor were already in his care, how and when would *he* deliver the news? It didn't seem fair to let Brooke deal with it alone considering that in a few days, a week, maybe, he'd pull the rug out from under her.

"What would you say to seeing an expert," he began, "before we break the news to Connor?"

When she didn't disagree, he added, "Just so we'll know the right way and the right time to tell the poor kid that…about…you know."

She was silent, which made him wonder if she was gearing up to blast him for saying *we*.

"Yeah," she said, "that's not a bad idea."

Relief sluiced over him. Why couldn't she be this calm and rational all of the time?

Hunter decided he wouldn't follow her to Connor's room; soon enough he'd be with the boy pretty much 24/7.

She met his eyes, a vacant, disconnected stare that, for a blink in time, took him back to the convenience store. Again. Right now he'd give anything to be as far away from her as he could get. This up-close-and-personal stuff was downright unnerving.

She left the room without a word, heightening his uncertainty.

If he knew what was good for him, he'd step up his boxing skills…because something told him that once she saw that DVD, he was in for the fight of his life.

CHAPTER FOUR

DEIDRE FROWNED. "First chance I get, I'm sending Felix over here to do something about this lawn before your neighbors start complaining." She shook her head. "That handyman of mine is an artist with hedge shears. I'll bet he can do something with that boxwood hedge. It was Kent's pride and joy. If he saw the mess it's in, he'd roll over in his grave." She clucked her tongue. "If he had one."

There were so many things wrong with her grandmother's statement that Brooke didn't know where to begin. First, this wasn't *her* neighborhood. Second, she'd tried starting the lawn mower during one of Connor's afternoon naps, but her arms had been too short for the pull cord. And that crack about Kent's grave! Brooke would blame it on advancing age…if Deidre hadn't always been so proud of her bluntness. Like during last year's Christmas service when Deidre spotted a sorority sister sitting with her new beau: "Do you think those two are having sex?" When heads turned to see who'd made the loud crude comment, Brooke said, "Gram! We're in church!" And Deidre, being

Deidre, blurted, "Oh, fiddlefarts. God *invented* sex!"

Now Deidre pointed at the ankle-deep grass beneath her Mary Jane–style sneakers. "You know what it means when dandelions bloom in March, don't you?"

What Brooke knew about dandelions could be summed up with a word: *weed*.

"This happened a few years ago. We had a terrible, fierce spring. Thunderstorms, derechos, tornadoes—"

Just what Connor needs, Brooke thought, *weather-related storms in his life, too.*

"—and a long humid summer that broke every weather record in the book." She turned toward Brooke. "Remember?"

No, she didn't, because she'd spent the past five years in Richmond, where every summer seemed endlessly sticky. But admitting that would only inspire another "if you had stayed home, *where you belong...*" speech. Her grandmother meant well and probably had no idea how upsetting it was to hear the list of hardships Brooke's move south had caused: she hadn't been there when one of Deidre's tenants left the garage apartment in shambles, when another forgot to close a window before a long business trip, and hornets built a basketball-size nest in the closet. She wasn't there to see Deidre's directorial debut in the little-theater production of *Our Town* and had never gone with her to place flowers on Percy's grave. Once, out of frustration, Brooke had suggested that Beth would probably love helping out. "Beth," Deidre had said, "has a family to take care of." Translation: Brooke had no responsibilities.

Well, she had her share of them now.

"Yeddow," Connor said, pointing at a dandelion. He squatted and picked the flower, then carried it to Brooke. "Yeddow?"

It was the closest he'd come to smiling in two days, and she felt like celebrating. She bent down to kiss his forehead. "Yes, yellow. And pretty, too!"

"Pitty," he echoed, toddling into the backyard.

His pronunciation of the word seemed beyond ironic, because losing his mommy and daddy at the same time *was* a pity.

He tripped on a clump of weeds and landed on his diapered rump. Ordinarily, he'd giggle, get right back to his feet and continue on as if nothing had stopped him. Not today. He cried for nearly ten minutes straight, quieting only after Brooke tossed aside the lid to the sandbox so he could play.

"Poor li'l guy," Deidre said.

"He senses something is wrong," Brooke agreed. "He just doesn't know what. It's as though he knows somehow that Beth and Kent should have come home before yesterday."

"You need to tell him. And soon."

"Tell him what, Gram? That his mom and dad are gone? He's only one and a half. Kids his age have no concept of death." She remembered Hunter's suggestion about talking with an expert who could help them explain things in terms Connor would comprehend. The idea was sounding better and better.

Deidre stared at Connor furiously banging his blue plastic shovel on a red fire truck. "I suppose you're right."

Once the funeral was behind them, she'd call Connor's pediatrician. Surely he could recommend a good child psychologist. For now, she'd just have to exercise patience as Connor expressed his confusion in the only way he could: tantrums.

"You look tired," Deidre said.

No surprise there. She hadn't had a decent night's sleep since before the deputy's phone call. Connor hadn't slept well since that night, either. If only she could blame a cold or the flu for his grumpy behavior.

"You're pushing yourself too hard. You need healthy food and a couple good nights' sleep."

"Once Beth and Kent are home and…" It might have been easier to say "once they're buried" if she knew that was their preference. Brooke had rifled through every drawer and cubby in the house searching for their will. With nothing but good intentions and guesses to go on, burial had won out over cremation. "Things will be over soon, and then I'll sleep."

"Soon, my foot. You're his mother now, like it or not, so stop feeling sorry for yourself and start acting like one. You'll have to learn to organize your time better so that you don't wear yourself out, because if you keep up at this pace, you'll topple like a tree in the woods."

The "If a tree falls, would anyone hear it?" adage came to mind, and for a moment, Brooke thought back to her critical-thinking class: if philosophers, poets and scientists like George Berkeley, William Fossett and George Ransom Twiss hadn't been able to solve the riddle, surely she never could. But...like it or not? Sorry for *herself?* Brooke hated the tragedy that put them all in this position, and she loved Connor more than life itself. What had she said or done to make her grandmother think she wasn't up to the job?

Deidre took her hand and led her to the sandbox. "Sit down before you fall down. I'm pretty spry for an old gal, but I'm not strong enough to pick you up."

Fourteen years ago Gram and Gramps opened their home to her and Beth after their father's death. It couldn't have been easy having his chil-

dren underfoot, reminding them that they'd lost
him forever, especially under such tragic circumstances, but they'd done it. Respect and gratitude
kept Brooke from snapping back.

Deidre picked up a tiny blue shovel. "What time
is your appointment with the bank manager?"

"Two o'clock. And at four I meet with the funeral director."

Sprinkling sand into a matching bucket, she
said, "I'm glad you're not bringing this munch-
kin with you...."

"No one could expect him to sit still and keep
quiet, least of all men in suits talking about balance transfers or coffins." Brooke scooped up a
handful of sand, watched it slowly rain from her
fingers. "Hunter volunteered to stay with him
while—"

"Hunter?" Deidre leaned closer. "Hunter *Stone?*"

That had pretty much been her reaction, too,
when she'd said yes to his offer.

"I didn't know you two were even on speaking terms."

Memories of the way she'd fallen into his arms
like a Victorian damsel in distress made her gri-
mace, but Brooke put it out of her mind. "He
stopped by the other morning. I'm not sure why.
To offer his condolences?" She shrugged again.
"We got to talking. One thing led to another. And

when he offered to help with Connor, I decided to let him."

Smiling, Deidre raised an eyebrow.

Good grief, Brooke thought. She loved her grandmother to pieces, but her notion that having a man in your life could right every wrong, well, that wasn't so easy to love.

Connor sighed and tossed his truck aside. "Look at those big sad eyes," Deidre said. "Why, it really is as if he knows. Did you tell him his uncle Hunter is staying with him? That might put a smile on his face."

At the mention of Hunter's name, Connor crawled over to Deidre. "Huntah?" And when she didn't answer fast enough to suit him, he leaned into Brooke's lap. "Huntah?"

"Yes, sweetie, he'll be here soon."

It had never sat well with her that Beth allowed Hunter to get close to her, and then to the baby. But as Beth had once pointed out, "Even you can see that they're crazy about one another. If it makes Connor happy…"

Being around him had made Beth happy, too.

"You're awfully quiet," Deidre observed.

"I was just thinking. Guess Hunter finally figured out how to stay awake on assignment. Otherwise Beth and Kent wouldn't have let him spend so much time with Connor."

Deidre aimed a bony forefinger. "Shakespeare

wrote that sarcasm proves a lack of wit, you know. I'm paraphrasing, but you get my drift."

Would Deidre be less sarcastic, Brooke wondered, if she hadn't memorized all those savvy lines during her years on the Broadway stage?

"I used to call them the Three Musketeers," Deidre continued, "because they were like siblings... until Beth came to her senses and married Kent."

The not-so-veiled hint wasn't lost on Brooke.

"Frown all you like. It's the truth and you know it."

It seemed her grandmother was determined to pick a fight. *She blamed it on the fact that,* just as Brooke had lost a sister, Deidre had lost a granddaughter...one she'd raised as her own child.

"These past years haven't been easy on Hunter, either, you know."

"They shouldn't have been easy!" And Deidre of all people should know why.

"Have you ever considered all that Beth gained when she forgave him?"

Brooke huffed. "A babysitter who lives just two doors down?"

"Tsk. Listen to yourself."

"I almost forgot. She got a babysitter who minds Connor for free. And someone who knows how to hammer nails into plaster walls without cracking them, fix leaky faucets, hang storm doors.

Oh. And wait. Beth also gained a confidant. A genuine friend."

"You sound as though you think those are bad things."

"They are…if you have to trade them for self-respect."

Deidre's eyes widened. "Is that what you think? That by letting go of the anger and bitterness, Beth and I handed over our dignity?"

Yes, that's exactly what Brooke thought. And it should come as no surprise to her grandmother, because they'd had this conversation no fewer than a dozen times over the years.

"If you knew the whole story, you wouldn't feel that way."

"I know enough. I know he couldn't stop that gunman in time because when the robbery began, he was asleep in the squad car."

Deidre harrumphed. "You talk as if you're the only one on the planet who ever suffered a loss."

Brooke didn't know how to respond to that. Deidre had buried two husbands. And when Brooke's dad couldn't face life without her mom, he'd closed himself in the garage and turned on the car. *And now, Beth.*

"But Hunter did stop that gunman, Brooke, permanently. And he's had to live with that, too, all these years. That's the truth, like it or not."

She did not.

Brooke glanced at her watch. "Well, I have just enough time to feed Connor and put him down for a nap before Hunter gets here."

"Aw, let him play. He's having fun for the first time in days. I'll keep an eye on him. You go on inside. Touch up your lipstick and mascara, run a brush through your hair. And if you have any of that dark-circle concealer in your makeup bag, you might want to use it."

"Wow. Aren't you good for the ego."

Deidre shrugged. "I calls 'em as I see 'em. Now go. Make yourself presentable for Hunter."

"I honestly don't care what Hunter thinks of my appearance. And since the bank manager and the funeral director are only interested in money, they won't even notice that I look like a worn-out old dishrag."

"Man," said a smooth DJ-like voice, "Beth hit the old nail on the head...."

Hunter...

"You really are too hard on yourself."

How much of the conversation had he heard? It annoyed her that Deidre hadn't given her a heads-up, since she'd been facing that direction. *Traitor,* Brooke thought as her grandmother wrapped Hunter in a welcoming hug. In reality, she was far more annoyed with herself: she'd come home from Richmond at least once a month. Had she really been so centered on her own trifling matters that she hadn't noticed how deeply he'd embedded himself into her family?

As if to underscore his importance in their lives, Connor ran to him. "Up," he said, clutching at Hunter's pant legs. "Conner up?"

Oh, how she'd love to tell Hunter that he had a lot of gall using feigned friendship with her loved ones to ease his guilty conscience!

But in the time it took to pick the baby up, his stance, his smile, even his voice changed. *Caring* was the only word she could think of to describe it. Which raised an important question: If someone else's child could incite such a transformation, why didn't he have children of his own?

"How's my li'l buddy?" he said, scrubbing his whiskered chin across Connor's palm.

The baby snickered, and envy coursed through Brooke. She'd done everything but imitate a monkey swinging from the chandelier and hadn't roused so much as a giggle. Jaws clamped and fists clenched at her sides, she stared at her shoes, remembering how Beth used to say that people could read her moods just by looking at her. She took a deep breath, then met Hunter's eyes.

"You're early."

He checked his watch. "You want me to go out the gate and come back in again?"

Beth had occasionally accused her of pettiness, but for all she knew, Beth had shared that with

Hunter, too, and Brooke had no desire to prove it to him.

"My watch must be slow, then."

"So tell me, Hunter," Deidre began, smiling sweetly at him, "what prompted you to offer your babysitting services today?"

"When my dad died last year," he said, propping Connor on one hip, "I was the only son who wasn't working swing shifts. So I made all the arrangements. Dad hadn't left a will, which put my mom in a tough position, legally and financially. It was hard for her." He caught Brooke's eye. "I just want to help."

Deidre nodded. "I seem to remember your sister-in-law telling me at your dad's memorial service that if it hadn't been for you, your mother would have lost everything."

"I wouldn't go that far," he said, cheeks reddening.

Bearing in mind how boldly he'd invaded the O'Toole world, his humble attitude surprised her. What invited it, Brooke couldn't say, but just as surprising was the way she remembered him, crawling around on all fours to help scoop up melting ice cubes. If Beth and Deidre knew of other messes he'd cleaned up, no wonder they had fallen so easily for his nice-guy routine.

Connor snuggled closer to him and whimpered.

"Aw, what's the matter, kiddo?"

It was all Brooke could do to keep from groaning out loud. She resented Beth for starting the "forgive and forget" ball rolling, resented Kent for keeping her at arm's length while letting Hunter get so close, resented Deidre for not understanding that she couldn't—wouldn't—let him off the hook as easily as they had.

Connor yawned, and like an indulgent dad, Hunter began rocking side to side. "I don't want you to worry about him," he told Brooke. "He'll be fine."

She only nodded.

"And don't worry about anything else, either. What you're facing is hard and painful stuff. But you'll get through it. And the sooner you put obituaries and grave markers and bank statements behind you, the sooner your life—and more importantly, Connor's life—can get back to normal."

"Normal? When I've lost my only sister? And the man I was going to marry deceived and humiliated me? When Connor and Deidre—the only family I have left—think *you* hung the moon? There's nothing normal about any of that!"

Hunter's eyebrows shot up and her grandmother gasped.

And she could hardly blame them. Even in her own ears, she sounded like the whimpering, self-centered women who'd always driven her mad; if they'd spent as much time counting their bless-

ings as they did cataloging all that was wrong
with their lives…

Maybe you should take your own advice.
Deidre, still mentally sharp at seventy-five, was
healthier and more active than people half her age.
Brooke couldn't remember the last time Connor
had suffered so much as a head cold, and the same
was true for her. Thanks to years of scrimping and
saving, Brooke had enough in her savings account
to make a year's worth of mortgage payments on
Beth's house. And moving in here meant she could
sell the furniture she'd put in storage, adding to
her account. So life had thrown her another curve.
She'd survived the others; she'd survive this one,
too. For the time being, anyway, it made more
sense to meet Hunter halfway. That wouldn't just
be good for Connor; it would please Deidre. And
if they were happy, she'd be happy.

She took Connor from him. "If you're still here
after I've fed him lunch and put him down for
his nap," she said over her shoulder, "maybe you
can share some of what you learned helping your
mom."

"Why wouldn't I be here?"

"Oh, I don't know," Deidre answered. "Maybe
because Brooke just talked to you as if—"

"Deidre," he said, holding up a hand, "it's okay.
Really. She's going through a lot. I get it." He faced
Brooke and said, "I'll be here."

She did her best to block him from her mind as she carried a squirming, whining Connor into the house.

The baby wouldn't eat, not even when she offered his favorite, macaroni and cheese. Well, he wouldn't starve skipping just one meal; he needed a nap more than food anyway.

But it took half an hour to get him to sleep, and once she did, Brooke rifled through Beth's desk. The funeral home would need pictures. She found fat envelopes stuffed with photographs: Beth alone; Beth with Kent; Beth as a little girl; Beth with Connor on her shoulders. Should she bring one? All of them?

Every day as a nurse at VCU's trauma center, Brooke had made snap decisions on behalf of patients, and more than a few had been literally life-and-death. She should be well equipped to handle the decisions that lay ahead, so why was selecting a few snapshots proving to be so difficult!

The overwhelming sense of dread reminded her a bit of the ski trip Donald had surprised her with just over a year ago. On the first lift up the mountain at Crested Butte, he'd crooned, "I love you for going along with this." On the second lift, it was "Of *course* the brochure made it sound scary— that's what draws so many tourists here!" And when he shoved off, howling like a madman from the third stage of their ride up the mountain, she'd stared down the 275-foot vertical drop, trembling and praying that she wouldn't find out the hard way why extreme skiers called the bottom "Body Bag." Terrifying as it had been, dodging the pines and ice-covered boulders on her way down paled in comparison to the responsibility of becoming Connor's substitute mother.

She dreaded the prospect of making decisions— about grave sites and headstones, bank accounts and deeds—that would impact her nephew for the rest of his life.

"Ah, here you are."

Brooke lurched and hoped he hadn't seen it.

"Deidre made a good suggestion just now, and I thought I'd run it by you."

If her grandmother was involved, Brooke shuddered to think what he might say.

"Connor's naps usually last an hour or two. He hasn't slept well these past few nights, so he's probably good for twice that. I figure your meetings will last an hour each, if that."

She almost told him to get to the point when he said, "So maybe I could drive you."

"Drive me? That's…very *neighborly* of you, but—"

He held up a hand to preempt her rejection. "Just hear me out, okay?"

Brooke sighed and slid a dozen photos into an envelope. As soon as she got rid of Hunter, she'd find frames and place them around the funeral parlor's viewing room.

She swiveled the desk chair so that it faced him. He pocketed both hands, shrugged one shoulder. "I know you're smart enough to figure this stuff out on your own, but since I went through it all just a year ago, it's real fresh in my mind. You'd be surprised how many ways those funeral guys have of trying to guilt-trip you into things you don't need or can't afford. I promise not to say a word unless you have a question."

Brooke's exploration of Beth and Kent's records made it pretty clear they couldn't afford anything pricey, and she wouldn't risk charging more than she could afford, because who knew what expenses might come up down the road. Besides, it would be a relief to put all of this behind them.

Standing, she shoved the chair under the desk. "Just so you know," she said, grabbing the envelope, "I intend to hold you to your word…about being quiet unless I have a question."

She couldn't decide if he looked more relieved than perturbed or the other way around, but as he followed her from Beth's office, she hoped she hadn't just made a huge error in judgment.

CHAPTER FIVE

HUNTER SHIFTED UNCOMFORTABLY in the too-narrow tweed chair facing the funeral director's desk, unable to escape the blinding ray of sunlight glaring off the man's polished brass nameplate.

"Sorry, pal," he said, turning it to face the guy, "but I left my welder's mask in the truck."

Turner shot him a puzzled glance, then went right back to yammering about granite versus bronze grave markers, available visitation parlors and background music, and the cost of opening the grave. Through it all, Brooke sat stiff-backed and unsmiling, alternately scribbling notes and pecking numbers into her pocket calculator.

The manager did some scribbling, too, before sliding a contract across his desk. Brooke took a moment to review it, and the minute she sat back, crossed her legs and cleared her throat, Hunter knew the guy was in trouble.

She pointed at the bottom line. "Correct me if I'm wrong, Mr. Turner, but you *can* provide a tasteful funeral without bankrupting me, can't you?"

Without missing a beat, Turner withdrew a fresh form from the file drawer of his desk and, after jotting down new services and prices, handed it to her.

"You'll see that I've reduced the total by a substantial sum," he said, looking very pleased with himself.

"I'll be the judge of that," she muttered absently.

Brooke had conducted herself the same way with the bank manager earlier, making sure the woman understood that while Brooke would assume all responsibility for the mortgage, insurance and taxes on Beth and Kent's property, the name on the deed should read Alexander Kent Sheridan. She quoted from Maryland's Uniform Transfers to Minors Act and informed the banker that her actions had been suggested by a reputable attorney. Had she been bluffing? If not, when had she found time to discuss all that with a lawyer? Hunter had pictured the DVD, tucked into a folder marked Connor in his filing cabinet, and an uneasy sensation had settled over him as he admitted the real reason he was with Brooke....

"You need to know that Connor was born with a heart murmur," Brooke had said to the bank manager. "If he needs medical attention, I'll need access to the accounts *and* proof of guardianship to get him the very best care, quickly."

Not surprisingly, the banker had given her word to rush the paperwork.

And just now Turner made the same promise.

"My next stop," she told Turner, "is the newspaper. So I'll need to know exact dates and times of the memorial service so that I can—"

"Oh, but we're more than happy to take care of that for you, Miss O'Toole." He flashed his best "the customer is always right" grin.

"For a fee," she said, pointing to a line on the contract that addressed obituaries.

Hunter had been on the receiving end of Brooke's hard-nosed inflexibility enough times to feel a little sorry for the guy. Where had Kent gotten the idea that she was scatterbrained and self-centered? Every smart decision she'd made, every astute word she'd spoken, had been on behalf of Connor, not herself.

Turner ran a finger under his collar, and Hunter was tempted to do the same.

"Of course we're happy to perform that service," Turner said, drawing a line through that charge on the contract. It was easy to see as he initialed it that the man wished he could lay his "To Serve As We Wish to Be Served" plaque on its face.

Brooke got to her feet. "If there's nothing more we need to discuss, we'll be on our way."

Turner stood, too, and handed her an elegant

black folder. "I'll be here for the afternoon viewing day after tomorrow. But if you have any questions or concerns between now and then, please feel free to call me."

She opened the file and finger-walked through pamphlets and brochures in the left pocket and checked the signature line of the contract in the right.

"Thank you, Mr. Turner. You've made these difficult decisions much easier." And just like that, she excused herself to use the ladies' room.

"That's some woman you've got there," Turner said, watching her walk away. "Quite a head on her shoulders." He stuck out his hand. And as Hunter grasped it, he added, "You're one lucky man."

Hunter had sat mum as a mime throughout the meeting. For all Turner knew, he was Brooke's brother, uncle, an old college friend, here to lend support. What gave the guy the impression they were a couple?

Yeah, he thought, heading for the door, *lucky me.*

He stepped into the hushed vacant hall and looked for the restrooms. A calligraphed sign pointed toward the curved plush-carpeted staircase. Hunter helped himself to a cellophane-wrapped peppermint, glanced at a few brochures, read the white-lettered blackboards that directed visitors toward the proper parlors. Nearly ten minutes passed before he saw her rounding the top step. Puffy red-rimmed eyes made it clear she'd been crying, and that surprised him a little. She'd seemed so in charge and unruffled through both meetings. But then, as a guy who'd spent years pretending he was okay with the past, he had no business criticizing her tough-girl facade.

He was hiding behind a facade of his own: once the miserable preparations were behind her, and her sister had been laid to rest, he could deliver the disc with less damage to his conscience.

"You did great in there," he said, falling into step beside her.

Brooke only harrumphed.

She kept her head down as they crossed the parking lot. Idle chitchat seemed stupid and inappropriate, so he revived his mime routine. They got into the car and traveled a mile or so in complete silence before he said, "Hungry?"

"Not really."

He'd no sooner braked for a traffic light than his stomach growled.

"Mind if we make a quick stop to shut this thing up?"

"Suit yourself." She glanced over her shoulder. "What's with the car seat?"

"It's Connor's."

She plucked a French fry from the console's cup holder.

"That's Connor's, too. He loves fries. Rita's ice cream. Donuts…"

"Our grandpa used to tease Beth, saying she had a nose like a bloodhound. How did you keep her from sniffing out all that junk food?"

"Pure dumb luck," he said, parking in the Kelsey's lot.

"When you said a bite to eat," she said, pointing at the restaurant's sign, "I thought you meant fast food, not a sit-down meal."

"Haven't had a decent meal in days, and this place serves the best corned beef cabbage for miles."

He parked beside a top-down convertible, and Brooke pointed at it. "They're rushing the season a mite."

"Maybe the owner is an Inuit."

She was already standing next to the truck when he went around to open her door.

"How's a guy supposed to earn any gentleman points around you?"

"I guess you can't."

Oh, he wasn't touching that one, not even wearing flameproof gloves. Hunter pushed the big brass handle and opened door to Kelsey's.

"Long as we're here," he said as she passed, "you might as well have a bite, too. As you pointed out the other morning, you need to stay sharp for Connor."

She was silent as the hostess led them to a table near the fireplace. "Jenna will be your server today," the girl said. "She'll be right with you."

Hunter picked up a menu. "Kind of a shame they didn't build a fire."

"Why?"

"Can I help it if I like a warm atmosphere?"

Brooke looked behind him. He was about to turn to find out what had captured her attention when a husky female voice said, "I'm surprised you even know what that means."

Jenna.

If he'd made the connection earlier, Hunter would have told the hostess, *Sorry, we changed our minds.* He hadn't seen Jenna since she'd hunted him down at a job site to ask why he'd been avoiding her. He'd almost told her the truth, that she reminded him too much of Brooke. During their short time together, he'd tolerated the verbal abuse Jenna had regularly dished out, put up with her erratic behavior. But on the night her car fishtailed away from his house after yet another tantrum, he had decided to call it quits.

She glared at him now the way she had in the construction trailer. It would no doubt make her day if he admitted that his guys still razzed him about the beating she'd given him that day...using the roses she'd brought as a so-called peace offering.

"Well, don't just sit there passing judgment," she said, unpocketing a pen. "Order something."

Passing judgment? She'd been a paralegal back when they were dating. Had her volatile temper forced her to swap legal pads for an order tablet? He glanced at Brooke expecting to find disapproval—or worse—on her face. Instead, he saw the hint of a smile. Would she pick up where Jenna left off?

"Waiting tables is good honest work," he said. "Did it myself in high school."

"Where was diplomacy like that when you were kicking me to the curb!" She'd barely finished her sentence before tossing her order tablet onto the table. "So how long have *you* two been an item?" she asked Brooke.

"Jenna," Hunter said, "maybe it would be best if you—"

But she ignored him. "Did he tell you that he was a cop before he took over his grandfather's big-bucks contracting firm?"

Brooke nodded.

"Did he tell you why…that his partner was killed in a robbery when he fell asleep on the job?"

Hunter couldn't decide where to direct his anger: at Jenna for behaving like a stereotypical scorned woman, or at himself for being fool enough to trust her with his shameful secret. He'd made a half-baked offer to help Brooke at the bank and the funeral parlor to make the process easier for her. Failed at that, he told himself, *but I can spare her this.*

He got up as Brooke said, "Hunter and I go way back, so there isn't much you can tell me about him that I don't already know."

Brooke stood, too, and met his gaze. "Ready to go?"

He watched her stride calmly toward the hostess station, where she turned and frowned at him, as if to say, *Well? What are you waiting for?*

He was tempted to tell Jenna to purge herself of hard feelings or she'd end up like Brooke… angry, spiteful, alone. But one look into his ex's eyes told him it was already too late. He peeled a five-dollar bill from his money clip and dropped it onto the table.

"That should cover the cost of changing the tablecloth and putting out fresh silverware," he said.

Jenna picked it up. "Wish I could say it was nice seeing you again. But I'd be lying."

Halfway to the door, he muttered, "Ditto."

When he caught up with Brooke, she said "So. You kicked Jenna to the curb, did you?"

Yeah, but only because she reminded me too much of you.

"Was it serious?"

"Thought it was."

"How long before you knew it wasn't, um, a match made in heaven?"

He unpocketed his keys, hit the alarm button by mistake. It took a moment of fumbling to silence the horn, and when he did, Brooke repeated the question.

"Too long," he said, opening the passenger door.

She waited until he slid in behind the steering wheel to say, "It's kind of ironic, don't you think?"

"What is?"

"Well, that scene wasn't exactly the fire you were hoping for, but you sure got your share of heat!"

Beth had told him her sister had a great sense of humor, but until this moment, he'd never experienced it personally.

"If you ever get bored with nursing, maybe you can try your hand at stand-up comedy."

She didn't respond. In fact, she didn't say another word for the next five minutes. As they sat at the traffic light at Route 40 and Rogers Avenue, his mind wandered. Why had she agreed to let him come with her if she wasn't going to ask him for help or advice even once? And why let him drive her to and from the meetings if she intended to stare out the window, silent as a stone? Just as confusing, she'd more or less stuck up for him when Jenna had pounced.

A horn blared behind him, startling them both. Hunter uttered a mild oath and took his foot off the brake.

Brooke glanced over her shoulder. "Don't let him get to you," she said as he blended into traffic. "Looks like a grumpy old poop to me. Hardly worth the breath it takes to insult him."

Man, but she was an enigma. Couple of hours ago in the Sheridans' yard, she'd blasted him with reminders of past mistakes…yet twice in fifteen minutes, she'd come to his defense. Sort of.

He wanted to do right by Connor, too—wanted that more than anything—but he hadn't seen any examples so far that backed up Kent's belief that Brooke wasn't capable of mothering the boy. If this kind of evidence kept stacking up, that DVD might never get delivered.

Maybe insomnia was a good thing after all, he thought as they rode along in silence, because he could put those hours of sleeplessness to good use…

…trying to figure out what really was best for Connor.

CHAPTER SIX

DEIDRE, CONNOR AND BROOKE were the only relatives in attendance at the funeral service. That might have been a sad fact if not for nearly a hundred others—coworkers, neighbors, folks from Beth's church—who crowded first into the funeral home and then into the tiny chapel. It touched Brooke to see how many people now stood under the green canvas tent that shaded twin graves, shivering in the raw late-March wind.

When the praying and singing ended, the pastor invited the congregants to step up and share memories of Beth and Kent. It amazed Brooke to see how quickly a line formed. As the first man started speaking, Deidre grabbed Brooke's hand. "Did you know about this?"

Brooke shook her head. During their brief meeting the day before yesterday, the preacher had promised to handle the services, in the church, at the funeral home and here at the cemetery. And since Beth had always refused to discuss anything even remotely related to death or dying, Brooke had quickly agreed to let him.

"I'm trying hard not to make a scene," Deidre said, "but I don't know how I'll hold it together if all these people share fond memories of Beth and Kent."

Brooke gave her grandmother's hand a gentle pat as the man at the podium cleared his throat.

"For those who don't know, I'm Isaac Nelson. Kent and I met when we were seventeen," he began, "and ended up in the same attic room at the Kardens' house. It was my first foster home, but Kent had been in the system for years...and had the scars to prove it. He taught me which rules I could bend and which would earn me a swift kick in the pants." He pressed a palm to the nearest casket. "This guy saved my bacon on more than one occasion. Yes, he did. He'd give you the shirt off his back and go without himself, he would. I loved this big galoot like a brother." He put his hand in his pocket, meeting Deidre's gaze, then Brooke's. "He was good people," he told them, "so I'm sure you'll miss him even more than I will." Then, head bowed, he quickly walked away.

Brooke recognized the young woman who took his place—Ivy McDaniels, her sister's across-the-street neighbor.

"Sorry," Ivy said, rummaging in her purse. "I would have sworn I put my notes in here...."

Amid the quiet laughter, Ivy searched her coat pockets...and Brooke remembered the day when

Beth called to share the news that Kent had proposed. "You've just got to come home," she'd gushed, "so you can meet him. I know you'll love him as much as I do!" Beth had spent the next half hour telling Brooke all about the man she planned to marry, but not a word was said about his years in the foster-care system.

Now Brooke looked around her at the dozens of friends gathered to mourn his passing. Had they seen a side of him that Brooke hadn't, or tolerated his brusque behavior for Beth's sake, as she had? Sadly, neither scenario freed her from the ugly truth: if she hadn't been so wrapped up with work, with her on-then-off love life, she'd know the answer.

Finally, Ivy found her notes.

"I can't tell you," the young woman said, "how many times I showed up at the Sheridans' house unannounced. No matter how busy she was, Beth always, *always,* made time to listen to my troubles, to deliver pep talks, to let me cry on her shoulder." Ivy bit her lower lip before continuing. "She'd set aside whatever puzzle she was working on—oh, how that girl loved word search!—or put down the newspaper and distract me with a news story, a weather alert, a recipe. And no matter how poorly the Orioles or Ravens were performing, Beth never said a bad word about them. Or about anyone else, for that matter, because that's just the way she was."

Half a dozen more speeches followed Ivy's, but Brooke barely heard a word. Her thoughts had turned to the days when she and Beth shared the back bedroom at Deidre's, whispering in the dark across the space between their twin beds about homework and chores, the latest movies, and the cute counselor at summer camp. When had Beth become a fan of puzzles and sports?

Tears pooled in her eyes as Brooke thought of all the time she'd wasted caught up in her own self-interests and mired in loathing Hunter Stone. *It's time you thought about someone other than him...other than yourself for a change.* Deidre and Connor were counting on her, she thought, swiping angrily at the tears, and she was no use to them this way.

And where *was* Connor? Last time she'd seen him, he'd fallen asleep in Hunter's arms...after crying nonstop for half an hour straight. How Hunter had quieted the baby, Brooke couldn't say. But Beth had been right when she'd said that Connor and Hunter shared a one-of-a-kind bond.

Brooke hadn't wanted to bring Connor here today, but Deidre had been unbending: "When he's old enough to ask questions, he'll never forgive us if he finds out we kept him away from one of the most important days of his life."

Brooke caught sight of Hunter and Connor standing side by side on the ornate little bridge across the way. Hunter pointed out a row of mallards bobbing beneath them on the water's surface, and for the moment, the ducks held Connor's attention. But the minute they floated out of sight, he began to wail again. Squatting, Hunter placed big hands on tiny shoulders and said something that captured the baby's full attention...and immediately calmed him.

Hunter looked up just then, caught her staring. She looked away quickly as Deidre jabbed an elbow into her side.

"Honestly, Brooke. I'll be long gone when Connor is old enough to ask what happened here today, and he'll be counting on you to tell him. Pay attention!"

Like an obedient child, Brooke faced front as those assembled near the coffins took turns at the podium.

"He was the most honest man I knew."

"She had a heart as big as her head."

"He was generous to a fault."

"Oh, how she loved her family, especially her big sister!"

The only way the woman in the red hat could know a thing like that was if Beth had told her. Brooke held her breath, determined not to cry.

A strong, warm hand rested on her shoulder.

Hunter....

He leaned near her ear. "I know you're holding it together for Deidre and Connor," he whispered. "Admirable."

When he straightened and walked away, regret throbbed in her heart. And right behind it, exasperation. She was behaving like a fool, unable to make up her mind whether she despised the man who'd let her mother die...or liked him.

She blamed exhaustion. Grief. Her constantly growing list of regrets. Blamed Hunter, too, because after thousands of bitter thoughts about him, she'd allowed a few kind words and gestures to soften her resolve.

The pastor led the mourners in song. Deidre gave Brooke's hand a tiny squeeze, the signal that had meant "behave, or else" since she and Beth were children. Connor wrapped his arms around her knees. "Conner up?"

She picked him up. "Shhh. It's okay," she murmured. "Everything's going to be all right."

He bounced in her arms, pointed at the closed coffins, where photos of Beth and Kent reminded everyone of happier times.

"Conner see Mommy?"

Her heart lurched as she realized what he was asking. "Aw, sweetie," she said around a sob, "how 'bout we go home instead, get you some lunch and a nap."

"*No* nap," he insisted. And pointing again, he repeated, "Conner wants Mommy!"

Even if she could get her feet to cooperate, Brooke wouldn't know what to say or do once she got him over there.

She felt Hunter's warm hand on the small of her back. "Want me to take him?"

Brooke thought of Deidre's earlier comment, that someday Connor would ask about this day.

"No, I'll do it." She could do this. Had to do this.

"Open," Connor said once they reached the front of the tent.

He looked away from the photos, and when he met her eyes, it felt as though he were looking straight into her heart, reading every memory and fear and regret written there.

He tilted his head slightly. "Aw, Brooke cry?"

"No, sweetie." Brooke blinked back the sting of fresh tears. "I'm not crying."

Connor touched a tear, then showed her the tip of his glistening fingertip.

She buried her face in the crook of his neck. *No more lies...not to you, not to myself.*

That seemed to satisfy him, and as Brooke prepared to walk away, he pointed over her shoulder. "No nap!" he cried. "Conner see Mommy! Open...open!"

Brooke looked up at Hunter. If he'd told Connor that his mommy and daddy were in these boxes...

"I didn't say a word," he told her, hands up as if in surrender.

She followed his gaze, saw that the wind had toppled Kent's picture.

Hunter righted it, and when he spoke, a fog of grief and confusion tinged his voice. "How does he *know?*"

Funny. Brooke wondered the same thing.

"Open," Connor repeated.

Brooke wrapped her free hand around his. "We can't open it, sweetie. It's…it's broken," she fibbed.

He looked up at Hunter, who agreed with a shrug and a slow nod. "Sorry, buddy. Broken."

For the longest time, Connor stared at the coffins. At the wind-rattled photographs atop the gleaming lids. At fluttering flower petals. As he stuck his thumb into his mouth, tears puddled in his eyes. He blinked, and one tracked slowly down his cheek. Then he inhaled a ragged, shuddering breath and quietly laid his head on Brooke's shoulder.

"Oh, look!" Ivy said, tilting her face to the slate-gray sky. She caught a snowflake on an upturned palm and showed it to Brooke. "You remember how much Beth loved the snow…." Looking heavenward again, Ivy smiled past her tears. "It's a sign," she whispered. "She's telling us that she's up there."

"Snow," Connor said, trying to grab a fat flake.

Yes, Beth had loved snow. And Kent had, too. Brooke remembered the big glass pickle jar where they'd tossed loose change, money they'd spend on a winter vacation at Wisp, where they hoped to teach Connor to ski.

"Snow," he said again.

She pressed a kiss to his temple. "Don't worry, sweet boy. I'll teach you—"

"Teach him what?" Deidre asked.

"Nothing, really, just—"

"If you'll let me," Hunter said, "I'll help."

Deidre piped up with, "Help with what?"

You don't have to explain was the message he sent Brooke by way of his hazel eyes.

Brooke couldn't have explained even if she'd wanted to as she swallowed over the lump in her throat. But since pretending that she'd accept his help—teaching Connor to ski—was the same as telling a lie, she couldn't do that, either. She'd made a promise to Connor and aimed to keep it.

She faced Hunter. "Thanks, but we've already imposed on you enough."

Hunter flinched as though she'd slapped him. In a way, Brooke supposed she had…with a dose of reality.

"Wish I could have done more."

Brooke had no reason to doubt his sincerity. "You did more than most neighbors would."

"Good grief, Brooke," Deidre said. "He's far more than a neighbor, and you know it." She linked her arm through his. "Let's go back to my house. I think we could all use a good strong cup of coffee."

Frowning, Hunter shook his head. "Maybe some other time. I have a punch list to check for a job that finishes tomorrow."

Deidre clucked her tongue. "All work and no play," she said, wagging her forefinger like a metronome. "Have you forgotten that you drove us over here in my car? You have to take us home, pick up your truck anyway."

Brooke held her breath, hoping he'd remember something else he needed to do.

"Okay," he told Deidre, "but just one cup." Then he faced Brooke. "I'll take Connor." And he did. "It's an uphill walk from here to the car, and he's a hefty li'l fella."

"I need to write your mother a thank-you note," Deidre said before Brooke had a chance to reply.

"Thank-you note?" He grinned slightly. "For what?"

"For raising such a bighearted, thoughtful young man." She looked at Brooke. "Isn't that right, honey?"

"Yes. Thoughtful."

As she and her grandmother trudged up the hill behind him, Brooke glanced over her shoulder. Two workmen were already busy disassembling the big green tent while another fiddled with the controls that would lower the coffins into the ground. The sight stopped her in her tracks.

"What's wrong?"

Brooke patted Deidre's hand. "Oh…nothing. Just tired, I guess."

"Don't give me that. You're having a hard time, same as me, leaving our girl here alone, aren't you?"

"She isn't alone, Gram." Brooke gave the graves one last glance. "Her husband is right there beside her."

By the time they reached the car, Hunter had buckled a kicking, screaming Connor into his car seat. Standing beside the open door, he shook his head. "First thing Monday morning," he said, "maybe we can make that phone call."

"What phone call?" Deidre wanted to know.

"To find someone who can help us explain things to Connor in language he'll understand," Brooke explained.

Deidre slid into the backseat beside her great-grandson. "That," she said, "is the best idea I've heard since this dreadful ordeal began."

"Hopefully," Hunter said, closing the rear door, "we won't have to wait too long for an appointment."

A week ago Brooke might have lashed out, told

him in no uncertain terms that he could drop the
we. Things were different now—though she didn't
quite understand why. Earlier she'd admitted to
herself that Connor adored him, that he felt the
same way about the baby. She'd also admitted that
it was time for her to start putting others first.

And she'd start, right now, by setting aside her
resentment, just far enough to make room for
Hunter in Connor's life.

CHAPTER SEVEN

DEIDRE CAME IN from the kitchen and groaned. "Sorry, but we can't have coffee after all. My cupboards are as bare as Mother Hubbard's."

"How's that possible, Mrs. Hollywood," Hunter said, "when your pantry is bigger than my entire first floor?"

"Mrs. Hollywood?" she echoed. "Brooke, will you please tell this handsome rascal the difference between Tinseltown and Broadway?"

Hunter tensed when Brooke pointed. At him. It had been a demanding day, physically and emotionally, and he had no idea how she might respond.

"He's right there," she said, smiling softly. "Why don't you tell him yourself?"

Earning straight As had been easy for Hunter until his English teacher added Yeats, Joyce and Whitman to the mandatory reading list. Allegory, hyperbole, onomatopoeia… Deciphering poetry wasn't easy, and he'd steered clear of it since high school. But when Brooke spoke just now, something clicked, and he understood what the poets meant when they described the music of a woman's voice.

"He's heard it all before, right, Hunter?"

"Too many times to count."

Deidre pulled Connor into her lap, and he quickly snuggled close. "Did I also tell you about the band I used to sing with—before my Broadway days?"

"That's a new one," he said, wondering how she'd connect the information to his retort.

"The drummer had a sign on his base. 'Nobody Likes a Smart Aleck,'" she said, drawing quote marks in the air. Smirking, she added, "Billy used a more colorful word, but I think I've made my point. Think about *that* next time you decide to sass an old lady."

"Guess I saved you the bother of writing that thank-you note to my mom, eh?"

She leaned back in her chair. "Silly goose." Turning toward Brooke, she asked, "How many people do you think showed up today?"

"I'm not sure. Ninety? A hundred? I'll have to ask Pastor Daniels when I drop off the check on Monday."

"The check?" Deidre asked, stroking Connor's rosy cheek.

"For the pastor. And the organist."

"How can they in good conscience take money at a time like this?"

LOREE LOUGH 77

Brooke shrugged, and Hunter said, "They gave up a big chunk of their Saturday to help us say goodbye to Beth and Kent. The church has bills to pay, too, don't forget."

Deidre harrumphed. "I thought that's what the dough people throw into the collection plate was for."

Out of the corner of his eye, he saw Brooke close her eyes. To block out another of her grandmother's inappropriate comments? Or to hide the misery and sadness of the day?

He watched her straighten already-straight doilies on the arms of her chair, adjust the folds of her gauzy skirt, finger the chunky turquoise pendant buried in the soft ruffles of her blouse. Then she crossed her cowboy boots at the ankles. What Hunter knew about fashion he could put in one eye, but he knew this: he liked what he saw.

"What will they do with all those beautiful flowers?" Deidre wondered aloud.

"I arranged to have them delivered to Howard County General," Brooke told her. "Mr. Turner told me the volunteers will give them to patients who haven't received any."

"That's so sweet. I remember walking the halls when Percy had his stroke, passing some rooms that resembled florist shops, others that were bare as…as my pantry." She looked at Hunter. "Isn't Brooke just the most thoughtful little thing?"

"That she is," he said. "Wish I'd thought to do something like that after my dad died."

He half expected Brooke would react with self-depreciating humility, shyness, anything but wide-eyed alarm. Hunter followed her gaze to Deidre's face. The woman had passed out. No wonder her last few sentences hadn't held their usual punch.

He crossed to her side of the tiny parlor in one long stride and eased the sleeping Connor from her lap. "Think she skipped breakfast again?"

"I wouldn't be at all surprised." He sat in the nearest chair. "How 'bout if I keep an eye on this li'l guy while you fix her a sandwich or something?"

First she frowned. Then she stood. "Skipping meals at any age is a bad idea, but all those medications Gram takes? On an empty stomach?" She groaned quietly.

"I'm hungry and tired," Deidre said, "not deaf… no thanks to our mini-human siren over there. So don't you dare wake him, because—much as I hate to sound like a grumpy old crone—the peace and quiet is a blessed relief."

Connor started fussing, as if on cue. But thankfully, he wasn't fully awake yet.

"Deidre, keep your voice down, will ya?" Hunter said, rocking back and forth, rubbing soothing circles on the baby's narrow back as Brooke disappeared into the kitchen.

"Remember what I told you about Billy's drum," Deidre said.

"Sorry. No disrespect intended. It's just—"

"Oh, no need to apologize. Or explain. These past few days have beat us all up pretty well. I can't wait until the black cloud that's been following us around fizzles out. I'm sick of all the moping and frowning!"

Hunter assumed she must have forgotten how long it had taken her to get back into the swing of things when Percy died.

Five minutes later Brooke returned carrying a snack-laden tray. "I made extra," she said, handing a plate to Deidre, "in case you're hungry...."

Hunter eased out of the chair. "Think I'll see if I can get him into his crib without waking him." He started for the stairs. Wish me luck."

"While you're up there," Deidre said, "give a thought to changing your pants, why don't you."

"Why?"

"Because somebody's diaper leaked. You're about Percy's size. Help yourself to a pair of his jeans. They're in my closet."

Odd, he thought, but he hadn't noticed the dampness until she mentioned it. On the way upstairs, Hunter pictured Deidre's third husband—the only one of three who'd earned Love of My Life title. He pictured himself wearing the man's trademark bib overalls and considered the possibility that he wasn't wet and Deidre needed comic relief.

As he eased Connor into the crib, Hunter felt the cold, clammy proof that the diaper really had leaked. He grabbed a fresh one and got to work. When the kid was fast asleep like this, nothing short of a shotgun blast would wake him. But just in case, Hunter took his time. As he cleaned up, the baby's eyelids fluttered. "Daddy?" He sighed. "Daddy-Daddy-Daddy."

If anyone had told him that a simple two-syllable word could hit him like a blow to the jaw, Hunter would have laughed it off. But the stark, quiet reminder of Kent's death hit hard. Leaning on the crib rail, he hung his head.

"Nothing would make me prouder than to call you son," he said, smoothing soft bangs from Connor's forehead. "But it won't be easy filling your dad's shoes." The admission made him wonder why Kent worked so hard to give some people—Brooke in particular—the impression that he didn't have a heart when in truth he had an immeasurable capacity for love.

"I'll do my best to fill your daddy's shoes, buddy."

Satisfied that the boy was safe, Hunter covered him with a light blanked and walked across the hall. Draped in gauzy lace, Deidre's four-poster bed was piled high with heart-shaped pastel pillows, and on the night tables, china dolls garbed in ruffly ball gowns wore lampshade hats. Ornate perfume bottles sparkled from the marble top of the mahogany makeup table, and in the closet, dresses of every fabric and hue hung in order by length. Beneath them a multi-tiered rack sagged under the weight of four, maybe five dozen pairs of shoes.

Up against the far wall, separated from the other clothes, one pair of coveralls had been draped over a padded hanger. Why had she discarded all of Percy's other clothes and kept these? A quiet reminder, perhaps, of happier moments spent with her husband, the former stand-up comic.

Hunter tucked his soiled trousers into a plastic bag found on the floor of Deidre's closet, then changed into the overalls and went back to check on Connor, who had turned onto his side and was cuddling a fuzzy teddy bear. Except for twin dimples—Beth's contribution to his facial features—Connor was the spitting image of Kent. Had he inherited his dad's "do everything by the book" nature, too, Hunter wondered as tears stung his eyes, or his mom's easygoing personality?

What was wrong with him lately? Seemed like every time he turned round, tears threatened. Connor sighed, and Hunter knuckled his eyes. "Don't be in too big a hurry to grow up, okay?"

"That's what I told him," Brooke said, stepping

up beside him, "when I tucked him in on the night of the crash. I guess it's a blessing that he's so young, because he won't remember how he lost his mom and dad."

"Yeah, but we'll make sure he knows what sort of people they were."

For a moment, Brooke stood, content, it seemed, to watch Connor sleep.

"So how's Deidre?" he asked.

"She's fine. I told her if she didn't eat that ham sandwich, I'd make her take a nap."

He chuckled as Brooke sighed.

"It won't be easy," she said, "admitting to Connor that I didn't know his dad very well."

It seemed she was thinking out loud, but that didn't stop him from saying, "Kent wasn't an easy guy to get to know."

"I'm not made of glass, Hunter. I can handle the truth."

Before those punishing meetings at the bank and funeral parlor before the graveside service, he might have disagreed, based solely on what Kent had told him about her. But he knew better now.

"All I meant," he defended, "is that I'll make sure Connor gets to know his dad."

"*You'll* make sure?"

"I'll help, I mean. If it's okay with you."

Brooke looked up at him through thick lashes. "Why wouldn't it be?"

Oh, I don't know...maybe because I killed your mother?

She avoided his gaze. "Beggars can't be choosers. I'm in no position to turn down any help that's offered."

She'd easily convinced both managers that Connor would soon become her son legally. If he hadn't had that DVD to tell him otherwise, she might have convinced Hunter, too.

Connor had kicked off his blanket. "You did a pretty good job," she said, pulling it up again, "diapering him."

Hunter hooked his thumbs into the pockets of Percy's overalls and puffed out his chest. "Yep, that's me," he drawled, "Old Put 'Em to Sleep Stone."

"No need to be modest." She raised an eyebrow. "I'm sure Jenna lost a few night's sleep over you, because…" She exhaled a groan of frustration. "Let's just say Connor seems very much at ease with you and leave it at that."

In the past, it seemed she'd worked at putting him in his place. This time, it seemed, the opposite was true. If she hadn't looked so uncomfortable, he might have kept her on the hook a little longer.

"I'm glad, because I couldn't love him more if he were my own."

A strange expression—something between regret and annoyance—flitted across her face, and he didn't know what to make of it.

"Well, in any case, I hope you'll feel free to visit him anytime."

Soon, I won't need your permission.

Connor stirred slightly, and Hunter said, "Guess we'd better get out of here before we wake him. And that would be a shame—the poor kid's plumb tuckered out."

He followed her toward the hall, and as he pulled the door shut, his stomach growled.

"Talk about good timing," Brooke said, jogging down the stairs. "I made extra sandwiches, so—"

His stomach rumbled again.

Brooke turned and looked up at him. "I'll pretend I didn't hear that." She grinned, but quickly suppressed it. "Just like I'll pretend that your pants aren't two inches too short."

Hunter peered down and realized if he'd worn white socks today, his ankles could have lit up the landing. He might have shared his absurd observation if she hadn't already disappeared around the corner. Just as well. In the weird mood he was in, he might blurt out something reckless and stupid, like, *It isn't nice to poke fun at a guy who's starting to like you...*

...maybe a little too much...

CHAPTER EIGHT

BROOKE GLANCED OVER her shoulder. "Look at him back there, fast asleep."

Hunter nodded. "Don't know how he does it, all cramped and confined by that contraption."

"I hope it's a sign he's beginning to come to terms with…" She shook her head. "I can't even say it. Not that it matters. Because he'll never get a handle on what happened. None of us will." On the heels of a ragged sigh, she added, "Wasn't it Deepak Chopra who wrote, 'It is the nature of babies to be in bliss'?"

He could tell that she'd almost lost it for a minute there, and he admired how fast she'd pulled herself together. Another of Kent's myths debunked, because Brooke could handle adversity.

"She's gorgeous and well-read," he said. "Be still, my heart."

The instant the words were out, Hunter regretted them, mostly because of the self-conscious flush they put on her face.

"I have to admit," he quickly added, "I envy the kid's ability to sleep." Was his comment enough to blot out memory of his verbal faux pas? Not likely. But with any luck, he'd sidelined it. "And I'm with you—I hope it's a sign that he's getting used to not seeing his mom and dad around every corner."

"Yeah," she said, staring through the windshield, "me, too."

They spent the last ten minutes of the drive between Deidre's and the Sheridans' in companionable silence. With any other woman, Hunter would have felt obliged to fill it with idle chitchat—commenting on landmarks and weather, complaining about some crazy driver who'd cut them off, pointing out another of the county's speed cameras—but with Brooke, the quiet seemed...right. He wondered about that, because before the crash, he'd always felt ill at ease and out of place in her presence. The sensation reminded him of his days in Bosnia, a full-out peacckeeping mission that left troops wondering where the next strike might come from.

The sun hung low in the late-March sky. Squinting, he decided a topic change was in order.

"Ever seen the green flash?" he asked, pulling into the Sheridans' driveway.

"I've never been in the right place at the right time."

He pocketed his keys and got out of the truck. Too late again to open the door for her.

"Yeah, if that isn't one of those 'the conditions are right' things, I don't know what is."

While she fiddled with Connor's seat restraints, he recalled a line from the 1882 novel *Le Rayon vert*. "Didn't Jules Verne say that the flash is a color no artist could duplicate on his palette?"

"He also said if there's green in paradise, surely it's that green."

Hunter slammed the back passenger door. "Sorry," he said when she lurched. "Darned thing needs a new latch."

"I know."

Had he told her about the faulty handle? he wondered, extending one hand.

Without a word, Brooke dropped her keys into his upturned palm. Hunter unlocked the front door and got a whiff of lilacs—or was it lavender?—as Brooke stepped past him and into the house. Following her, he watched as she removed Connor's hat and jacket.

"I'm surprised…"

She tucked the baby's hat into his jacket sleeve. "About what?"

He raised his voice so she could hear him over Connor's wailing. "That you're a sci-fi fan."

"I'm not. But I had a professor in college who was, and it didn't take long to figure out that an occasional Verne quote could make the difference between a B and an A."

"Hmm…"

"Now what?" she asked, hanging the jacket on the hall tree.

Things between them had been fairly harmonious. No way he intended to sour things by sharing his thought: *Are women born manipulators, or do they work at it?*

"I aced a high school literature class," she added, "thanks to extra-credit papers I wrote on the elusive green flash. Unfortunately, that didn't get me to Hawaii. And chances of ever getting there are slim to none."

"But I've seen it in the Alleghenies, on a Florida beach, even from the fishing pier in Ocean City." Pausing, Hunter then added, "What's stopping you from going to Hawaii?"

"Time, mostly. Connor is too young for a trip like that."

Still mapping out his future, was she? But that was an issue for later, after she'd had a chance to recover from the crash.

"What kept you from going before now?"

She gave the question a moment's thought. "Never met anyone I wanted to spend that much time with, I guess. Don't like the idea of vacationing on my own."

The image of her with another guy put every nerve on edge, and he didn't get that. Didn't get it at all. She held Connor closer and said over his whining, "I'd much rather stay home with this little guy than jet off to some white-sands island."

He pictured Brooke walking hand in hand with him on a sunny beach as Connor splashed in the surf beside them. "Maybe someday," he said distractedly. Kent had told him all about Brooke's bad luck with relationships....

She headed for the stairs. "I'm going to run a bath for Connor." Looking into the baby's face, she added, "And after he's all clean and shiny, I'll put on his pj's." She nuzzled Connor's neck. "Early to bed, early to rise, young man." Any second now she'd say something like *Lock up after you let yourself out.*

Halfway up the stairs, she stopped. "Would you like to stay, help me tuck him in?"

Good thing he wasn't a betting man. "I'd love to."

If he had a lick of sense, he'd follow her up the stairs.

If he'd never seen the disc, he wouldn't be in this untenable position now, trying to forget the years she'd spent exploiting his guilt. He should feel justified using Kent's tirade against her. But he didn't.

If he could find more proof that Kent had been wrong about her, he wouldn't need to go forward with his plan to adopt the boy. And if Connor's well-being didn't hang in the balance, he'd take a hammer to the DVD.

Doing the right thing for Connor shouldn't be this hard.

So, then, why was it?

Because, you idiot, you're falling for her.

Which was beyond foolish. The occasional bursts of cordiality he'd witnessed over the past few days were probably nothing more than Brooke feeling obliged to show gratitude for the chauffeuring and Connor-hauling. If he didn't watch himself, Hunter would be in for a world of hurt, because chances that she'd ever feel anything but hostility toward him were slim to none.

If. The most powerful little word in the English language.

Then he remembered that Beth had loathed him, too, until he put some of his mother's advice into play, and put everything he had into showing Beth how sorry he was about his part in what had happened to her mother. And in time, she'd forgiven him.

How would Brooke react if he tested that theory on her?

Only one way to find out.

Brooke was fastening the top snap of Connor's pajamas when he joined them in the nursery.

"You know," he said, "until I met this little guy, I had no idea they made long johns this small."

She lifted the freshly powdered and pj'd toddler from the changing table, carried him to the big wooden rocker beside his crib. "Tell your uncle Hunter that long johns are for lumberjacks, and blanket sleepers are for babies."

"Baby," Connor echoed, rubbing his eyes. "Brooke sing?"

"You betcha, cutie-pie, any lullaby your little heart desires." And then, blushing, she looked at Hunter. "Connor probably won't mind if you stay, but I don't perform well in front of an audience."

"Gotcha," he said, backing into the hall. "Take your time."

And then he hotfooted it down the stairs as an idea took shape.

In the living room, he scrolled through the numbers in his cell phone's contacts list and highlighted his favorite pizza shop. Not knowing if Brooke preferred hers fully loaded or plain, he ordered both. And while waiting for the delivery guy, Hunter slipped out the front door and hurried over to his place. After grabbing the bottle of Beaujolais nouveau from his pantry and a couple of wineglasses, he went back to the Sheridans' and set the stage.

Too much light, and not even the wine would relax her enough to listen to his confession; not enough light, and who knew what she'd think he was up to.

Last summer he'd helped Kent install a dimmer and pot lights above the fireplace. He'd never used it himself but soon realized that Beth had been right: it took an excessive amount of fiddling to achieve a soft, relaxing glow. If he'd paid more attention to Beth and less to Kent's "it's fine the way it is" assessment, he could have tweaked the switch months ago.

Hunter made a mental note to fix it, then he checked the cable TV movie guide. *Roman Holiday*...too romantic. *Casablanca*...too depressing. "Where's a good old-fashioned Western when you want one?" he complained.

Cat Ballou flashed in the list, and he clicked on it. If things worked out as planned, he would know where he stood with Brooke by the time the credits scrolled down the screen.

He'd barely finished pouring the Beaujolais when a car door slammed. Hunter stepped onto the porch to catch the delivery boy so the doorbell wouldn't startle Connor. He slid the pizza box between the goblets on the table and he headed back upstairs to see how much longer it would take her to get Connor down for the night.

A familiar melody stopped him just outside the baby's bedroom door, but it had never sounded like this.

"...toora, loora, loora, hush, now, don't you cry..."

Suddenly, it wasn't enough to hear her voice. Hunter needed to see her sing, too. He eased into the doorway in time to see her form the final notes.

"...that's an Irish lullaby."

The affection she felt for Connor was visible even in the dim glow of the Thomas the Tank Engine night-light. The baby looked so peaceful and content, and it was clear that he trusted his aunt Brooke almost as much as if he'd been born to her. What kind of monster would even think about separating them?

"How long have you been standing there?" she whispered, rising slowly from the rocker.

"Uh…"

Brooke laid Connor in his crib and tiptoed toward him. "Did I hear the front door open and close just now?"

"Pizza delivery guy."

When she looked up at him with that blank brown-eyed stare, he wished he could read minds.

"I didn't know how you like yours, so I ordered two. One with cheese. One with pepperoni and mushrooms."

"Perfect. For the first time in days, I actually have an appetite."

He breathed a sigh of relief and followed her down the stairs.

"Oh, wow," she said, entering the living room.

"I haven't seen this movie in—" Brooke looked from the TV to the goblets to Hunter. "Where did the wine come from?"

"It was a thank-you gift from one of my clients. Thought it might go well with the pizza."

She disappeared into the kitchen as Hunter sat on the love seat. If Brooke wanted a clear view of the television, she'd have to sit beside him...the only way he knew to guarantee she'd see him. He could hear her in there happily humming the lullaby. If Lady Luck was on his side, she'd still be in this mood after he'd said his piece.

Brooke deposited two paper plates and napkins on the coffee table and flipped open the nearest pizza box. Somewhere between the kitchen and living room, she'd kicked off her shoes, and Hunter tried not to stare at her shiny red-painted toenails.

"Your favorite," she said, sliding a slice onto a paper plate and holding it out to him. And when he took it, her fingers grazed his, sending a shudder down his spine.

"How'd you know pepperoni and mushroom is my favorite?" he asked.

"Beth," she said matter-of-factly. "She also told me you don't like lima beans and that you put catsup on everything."

He couldn't imagine why his food preferences had come up during the sisters' conversations, but he wasn't about to muddy the atmosphere by asking for an explanation.

"Beth was wrong," he said.

Brooke bit off the point of her slice. "Oh?"

"I don't put catsup on everything. I like my steak plain," he said. "And chocolate sauce on my ice cream."

"I heard that you put catsup on birthday cake."

"Once, and only because your sister dared me."

"Uh-huh," she said, sitting cross-legged on the sofa. "So…is it back to the old grindstone on Monday?"

"Nope. Took off the whole week. I have a very indulgent boss. What about you? You're due to start the new job soon, right?"

"Lucky me. I have a very indulgent boss, too. She told me to take all the time I need. But don't worry…I won't hit you up for a loan. There's enough in my savings account to tide me over for a while."

"Never crossed my mind." And it hadn't. Plenty of other things to worry about, he thought, but not that.

"Connor did pretty well today," she said.

He nodded. "He did great, all things considered."

"You have projects to do around your house?"

Her question caught him off guard. "No. Why?"

She shrugged. "You've already taken off three days...."

He'd put everything on hold in case she needed him. Correction: in case Connor needed him. "It's a good test for my newest foreman," he fibbed. "Poor guy hasn't had a chance to prove himself since I hired him."

Brooke downed her wine in two big gulps, re- filled her glass and held the bottle aloft.

"Thanks," he said, "I'm good." If he hoped to make any headway in a few minutes, he'd need his full wits about him.

"Is it just me, or does Jane Fonda play herself in every role?"

Grabbing the remote, he hit the mute button and didn't give her time to object or ask why.

"Listen, Brooke," he said, "there's something I've been meaning to tell you for a long time...."

CHAPTER NINE

THE DOORBELL RANG before Hunter could tell Brooke more.

"There's only one person who'd drop by unannounced at ten o'clock."

Beth had told him all about Brooke's ex, but for the life of him, Hunter couldn't remember the guy's name. "Who?"

"Donald," Brooke said. "The biggest mistake of my adult life."

Hunter started for the door. "It's probably just the pizza guy. Maybe I shortchanged him. Or overpaid him."

The man on the other side of the storm door adjusted the Windsor knot of his red silk tie. "I was told I could find Brooke O'Toole at this address?"

Hunter crossed both arms over his chest and did his best to block Donald's view of the living room...and Brooke.

"Who told you that?"

Donald's gaze traveled from Hunter's eyes to his shoes and back again. "Not that it's any of your business, but her grandmother sent me over here."

Brooke stood beside Hunter. "What were you doing at Gram's?"

"Looking for you, of course."

She stood so close that Hunter got another whiff of her flowery shampoo. Did that look on Donald's face mean he noticed it, too?

"You're not going to make me stand out here in the cold, are you?"

"I told you before I left Richmond: We. Are. Done. And I meant it."

Attagirl. Now slam the door.

"Aw, babe, don't be like that. I would have been here sooner, but I just found out about your sister."

Hunter could hardly believe his ears when she stepped aside and said, "You have five minutes." Couldn't believe his eyes, either, when Donald wrapped his arms around her…and she *let* him. He wanted to step in like a refercc at a boxing match and pry them apart. After what seemed like ten minutes, she untangled herself from her ex-fiancé's embrace.

"Who's the guy doing the Mr. Clean impersonation?" Donald said, pointing with his thumb.

Brooke blushed. "Hunter Stone, meet—"

"Not *that* Hunter Stone…."

So. She'd told the guy about him, had she?

Brooke's blush deepened. "If you're hungry," she told Donald, "there's pizza on the coffee table."

Hey, wait a minute, Hunter wanted to say. *I paid for that pizza.*

Donald patted his flat stomach. "Came straight from a shindig at the downtown Marriott," he said. "Couldn't eat a bite." As he walked beside her into the living room, he leaned close and whispered, "Seriously. Brooke. Have you taken leave of your senses? I mean, after what he did? I can't believe you'd let him get within a mile of you!"

Hunter tensed as Brooke returned to her cushion on the sofa. He quickly took the other one as she said, "A meeting in Baltimore. I should have known you didn't come all the way from Richmond just to extend your sympathies."

"Well, to be fair, I haven't exactly been your favorite person these days." Donald aimed a phony grin Hunter's way. "Guess we have that in common, too, eh, buddy?"

Too? Hunter bristled. *The only thing we have in common,* buddy, *is our gender.* He took a gulp of wine.

"So. Hunter. I wonder if you'd be a good egg and give me and Brooke a few minutes alone to, ah, catch up and, ah, talk…."

Hunter was itching to correct Donald's grammar. And find out why he'd put so much emphasis on the word *talk.* "It's up to Brooke."

It seemed like an eternity before she looked at

him. "It *has* been a long day, and I'm sure you're tired, too."

Jaw clenched, Hunter pretended not to notice Donald's self-satisfied smirk. Did his best to hide his disappointment, too, as Brooke walked him to the door. Once there, she held his gaze for a moment. Would she change her mind, show Donald the door instead? A guy could hope....

"Thanks for everything today, Hunter...the ride to the church and home, keeping Connor occupied at the cemetery, the pizza and wine...."

The wine. His plan—to help her relax after a long heartbreaking day—could very well backfire, make her easy pickings for Donald instead. Hunter moved closer and lowered his voice. "He steps out of line, even a little bit, I'm as near as the phone."

"I'll be fine."

She'd forced a feeble smile, but he wasn't convinced. "I could sit in the kitchen while you two, ah, talk. You won't even know I'm out there."

Brooke glanced toward the living room, where Donald had just helped himself to a slice of pizza. "He's a royal pain," she said, opening the door, "but he's basically harmless."

"Oh. Right. I forgot." He frowned. "That's why you left a great job, a nice condo, friends in Richmond after he—"

"I can handle him."

Lucky for him, she had interrupted, because he

didn't know how she might have reacted if he'd finished with "...after he dumped you."

"Okay, but I'm only two doors down."

"I know. Thanks." And when she nodded, a curl fell over one eye.

"I own a contracting company, don't forget." And without thinking, he tucked her hair behind one ear. "Meaning...I have access to a huge collection of dangerous tools."

She laughed softly and, for a tick in time, nestled her cheek against his palm. Under normal circumstances, Brooke never would have done such a thing. Knowing that, Hunter slowly withdrew his hand.

A cool blast of air whooshed through the screen, and she cupped both elbows to fend off the chill. He felt like a heel, making her stand in the cold foyer. Felt even worse about leaving her alone with the guy who had broken her heart. Who might break it again. But she hadn't given him any other option.

"Call you tomorrow?"

"Okay," she said and, giving him a tiny wave, closed the door.

Head down and hands pocketed, Hunter walked toward his house. Halfway there he stopped, trying to think of a logical excuse to go back...

...and there in the picture window saw Donald pull her into another hug.

He held his breath, waiting. Any second now she'd slap him silly and send him packing. Hunter would bet his next renovations contract on it. Instead, he watched as she let the guy rock her to and fro, back and forth, as if offering comfort and support.

He stalked the rest of the way home and unlocked his front door. Good thing he wasn't a gambler, he thought again.

Maybe Kent had been right, and Brooke really was scatterbrained and impulsive. And maybe her brother-in-law had been wise to ask Hunter to protect Connor from her reckless knee-jerk decisions.

Hunter had some decisions of his own to make, starting with finding a way to spend time alone with Connor until the time came to hand over that DVD.

He tossed his keys onto the kitchen counter and grabbed a soda from the fridge. The label said Decaffeinated. Not that it mattered. Between admitting how powerless he was to look out for Connor and wondering if Donald was putting the moves on Brooke, he wouldn't get a wink of sleep anyway.

Though for the life of him, he didn't know why he cared *what* Donald did.

CHAPTER TEN

LAST TIME HUNTER checked the time, the clock face said five forty-five. When the doorbell rang, he opened one eye. Maybe he was dreaming, because now it said ten minutes after nine. Nearly four straight hours of sleep? Yeah, he was dreaming, all right.

The bell dinged again. He dropped the recliner's footrest, then worked the kinks from his neck as he walked toward the door. He'd get rid of the magazine salesman, then change the battery in that clock.

He peeked through the curtains. Brooke and Connor? Now he knew he was dreaming, because not once in all the years since he'd lived two doors down from Beth and Kent had she come to his house. Oh, what the heck, he thought, running a hand through his sleep-tousled hair. Might be interesting to see how this dream played itself out.

"Morning," he said, opening the door.

She took one look at him and said, "Oh. My. We woke you. Sorry. I had a feeling I should call first."

"You did me a favor. I should have been up hours ago."

"But I thought you took this week off."

"True," he said, stepping back. "I just hate sleeping the day away." With a sweep of his arm, he invited her inside.

As she passed, he took note of her snug jeans and white sweatshirt jacket and the flushed cheeks that made her look more like a high school kid than a full-grown woman. Had she deliberately chosen a similar outfit for Connor, or had it been a happy accident?

"I need coffee," he said, leading the way to the kitchen. "Can I interest you in a cup?"

"Thanks, but I can't stay," she said, placing a bag on his counter. "I only stopped by to return your wineglasses. I rushed you out of the house so fast last night that I forgot to wash them up and give them to you."

"I don't do much entertaining, so no rush." What he really wanted to say was, *Last time I checked*—at quarter past one—*Donald was still there. You must have had a lot to hash out....*

"Cookie?" Connor said, pointing at the cupboard above the toaster.

Hunter grinned and grabbed a box of vanilla wafers. "He knows I keep his favorites up there."

Brooke raised an eyebrow. "I know Beth was a

little extreme with her 'natural foods only' rules, but do you think maybe you're—"

He knew where this would lead. Straight into a lecture about how he'd gone to the other extreme.

"You're right," he said, giving Connor a handful of cookies. "Beth did go overboard." Way overboard, he thought, filling the coffee carafe. "But it isn't like I spoon-feed him sugar or anything."

He didn't have to turn around to know that Brooke was frowning.

"I suppose there's nothing wrong with junk food once in a while."

Mighty generous of you, he thought, pouring water into the reservoir. Maybe he'd nominate her for the Mother of the Year award. "I noticed the stroller on the front walk," he said, jamming a filter into the basket. "Were you two headed for the park?"

"Yeah," she said, nodding. "I thought maybe some fresh air and a change of scenery would be good for him."

"Nice day for it," he said, adding the grounds.

She sat in the chair nearest the high chair and, tapping the tray, said, "Did you buy this just for him?"

"That and the crib in his room upstairs, the playpen in the living room, clothes, diapers and a mountain of toys." He hit the on switch. "He's over here a lot, and it was a pain dragging stuff back and forth."

"But you only live two doors down...."

He leaned his backside against the counter and crossed one white-socked foot over the other. "Do I hear an *and* in that sentence?"

"It's just...well...Beth quit her job when Connor was born. Went on and on about not wanting to leave him with sitters. It's a little confusing, is all."

"Why? Because choosing to be a stay-at-home mom meant she didn't deserve an hour or two all to herself once in a while? Maybe dinner or a movie with her husband every now and then?"

Brooke blushed. "That isn't what I meant at all!"

"Oh. Wait. I think I get it. You're surprised that a woman who loved her kid too much to stick him in day care was okay leaving him with a guy who falls asleep on the job."

Well, that shut her up in a hurry. Because she was sorry for leading him to believe such a thing? Or because she agreed?

He dropped a few more cookies onto Connor's tray. "Seems like he's in a good mood today. Did he sleep better last night?" He was becoming an old hand at changing the subject.

"I wish. He was up half the night fussing and fretting. First thing this morning, I called his pediatrician, who recommended a child psychologist. She's usually impossible to see, especially on such short notice, but Dr. Miller talked her into squeezing us in."

Us *as in the three of us?* he wondered. *Or* us *as in Connor and Brooke?*

"What time?"

"Two, right after his afternoon nap." She groaned. "If he takes a nap, that is."

If Brooke couldn't muster the patience to handle Connor's behavior a mere week after the funeral, how did she expect to cope if it continued…and she added a job to her responsibilities?

"I'll drive," he said. And then he waited, knowing if she had a notion to exclude him, she'd do it now.

"All right," she said. And glancing around the room, Brooke added, "Who does your housekeeping?"

"I do." He filled a sippy cup with juice. "Leftover habits from my days in the army."

"And I suppose the army taught you to choose curtains that match the wallpaper."

Hunter chuckled. "The woman who owned the house before me is the one with good taste. Keeping it clean, that's all I can take credit for." He took two mugs from the cabinet above the coffeepot. "But I'm glad you approve."

By now he knew that the rise of her left brow meant one of two things: she was angry…or confused. He answered her unasked question with "So you'll be comfortable leaving Connor with me. If you need to run errands or whatever."

"Of course."

He shrugged.

"I told you that you could see him anytime you wanted to." She met his gaze. "You didn't believe me?"

He resisted the urge to tell her that if things went as expected, he wouldn't need her permission much longer. Last night—between stewing every time he saw Donald's car still parked in front of the Sheridans' house and walking the floor—he'd emailed instructions to his attorney. First chance he got, Harry would put the petition for adoption in motion. According to Hunter's internet research, the court would have 180 days after the pleading was filed to grant or deny it. Providing no one contested it, that is. When faced with official documents that backed up Kent's DVD, would Brooke fall back on her typical behavior and run away again…or stay and fight for Connor?

"I believe you," he said. "But there's still an elephant in the room."

He wasn't totally convinced she was fit to raise Connor, but he wasn't sure he was, either.

Soon it would be up to professionals who earned a living making decisions like that. If the gavel fell in his favor, Hunter would include Brooke at every stage of Connor's life. If it landed on her side, he hoped she'd do the same.

She had built a tower of vanilla wafers, and Connor wasted no time toppling it. Normally, it would have kindled a fit of giggles. When it didn't, Hunter decided two o'clock couldn't get here soon enough.

"Would you believe I have a friend," she said, restacking cookies, "who works at the National Zoo in Baltimore?"

"The zoo," he echoed. What did that have to do with anything? "Sorry. I'm a little dense before my first cup of java."

"I'm sure he'll help us get rid of it. The elephant, that is."

So her friend was a he. Did she know any women? Not that it mattered, since Connor was the magnet that held them together.

"Pancakes," the baby said. "Conner want pancakes."

"No, sweetie," she said, "Uncle Hunter doesn't have time for that."

And Connor pouted. "Pancakes?"

"It's no trouble," Hunter said. "I froze the leftovers last time I made him breakfast. It'll only take a minute to nuke 'em." He kissed the top of Connor's head. "Pancakes coming up, buddy."

"He already had oatmeal," Brooke said. "But I guess it's okay. Just this once."

He pulled a zipper bag from the freezer and emptied the contents onto a paper plate.

"I hope Dr. Rosen can help us," she continued, "because I'm at my wits' end trying to figure out how to make him happy."

Hopefully, family court would soon relieve her of that obligation.

Hunter set the microwave timer as Connor held a cookie near Brooke's lips. She took a tiny bite. "Yum!" she said. "Thank you!" But not even her exuberance inspired a smile.

She looked at Hunter. "Two o'clock can't get here soon enough for me."

Great minds think alike?

"My mom spent months in therapy after Dad died," he said, "and nearly quit half a dozen times because things weren't happening fast enough to suit her."

"Depression, huh?"

"That's putting it mildly."

"How long were your folks married when...before he passed?"

"Forty-two years."

"Wow."

"Yeah."

The microwave dinged, startling them both.

They shared a quiet chuckle, and as he cut up a pancake for Connor, Hunter said, "I only brought it up to make the point that we shouldn't expect too much from the first couple of sessions." He dropped the squares one by one onto the high-chair tray.

"Dr. Rosen's office is near the mall in Columbia. What time do you think we should leave?"

"One-thirty ought to get us there in plenty of time."

She nodded. "Can I ask you a question?"

Hunter tensed. "Can't promise I'll answer, but… shoot."

"I'm surprised that you didn't ask how long Donald stayed last night."

"That's a statement, not a question." And when that left brow rose, he added, "I figured if you wanted me to know, you'd tell me."

He already knew that the sleek convertible had been parked at the curb until well past one. It shouldn't matter what Donald did. Or what she did…unless it affected Connor. But it mattered. A lot. And he had no idea why.

"After he left, I read Beth's diary."

He'd never heard Beth mention a diary. "Didn't realize she was into journaling."

"Neither did I." She sighed. "Just one more thing I didn't know about her." Brooke went to the sink, turned on the water and grabbed the sprayer nozzle. "It's sort of your fault that I found it."

"My fault…"

"Well, I got to wondering why you brought your

own wineglasses over. I knew Beth had her own someplace, so I went looking for them. They were still in the original boxes on a pantry shelf. And right on top, her diary."

Her voice cracked on that last syllable. Because reading it eased the pain of losing her sister...or added to it?

"Did you know that Kent was jealous of my relationship with Beth?"

A pang of guilt shot through him. "Yeah, I kind of suspected."

"Well, it came as a total shocker to me. I would have expected to read about the way she and I used to squabble over..."

She bit her lower lip, and Hunter knew why: *he* had been the cause of most—if not all—of the sisters' arguments.

"So what was it like," she asked, "growing up with three older brothers?"

It was odd, hearing her alter the subject for a change.

"I took my share of big-brother bullying, and by the time their hand-me-downs made it into my closet, the other kids thought I was trying to set new trends." He laughed at the memory. "Mostly, though, it was good. Real good."

"Sounds like you looked up to them."

"Still do." He winced. "For the most part."

Brooke stopped chewing. "You mean...you

didn't want to be a policeman, like the rest of them?"

He didn't think anyone, not even his mom, knew that. How had she figured it out from the little he'd told her?

"From the time I was old enough to hold a hammer, I wanted to be a carpenter, like my grandpa. My mom's father taught me everything I know. Including how to run a business." He had never admitted that out loud, not even to himself. Did her sudden silence mean she thought he was using this minor disappointment as a way to excuse his part in her mother's death? As if he could forget, even if he didn't picture her mother every time he looked into Brooke's eyes…eyes the exact same shade of brown as her mom's.

A minute, maybe two, passed before she said, "As long as we're admitting things—"

His heart tensed, wondering what she might say.

"—when I was talking to my new boss this morning, she said all the right things—that I should take my time, as much as I need—but of course she didn't mean it. And I can't say I blame her. I was a floor nurse years ago, and scheduling was my biggest headache. My new boss hinted around, hoping I'd have some idea when I could start. But with Connor in the shape he's in…"

"The *Is* are dotted and the *Ts* are crossed," he said. "You worried he'll get worse in day care?"

"In a word, yes. Beth was a good mom, maybe a little too good. She sheltered him so much that he'd probably have trouble adapting to day care even if she hadn't..."

Hunter wondered how long it would be before any of them could say the word: *died.*

"I have a friend who heads up the day-care program at Hopkins," he said. "Don't know much about the place, but if I know Stacy, it's great. Want me to give her a call? Set up a meeting? If she's available, maybe you can meet with her after we've had a chance to meet with Dr. Rosen."

She hesitated, but only for a moment. "Okay, but—"

"Don't worry about Connor," he said, looking at his cell phone and scrolling to Stacy's number. "If she can't see you today, I'll keep an eye on him. Whenever."

Nodding, she frowned. "But what if Dr. Rosen says day care is too much for him to handle right now?" She shuddered. "I can keep the wolf from the door for eight or ten months, but what if that isn't enough?"

She must be under a lot of pressure to voice her concerns...to him of all people.

"How about we cross that bridge when we get to it?"

Okay. So she loved Connor. Enough to give up her career if necessary. Enough to run through her savings to do right by him. But her hands were trembling and her voice shook; if she got this rattled before meeting with Rosen, how would she behave when Connor got older, and doing normal boy stuff that might land him in the E.R.?

Until this moment, he hadn't considered that his adopting Connor might relieve her of an enormous burden. Suddenly, he felt less like an ogre.

"Guess I'd better get him home," she said, "so he can get some sleep before the appointment."

"He always sleeps in the car," Hunter reminded her. "Worst-case scenario, he'll catch a twenty-minute nap on the way over."

Brooke shot him a look that was somewhere between astonishment and a scowl, and he read it to mean that she didn't like taking child-care advice from a bachelor. He started to explain when Connor started squawking. Hunter could hardly blame the little guy. He'd been perfectly content sipping juice and eating pancakes and vanilla wafers.

"Why don't you leave him here with me?" he suggested as she removed the high chair tray. "You said yourself that he kept you up half the night. Go home. Catch a few Zs. I'll give him a bath, then take him for a drive. The purr of that motor always puts him right to sleep. We could pick you up at, say, 1:15?"

"I don't need a nap," Brooke said, zipping the baby's sweatshirt jacket. "And there's no need to pick us up. We'll meet you here, and we'll leave at one-thirty, as planned."

With that, Brooke carried the baby out the door and down the porch steps. She didn't put Connor into his stroller. Instead, she rolled it behind her and half ran toward the Sheridans' house, as if trying to outrun a criminal.

He cringed slightly, because in her mind, he was that criminal.

CHAPTER ELEVEN

STACY COULDN'T MEET with Brooke after the appointment with Dr. Rosen, but she did have a half hour between Book Time and Art the following afternoon. Brooke arrived ten minutes early and, rather than interrupt story hour, sat quietly on a purple plastic stool, leafing through a Golden Book. Remembering how she'd felt before talking with the psychologist, Brooke empathized with the little Billy goat, facing the ogre on the bridge. As it turned out, her fears had been unnecessary. With any luck, the meeting with Stacy would go just as well.

Connor was far too young, the doctor said, to be told that his parents had been killed. He'd seen dead worms in the flowerbeds and dead bugs on the sidewalk, but at his age, he couldn't understand that in death the body ceases to function. And it wasn't at all unusual, Rosen added, for children who once slept well—like Connor—to have trouble falling asleep. Or staying asleep. Those with healthy appetites might develop an aversion to food, and cheerful kids could become sullen.

And Deidre had been right, the doctor said, insisting that they bring Connor to the funeral. Though he couldn't fully comprehend the meaning of loss and mourning, memories of these days would help him cope years down the road. "Even the youngest infants remember their parents," the doctor had said. "It's a powerful bond, and believe me, they notice when something as permanent as death interferes with it."

To avoid attachment disorder—which could result in an inability to trust people in the future—it was important for Brooke, Hunter and Deidre to give Connor as much attention and affection as possible, particularly when he acted out with tantrums and crying jags. Above all, it was imperative that they keep change to a minimum. "Stick to routines, like baths and meals and bedtime," the doctor said, "and if at all possible, don't expose him to something as out of the realm of his routine as day care. At least not until we see how he progresses during the next few months."

Brooke had kept her meeting with Stacy for two reasons. One, out of gratitude that she'd set aside time on such short notice, and two, to get Connor's name on the waiting list. That way, when he was ready, she could trust that his environment would be safe and the staff reliable.

A little boy sneaked away from the reading circle and peered over Brooke's shoulder.

"Hi," he said. "My name's Tony. Who are you?"

"Nice to meet you, Tony. I'm Brooke."

"You should get a different book. That's a dumb story."

Smiling, she met his dark eyes. "Oh? Why do you say that?"

"Well, first of all," he began, crossing both arms over his chest, "there's no such thing as talking goats. And there's no such thing as ogres, either."

"You make some very good points," she admitted. Before changing her major to nursing, she'd considered teaching English, and during her college literature class, Brooke read the original story, translated in 1859 by George Webbe Dasent in the collection *Norske Folkeeventyr.* "I wonder what lesson the writer was trying to teach children?" she asked, leaning toward Tony.

"That grown-ups think kids like boring stories?"

Brooke laughed, and before she could share her opinion, he added, "Did anybody ever take something that was yours?"

A schoolyard bully had stolen her two-wheeler. Her Richmond neighbor regularly "borrowed" the morning paper. An ingénue had stolen Donald. But Brooke couldn't explain all that to a five-year-old boy.

"Someone took something of yours?"

Tony glared and pointed at the little blonde front

and center in the story circle. "That's Madison," he said. "She thinks everything is hers. This morning, she took my dollar. And I was going to use it to buy a book from the book lady."

"That wasn't very nice. I wonder what made Madison do such a thing," Brooke said. "Did you tell your teacher?"

"No. Because my mom told me to be nice to Madison. She said Madison is acting out because her mom got in a car wreck last month."

Brooke thought of Connor acting out his frustrations over his mother's accident in a completely different way.

"You're a sweet boy to be so kind and patient with Madison." She couldn't tell him to try and empathize with the girl. Doing that would only give the poor kid nightmares and who knew what else. "I'm sure Madison will be nice again after a while. But I'm also sure it wasn't easy for you letting her get away with taking your book money."

He pouted, looking at Madison, but when his gaze met Brooke's his expression brightened. "But it's okay. I can always get another dollar. She'll never get her mommy back."

Brooke's hand tightened on her purse.

She opened it, handed Tony two crisp one-dollar bills. "You deserve two books," she said. "One for being such a thoughtful boy and one for not being mean to Madison."

"Wow," he said, grinning. "Thanks, Miss Brooke!"

A pretty young woman approached. "Sorry to keep you waiting, Miss O'Toole." She held out a hand. "I'm Stacy, Hunter's friend?"

"Please, call me Brooke. And you didn't keep me waiting—I got here early. Thanks to this young man," she said, winking at Tony, "the time passed quickly."

"This young man," Stacy said, smiling, "should be over there, drawing a picture to explain what this morning's story was about."

Tony pocketed his dollar bills. "I've heard *Never Tease a Weasel,* like, a hundred times." He trudged toward the big round table where his classmates sat scribbling. "And anyways, I never drawed a weasel before."

"Drew a weasel," Stacy corrected. But Tony didn't hear her, because he'd already grabbed a box of crayons from his cubby and started on his picture. Facing Brooke, she said, "Do you mind if we talk in there?" Stacy led the way to the small glass-walled office that connected four classrooms. "My assistant had a dentist's appointment this morning, so I'm keeping an eye on her kids, too, just for a few hours."

She cleared a stack of file folders from the chair beside her desk and as Brooke sat down added, "I heard the tail end of your conversation with Tony.

If you ever want to leave nursing, you'd be perfect for this job. I love the way you helped him see Madison's point of view!"

"I asked a couple of questions. Tony did the rest himself."

"Oh, trust me. You did more than that. A lot more. You're a natural with kids."

It felt good hearing a child expert say such a thing. Maybe she could get Connor over this hump and help him transition into life without his mom and dad. It would help him adjust to a setting like this, too, and at the park, or anywhere he'd interact with other kids…when he was ready.

"Don't mind me," Stacy said, laughing. "As Hunter can tell you, I have a tendency to dream out loud."

Few things could have surprised Brooke more than the jolt of envy that shot through her at the suggestion that Hunter and this lovely young woman had been more than friends. She didn't have time to dwell on it, though, because Stacy launched into a recitation of a typical day at the facility, handing Brooke page after page of information as she talked: drop-off and pickup times, payment options, immunization requirements, and permission forms she'd have to fill out and sign before Connor's first day of school.

Brooke explained what Dr. Rosen had said, and asked if filing the paperwork now would save time when Connor was ready to enroll. Comforted by the young woman's assurances, she said, "Sounds like you love this work."

"Oh, I do," Stacy said, "I really do! And you know, it's funny, because I wouldn't even be here if it hadn't been for Hunter."

"Oh?"

"Once upon a time, he and I had a 'thing.'" Grinning, she leaned closer. "The truth is, I'm the one who had a 'thing.'" Stacy laughed again. "He's a sweetheart, don't get me wrong. But…I wanted the whole nine yards. Fairy-tale wedding, island honeymoon, then home to a house with a white picket fence that we'd fill up with chubby-cheeked kids. Hunter? I think the only time we exchanged cross words was when I forced him to admit that he didn't want any such thing."

Didn't want a life like that with Stacy? Or with anyone, ever?

Stacy laid a hand on Brooke's forearm and gave it a gentle squeeze. "Don't look so surprised, hon! I think I knew all along that I wasn't his type. And as it turns out, he wasn't what I was looking for, either."

She went on to explain how after the breakup, she dated a few guys on the rebound. "And then I met the man of my dreams. A pediatrician— Connor's doctor, as a matter of fact. We met at one of the Stone family parties. Josh and Hunter were best buds in high school. Went their separate ways for a while but stayed in touch. So imagine my surprise when I helped my sister bring her twins in for a checkup, and Josh was the great Dr. Miller she'd been raving about. I mean, Miller is one of the most common names in the phone book, y'know?"

Brooke hadn't made the connection, either.

A dreamy smile lit Stacy's face as she continued, "Anyway, the rest is history." She pointed at the young girl and boy sitting on either side of Tony. "Those are mine. Ours, I'm proud to say. When this job opened up, I put my degree in early childhood development to use and applied for the position. Lucky me, I got the job!"

"I'm sure luck had very little to do with it," Brooke said. "It's easy to see you're very good at what you do. This place runs like a top."

Stacy studied Brooke's face for a second or two. "Just so you know…if you ever need a letter of recommendation for any reason, Hunter is your man."

The comment came so far from left field that Brooke didn't know how to react.

"Josh and I both value his opinion. And the kids—oh, you should see their eyes light up when they hear their uncle Hunter is coming over. When he called to get us together, he said you're good people, and that's good enough for me."

Brooke tilted her head, knowing that she hadn't earned his loyalty or his words of praise.

"Oh, there you go looking surprised again. He told me why you've mostly avoided him. In your shoes, I might have done the same."

Might have done the same, meaning at some point over the years, Stacy would have accepted the olive branch.

"I didn't intend to tie up your whole morning," Stacy said, standing. "But it's your own fault for being so easy to talk to!" She smiled. "Looks like Hunter was right about that, too. I just hope I haven't made you late for your appointment with Adele."

"No," Brooke said, checking her watch. "No, I have plenty of time." It wasn't as though she were in any hurry to tell her future boss that she didn't know when—or if—she could start work.

Stacy walked with her as far as the door. "No huge rush getting all those forms filled out, signed and delivered. Whenever Connor is ready, give me a call, and we'll see what we can do about moving him to the top of the waiting list."

"I appreciate that. And thanks for seeing me on such short notice. It's been a genuine pleasure meeting you."

"Believe me, the pleasure is all mine. Tell Adele I said hi."

She remembered from her days at Johns Hopkins School of Nursing that the hospital was the size of a small city—big enough to require its own zip code and post office. Brooke made good use of the long walk between the day-care center and her future boss's office by trying to figure out how she'd phrase things…and hoping that by asking for what could be months of patience, she wouldn't lose the job altogether.

She arrived with two minutes to spare, barely time to grab a magazine from the table in the waiting room before Adele Mitchell opened her office door. After exchanging pleasantries, she invited Brooke to have a seat.

"Thanks for agreeing to meet with me on such short notice, Ms. Mitchell."

"No thanks necessary. And please, call me Adele." She sat behind her desk and opened Brooke's application folder. "So how are things going at home?"

This was hardly the time for full disclosure; Adele wanted proof that Brooke could balance work and family even during difficult times. "For the most part, we're all adjusting fairly well," she said, choosing her words carefully.

"Remarkable, all things considered. Did the plant we sent arrive in time?"

"It was lovely. I mailed the thank-you notes last week."

Adele leaned forward and lowered her voice to

say, "It was my first time using that florist, and I just wanted to make sure you liked the arrangement." Sitting back again, she said, "Have you had a chance to find a place of your own yet?"

"Yes and no. I've made arrangements to take over my sister's mortgage so that Connor won't have to adjust to a new home in addition to everything else."

"Makes perfect sense." Adele handed Brooke a chart. "That's your schedule for the remainder of April. Take a few minutes to look it over, and if you see anything that looks unreasonable, I can probably make adjustments."

Brooke didn't need a few minutes. "I hate to be difficult," she began, "especially after you've been so patient and understanding, but my nephew is only eighteen months old. I'm afraid he isn't coping well with the loss of his parents. We've started seeing a child psychologist, who made it pretty clear that I need to protect him from any drastic changes in his routine right now." She tapped the schedule. "I'm afraid swing shifts are out of the question. At least for the time being."

Adele folded her hands on the desk, nodding.

Brooke didn't know her well enough to tell the difference between thoughtful contemplation and well-controlled annoyance.

"Exactly how much more time will you need?"

"I wish I knew. A couple of months, maybe?"

Adele sighed. "I was afraid you'd say that. Problem is, I should have filled this position weeks ago and my nurses have about had it with all the extra hours."

Brooke's heart sank. "I understand." And she did. In Adele's shoes, she might not have been as tolerant. "I don't suppose there's a part-time nursing position open. Maybe I could relieve some of the nurses on the day shift, just until Connor has settled in and can handle day care?"

Adele typed something into her computer. "No, I'm afraid our only open jobs right now are full-time."

And then she brightened. "I do have one part-time job open, though. It's a thirty-hour work week, days, mostly, but the salary isn't anywhere near what we promised you as a trauma nurse." She printed out the job description. "As you'll see," she said, giving it to Brooke, "your hours would be far more flexible."

Patient advocate, Brooke read. And when she reached the salary paragraph, she inhaled sharply.

"I know," Adele said, frowning. "Far less than what you'd make as a trauma nurse." She brightened slightly to add, "But you'd qualify for benefits, and I'd throw in a parking pass. And since it's days, I'm hoping day care won't be a major issue. You have family to help out, right?"

Nodding, Brooke scanned the first paragraph of the job description:

> With duties comparable to that of a social worker, the ideal candidate will possess knowledge of medical terminology, and excellent communication skills are a must. The ideal candidate will act as a collaborator between patients and hospital staff, as well as between patients' family members and hospital staff.

"You've been very up-front with me," Adele continued, "so I feel it's only fair to be honest with you, too." She pointed at the nursing schedule, then at the job description. "It's one or the other, and in either case, it's ASAP."

"If you don't mind my asking, why is the current advocate leaving?"

"Her husband is taking a transfer to Chicago. But they aren't leaving for another three weeks, so she'll have time to train you."

Brooke knew she had no choice but to accept the job. She also knew that in addition to becoming an emissary between hospital staff and patients and their families, she'd be a juggler-in-training, too, as she learned to balance house- and yard work, caring for a troubled toddler and the demands of a brand-new career.

"If it's any consolation, Brooke, I was in a similar position not long ago. Divorced, hadn't worked outside the home in years, faced with providing for my daughter on the next-to-nothing child support my ex paid...when he was in the mood. It took a few months to figure it all out, but eventually it all came together."

Brooke nodded again. "How soon would you need me to start?"

"Monday? Wednesday at the latest."

That didn't leave much time to find someone to care for Connor while she worked...someone he already knew and felt comfortable with. Someone like Hunter?

CHAPTER TWELVE

"So? What do you think? Can you help out?"

"You know I'll give you as much time as I can, honey."

Brooke heard the hesitation in her grandmother's response, and listed all the unspoken reasons behind it: *The play only just opened. I have half a dozen fund-raisers lined up. I'm seventy-five years old....*

"I promise, Gram, it'll only be a few hours a day, for a few weeks. I've already started interviewing sitters. When I find one that Connor seems comfortable with, I'll have her over—a lot—so he'll get so used to her that he won't think a thing of it when I'm at work."

"I'll talk with Felix. That old handyman of mine loves that baby almost as much as we do. And the feeling is mutual."

"That's true." And it was only temporary.

"So what does a patient advocate do, exactly?" her grandmother wanted to know.

Brooke did her best to quote the job description Adele had given her.

"Ah, like that sweet young thing who stepped in to help us when your grandfather was so ill."

Brooke remembered the woman who went to bat for Deidre half a dozen times, easing her worries and fears and resolving misunderstandings between her and the medical staff.

"Do you really think you have the personality for a job like that?"

Wondering if she'd fail or succeed in the job already had her nerves on edge. "Good grief, Gram. Why would you ask such a question?"

"Because as a trauma nurse, you never had to get involved with patients. They were flown in from one emergency or another, you fixed them up and off they went to the coronary unit or Pediatrics...or the morgue. There wasn't time to get caught up in family dynamics. And if the hospital lost a patient, you weren't responsible for delivering the bad news, either. But this job? It'll require you to make personal connections, to sooth fears and ease grief, and not just for a few hours, either."

Thanks for the vote of confidence, she thought. "Gram. Please. I can handle it."

"Don't make me laugh," Deidre said. "You. With your intimacy issues."

Brooke didn't need to ask for an explanation.

"Need I remind you that except for the Donald debacle, *you* ended every relationship you were involved in?"

No, you needn't remind me.

"Oh, now, don't look hurt. You know I love you. If I don't tell it like it is, who will?"

"Well, you've got me there," Brooke said, grinning.

"Have you told Hunter yet?"

"No. Not yet."

"After all he's done for us lately? Why not?"

"Yes, he's done a lot for us, but he's also grown territorial." And before Deidre had a chance to launch into another Hunter the Wonderful speech, Brooke said, "I realize he and Connor were close before the accident and that they need to go right on seeing one another as often as possible to help the baby adjust to life without Beth and Kent. And that they'll almost definitely stay close, indefinitely. I get that. In fact, I approve of it. But that doesn't mean I have to get involved in all the... closeness."

"Mmm-hmm," Deidre said to the ceiling. She clucked her tongue. "Honestly, Brooke. How do you hope to meet strangers' needs—when they're at their most vulnerable—when you're completely blind to what Hunter needs? Or...are you just so heartless that you refuse to see it?"

Brooke had long ago accepted that Deidre would always believe Hunter could do no wrong. That didn't mean she had to like it. Or agree.

"All he needs is access to his 'little buddy,'"

she said, drawing quote marks in the air. *And you singing his praises at every turn.* "I'll make sure you have everything you need," she said. "Diapers, sippy cups, juice and snacks, toys… Thank goodness I have until Wednesday to get ready."

"I have to say, it isn't like you to leave things until the last minute."

"I just got word about my start date."

"Mmm-hmm."

Brooke closed her eyes and summoned patience. "Well, I'd better get home and relieve Hunter. Thanks for agreeing to help out, Gram." She kissed her cheek. "See you Wednesday morning."

She was halfway down the walk when Deidre called out, "Bring earplugs, or the deal's off!"

Brooke kept walking as if she hadn't heard the remark. Her grandmother was probably kidding. "But just in case," she muttered, "I'd better test my earphones, see if they'll do in a pinch."

Hunter was out back when she arrived at Beth's, walking the backyard fenceline with Connor on his shoulders.

"This," he said, pointing, "is called a picket. And that," he added, "is a knothole." In the corner of the yard, he stopped, grabbed a low-hanging tree branch. "And this," he said, breaking off its tip, "is a twig. Can you say that? Too-wig."

"Too-wig," Connor echoed, inspecting it.

Hunter showed Connor the gate, its hinges and

its latch, enunciating the words, then waiting patiently while the baby repeated them.

"Any minute now," Brooke said, joining them, "I expect to hear the Mr. Rogers theme song."

Turning, Hunter smiled. In one tick of her watch, it looked as though he was glad to see her. In the next, his smile faded as guarded realization set in.

"Look who's here," he said, taking Connor's hand, waving it at Brooke.

The baby studied her face for a moment and rested his head on Hunter's shoulder...facing away from her. Surely the baby wasn't old enough to punish her for leaving him with other people.

Was he?

Hunter was watching her. Closely. Brooke did her best to hide how much it had hurt seeing something akin to rejection on Connor's face, and in his body language.

"Poor kid is exhausted," Hunter said, taking a step closer. "Tried to put him down for a nap, but he wasn't having any of it. After three tries, I cried uncle. Thought maybe some fresh air would make him sleepy." Now he looked at Connor. "But no dice, right, buddy?"

It annoyed her that he was behaving like Connor's dad. And that he felt it necessary to make excuses for the baby's obvious rebuff. But she couldn't, wouldn't let it show.

"Stacy is terrific," she said, forcing cheerfulness into her voice that she didn't feel. "She put Connor on the waiting list and said that whenever he's ready, she'll make sure there's space for him at the day-care center."

"That's great." He took the porch steps two at a time, then held the screen door for her.

"Aren't you afraid you'll trip or lose your balance climbing the stairs that way?"

His eyes narrowed, but only slightly, before he said, "I'd never do anything to put Connor in harm's way. You can take that to the bank."

She followed him inside feeling very much like a chastised child. But she wouldn't give him the satisfaction of knowing how self-conscious it made her feel. After hanging her purse and jacket on a hook beside the door, Brooke shook the teakettle.

"Good," she said, firing up the burner, "a full pot." She grabbed two mugs. "Coffee or tea?"

Hunter held up a hand. "I'm good. But thanks." He strapped Connor into his high chair and dropped some Kix cereal onto the tray. "So how did your meeting with your future boss go?"

She told him about the patient-advocate opening and how she'd agreed to give it a try. "Deidre was all over me about it earlier," she admitted, popping a tiny cereal ball into her mouth. "She thinks I'm all wrong for the job. Or it's all wrong for me."

He frowned. "No disrespect to your grandmother, but sometimes she can be harsh."

Yes. She could. But admitting it would be disloyal.

"So what's her problem with the job?"

Brooke hesitated, because if he agreed, she didn't know what she might say.

"Not that my opinion counts for much, but I think you'll be great at it."

That surprised her. "Why?"

"Well, you're usually outgoing and friendly—"

Was it her imagination, or had he verbally underscored *usually?*

"—organized and smart. With your background in the medical field, it seems like a job that's tailor-made for you."

"When do you start?"

"Wednesday."

Frowning, Hunter leaned back in the chair. "Yeah? And who's gonna mind this li'l guy?"

"Once I'm fully trained, I'll work thirty hours, but until then it's half days. Deidre and Felix will take turns watching him."

"Deidre?" he asked, raising a brow.

He was probably echoing her own concerns: Deidre was seventy-five, Felix just shy of that. Could they handle an active toddler? Especially one with emotional issues?

"I've already started looking for someone to

pick up the slack. Once I find a reliable care-giver—one who gets along well with Connor—she—or he—will stay here at the house with him until my hours increase. If things work out, he may never need to make the adjustment to day care."

"Sounds like you have things all figured out."

He sounded peeved, no doubt because he'd been a regular part of Connor's life, almost from day one. She understood that Hunter expected her to include him in the final decision. But did he really expect her to inform him of every detail about the search and the interviews?

"I have some bad news," he said.

"What kind of bad news?" Brooke asked slowly.

"Tried to make a pot of coffee while you were gone and blew a fuse. And when I went into the basement to replace it, I saw that the wiring is shot. If we don't bring it up to code, this whole place is pretty much a fire trap."

A fire trap? "Not the whole house…"

"Afraid so."

She could keep up with the mortgage and regular household bills, thanks to her savings account, but with the cut in her salary, Brooke wondered how she'd pay to have the place rewired.

"I have skids of materials left over from other jobs just sitting around taking up space at the shop. Say the word and I'll get started."

"I guess I should be grateful the place didn't go

up in smoke." Her hands were shaking, and she clasped them together.

"You'll do the work yourself?"

"My crew, working alongside a licensed electrician."

She sighed. "How long will it take?"

"Depends on what we find when we tear out the walls. If we're lucky, *all* we'll find is outdated wiring. Could take a couple months."

"Months?" She groaned softly.

"Keep in mind that this place is pushing a hundred and twenty-five years old. I'll work the guys as hard as I can, but to preserve the historic integrity and make it safe for you to live in, we'll have to approach with caution."

Eyes closed, she tilted her head toward the ceiling.

"Look at the bright side."

"What bright side?"

"You're paying the bills around here now. You're well within your rights to turn it into the home of your dreams."

Chin on her chest, she inspected her fingernails. "I'm not sure I can handle that much change right now."

Connor threw a handful of Kix, then whined because his tray was empty.

"And neither can Connor," she said, adding another handful of cereal to his tray. "But that's beside the point."

"Well, you'll have some time to think about it. Last I heard, Deidre's garage apartment was available, but if it isn't, you guys are welcome to stay with me during construction. I'll hole up in the den and you and Connor will have the whole upstairs, all to yourselves."

Oh. Right. Move in. With the guy who'd played a role in her mother's death.

"That's very thoughtful, but last I heard, Gram's garage apartment was vacant. Connor has been up there dozens of times, so it won't feel like a strange new place." On her hands and knees, she started picking up the cereal he'd thrown. "How soon do you want to start?" she asked without looking up.

"The sooner, the better. I can probably line up a crew by day after tomorrow."

On her feet now, Brooke dumped the cereal into the trash can, starting up a whole new round of wailing from Connor.

"Mine!" he shouted, pounding his tray. "My Kix!"

She rummaged in the cupboard and found the box of teething biscuits. Today was Monday…for a few more hours, anyway. She'd start a new job on Wednesday and had three interviews lined up with potential sitters tomorrow. What choice did she have but to postpone them and move her things and Connor's from the house to the apartment instead?

"I have enough in savings to pay for the move," she said, mostly to herself. "Gram puts on a good show, but she's not as well off as she likes people to think." She sighed. "I'll need to pay rent while making mortgage payments. And utilities and—"

"Well, you can cross construction materials off the list. I already told you. I have everything we'll need over at the shop. Stuff left over from other jobs. Rehab won't cost you anything but time and patience and the inconvenience of living in a three-room apartment until we're finished here." He hesitated, then added, "You could cross rent off the list, too, if you and Connor moved in with me."

She shook her head. "No offense, Hunter. I'm grateful for all you've done for us these past few weeks. But we can't move in with you, because..." It was her turn to hesitate. "Because—"

"Because I killed your mother."

"No. It's... Seriously. How would it look...me living in your house?"

Hunter nodded. "Okay," he said, drawing out the word. "I hear ya. Loud and clear." He put his mug in the sink, none too gently. "We need to get Connor out of this place, the sooner, the better." He walked toward the door. "I have some cartons at the shop. I'll drive over and get them, and while

I'm gone, maybe you can sort through the things we'll box up when I get back."

He opened the door, started to leave but changed his mind. "How long since there was a tenant in that apartment?"

"I don't know. Six months? A year, maybe?"

"Then it's probably a pigsty." He ran a hand through his hair. "Soon as Connor has something to eat, I'll drive you both to Deidre's. After you put him to bed at her house, meet me at the apartment. We'll get the place cleaned up, and then I'll bring your stuff upstairs."

She started to object, but he didn't give her a chance.

"You start a new job on Wednesday. If we don't get this done tonight and tomorrow…" He shrugged, as if to say, *When* do *you expect to get it done?*

Did he always have to be *right?*

"Look. I know you're determined to walk in Beth's organic shoes, but Connor can't have cereal for supper and I don't have time to hunt for a health food store. So I'll pick up chicken nuggets for him, and burgers and fries for you and me—"

Though she hadn't said a word, he held up a hand.

"—and I'll bet Stone Contracting on this—one fast-food meal won't kill any of us."

Then he stomped out and slammed the door behind him.

Hunter probably hadn't made it to the corner stop sign before it hit her: he loved Connor as much as she did.

Why else would he be so angry?

CHAPTER THIRTEEN

THE BREATH CAUGHT in her throat when she heard the rumble of his truck's motor.

For Connor's sake, she had to find a way to put the past behind her.

Starting now.

She opened the door for him, and when Connor saw the tower of cartons, he jumped up and down in his playpen. "Uncle Hunter!" he said, pointing. "Big blocks? Blocks for Conner?"

Chuckling, Hunter peeked around the stack. "They're boxes, buddy, not blocks."

His expression went from pleasant to dour as he shifted his attention to Brooke. "Where do you want these?"

This didn't seem the time to issue a half-baked apology. She cleared a space near the closet. "Just drop them here."

And when he did, Connor said, "Boxes go boom."

One glance at Connor was all it took to soften Hunter's hard expression.

"C'mere, you li'l pip-squeak," he said, lifting

Connor high into the air, "before your jumping tears that playpen apart at the seams!"

"Fuzzy?" Connor said, patting Hunter's cheeks. "Uncle Hunter fuzzy."

"Yeah, I guess you could call me that." He grabbed Connor's hand and gently whiskered his palm. "Fuzzy Wuzzy was a bear," he said as the boy giggled. "Fuzzy Wuzzy had stubbly hair."

It was good to hear Connor laughing, good to see Hunter happy, too, and she hoped the contented mood would last.

"What're you grinning about?" he asked her.

Until that moment, Brooke hadn't realized she was grinning. An opportunity to bridge the gap her recent rudeness had put between them? Only one way to find out....

"I was just thinking—"

"Uh-oh," he said, left brow rising slightly.

Her college psych professor used to do that... right before launching into a humdrum lecture. She didn't like the class, but it had been a requirement for her nursing degree. The comparison of Hunter to the teacher seemed weird on a couple of levels. For one thing, Mr. Delano had been short, chubby and mostly bald, and thanks to the fluorescent glare on his thick horn-rimmed lenses, she'd never seen the color of his eyes. Something told her they hadn't been long-lashed and hazel like Hunter's. For another thing, Hunter had never lectured her, even when she'd been wrong.

"I was thinking—that you look as good in jeans and a T-shirt as you did in a suit and tie."

The eyebrow returned to its normal position. "Thanks." He pursed a corner of his mouth. "I think."

Not his usual soothing DJ voice, but what did she expect, making up an answer on the spot that way?

"Be right back. The burgers are in the truck."

Minutes later, as she doled out paper plates, he put the paper sack on the table.

"I didn't take you for a cheeseburger kind of gal, so I got you a regular burger."

"You figured right."

He put Connor into the high chair. "So this no-cheese thing of yours," he said, sprinkling a few fries onto the tray, "is it a diet thing?"

She placed a napkin beside each plate. "It's more a texture thing."

"Good, because you're the last person who needs to watch her weight."

So he'd noticed something other than her bad manners, had he?

"Guess I made the right call, then, getting you regular instead of diet soda?"

"Hunter, I need to explain. No, not explain. I need to say…I'm sorry."

"Sorry?" he repeated, wiping crumbs from Connor's chin. "Sorry for what?"

"For taking my bad mood out on you earlier. You didn't deserve that. Especially after all you've done for us lately."

"No big deal." He unwrapped his burger. "It's been a rough few weeks. Guess you're entitled to be a little short-tempered." He slid the pickle to the middle of the burger and put the top bun back on. "Besides, I've had years to get used to having you mad at me."

Brooke flinched. She'd left herself wide open for that one.

Connor held up a chicken nugget. "Dip?" he said. "Conner dip?"

She watched Hunter peel back the cover of a sweet-and-sour container, then hold it tight as Connor dunked.

"It's been rough for all of us," she continued. "That doesn't give me the right to behave like a spoiled brat."

He leaned back in his chair and took a big bite of his burger. "So what're your thoughts about leaving Connor with Deidre," he said around it, "while we get your stuff moved up there?"

She glanced at the baby, who seemed satisfied... for the moment. "We can probably let him stay here in his own bed for just one more night." Now he had her saying we, too.

"My thoughts exactly."

"Tomorrow once we've moved the boxes from your truck to the apartment, you're welcome to get back to work. Or relax at home. I can handle the unpacking."

Hunter only nodded as Brooke listened to the steady tick of the wall clock and Connor's nonstop mumbling. A jet roared overhead, and in the distance the rumble of a lawn mower competed with the whine of a weed whacker. And paper crinkled as Hunter wadded burger and fry wrappers into tight balls and bank-shot them, one by one, into the trash can.

With all that going on, why did the room seem strangely silent?

An hour later, Brooke packed towels and bed linens while Hunter emptied the baby's toys into a box. He'd barely said a word since she'd tucked Connor in for the night. Maybe a joke would break the somber mood.

"Look at these," she said, holding up a pair of tiny tasseled bedroom slippers. "Did his feet graduate or something?"

It might as well have been Donald hunched grimly over that carton. Except…Donald wouldn't have offered to help her pack. Or make the repairs at Beth's that inspired the move in the first place.

Brooke tried again and held up a blanket sleeper

emblazoned with a big yellow crown. "Where does a baby king keep his armies?"

Hunter glanced at the pj's and frowned. "Where?"

"In his sleevies, of course!"

"I'd laugh," he said around the hint of a smile, "but...I wouldn't want to wake Connor."

"I don't know why, but I'm reminded of something Donald said the first—and only time we played chess."

"I'll probably regret asking, but what did he say?"

"Half an hour into the game, he said, 'I know how to make this game more interesting!'" She gave him a moment to consider the possibilities, then added, "He packed up the game pieces and put the board away."

Hunter's eyes narrowed slightly. And then he said, "Looks like we're finished here. How 'bout we head into your room?"

On the day Brooke arrived from Richmond, she'd put her suitcase on the extra twin bed in Beth's guest room...and that was where it sat now.

"It won't take long, since I never really unpacked."

"But you've been here for more than a month."

"It didn't make sense to go to all that bother for just a few days, since I expected to move into my own place after..."

Hunter sat on the stool of the gliding rocker beside the playpen. "After Beth and Kent came home," he finished, patting the chair's cushion.

She'd decided to be a little more polite, but it seemed a bit extreme to start by sitting nose to nose with him.

Then why was she doing it?

He leaned back a bit as she stepped between him and the stool, waited until she was settled and took her hands in his. "You're shaking like a leaf. Are you cold?"

"I'm fine."

Hunter blew a stream of air through his lips. "There's no shame in admitting you're scared. Letting your guard down once in a while is healthy."

Brooke had been cynical and cautious for so long she didn't know if she remembered how to let down her guard. Those who knew her best said she'd been mistrustful almost from birth. But they were wrong. And the proof could be found in her personal phone directory, where half a dozen former boyfriends' names had been crossed out. She'd trusted every one, and look where it got her.

"I know you're tough," Hunter continued, "but even you have a breaking point."

"I'm fine," she said again.

"Do you have a girlfriend? A guy friend? Someone you can talk to about all of this? Who can maybe help you make sense of—"

Brooke withdrew her hands. "I don't need to talk to anyone." And even if she did, where would she find the time!

"Okay," he said, nodding. "But…if you change your mind, if you ever need a sounding board…" He extended both hands palms up.

Deidre, Beth, Kent—they all felt she'd overreacted that night in the O.R. waiting room, when she'd accused Hunter of killing her mother. Even if he had walked into the store with his partner, they said, the outcome would have been the same. Brooke's rational mind knew they were probably right. But what if they weren't? What if instead, her *ir*rational side had been right: If he'd been where he was supposed to be, might he have stopped the gunman sooner, saving his partner and her mom and the others who'd been there that night?

"Why don't you put your feet up for a few minutes and let me finish up in here?"

"No, you've already done—"

"Brooke, Brooke, Brooke," he said, shaking his head. "Why is it so all-fired hard for you to let people do things for you?"

"You're kidding, right?" She pictured him on all fours, helping clean up the mess on the porch, on the kitchen floor. And sitting beside her at the bank and funeral parlor, lending moral support. He'd taken charge of Connor at the cemetery so that she and Deidre could participate in the memorial, though he'd experienced a double loss, too.

"You've been doing things for me since that awful morning. Maybe you're the one who has a hard time letting people—"

"Not 'people,' Brooke. Just you."

"Me? But why?"

"Because of what I did—or rather, what I didn't do that night. I turned your life upside down. Along with your dad's and Beth's. And ultimately, Kent's and Connor's, too." He exhaled a shaky sigh. "I know I can never make it up to you—"

A lot had changed in a few short weeks, she thought.

"—but I will do everything in my power to make your life a little easier. If you'll let me."

She wanted to believe him. Wanted to put the past behind them, let bygones be bygones. Easier said than done, she thought, remembering how many times she'd put her faith in a man's empty promises and ended up feeling stupid and used.

Brooke should have stood up right then and there. Might have summoned the nerve to put a safe distance between them…

…if he hadn't chosen that moment to wrap her in a reassuring hug.

CHAPTER FOURTEEN

IT HAD BEEN a knee-jerk reaction, pulling her close. He'd had no one but himself to blame when she gave him a gentle shove that left him feeling a little confused and a whole lot like a villain. He'd been up half the night thinking about that moment. Wondering why he kept putting himself in that ridiculous position.

With Brooke, it was three steps forward and two steps back. Just when he thought he was getting through to her, she hit him with a stinging reminder of the past. Every time it seemed he'd removed a brick in the wall between them, she added another instead. If the plane crash, if sharing Connor's care all these weeks, couldn't tear it down, what could?

Now, Brooke was on her knees in the passenger seat, fetching the toy Connor had pitched onto the floor yesterday. That kid was the only reason Hunter put up with her mood swings. But he had no room to talk about moods. Half the time, he resented the way she treated him. The other half, he felt like a goofy kid plucking petals from a daisy, chanting, "She likes me, she likes me not." Trouble was, the ritual game accomplished nothing... except to destroy the flower.

At least one good thing had come of last night's pacing. He'd decided that he'd keep his hands—and his feelings—to himself from now on. And that he'd check in with his lawyer just as soon as she and Connor were moved into the apartment. A week from now, *he'd* add a brick to the wall. Because he was tired of trying to protect her from stress and angst when she clearly didn't give a fig about him...unless he was doing something to make her life easier. Like minding Connor when she couldn't. And hefting boxes so she wouldn't have to.

"You're awfully quiet this morning," she said.

"Didn't sleep well last night." *Thanks to you.*

"Oh. Sorry."

"No big deal. After fifteen years of insomnia, I'm used to it."

Was it his imagination, or did he sound like a whiny, sympathy-seeking brat to her, too? Would she put two and two together? Realize that his inability to sleep started on the night her mother's life ended? Hunter had no answers. Didn't need them. Because after today, he was done. D-O-N-E, done.

He parked in the driveway, as close as possible to the long narrow staircase that hugged Deidre's garage wall. Connor had nodded off in the back-seat, so he said, "Might as well let him sleep, since one or both of us will be able to keep an eye on him until we've off-loaded your stuff."

Before she had a chance to object, he added, "How 'bout you unlock the door while I grab a few cartons." He got out of the truck and took care not to slam the door. She sat in the front seat for a moment, probably mulling over the message his attitude had just sent her: *you're not holding the reins anymore.*

He'd never seen her move at anything less than breakneck speed, so it didn't surprise him when she raced up the stairs in less time than it took him to drop the pickup's tailgate. Hunter slid three car-tons from the truck bed and, peering around the tower of boxes, saw Brooke standing stock-still on the white-painted 5 x 5 landing.

"What's wrong?" he called. "Did you lose the key?"

She came to life, but only enough to shake her head. She said something, too, but he couldn't make it out from this distance. He left the boxes on the tailgate and jogged across the lawn. It sure would be a blessing when he didn't have to baby-sit her anymore.

When he reached her, she pointed, and he knew in a blink what she had muttered earlier: *Spider.*

In his work as a contractor, he'd found raccoon dens, bats, bird nests, snake skins—some with the snakes still in them—and rats the size of small dogs during the demolition phase of home-improvement projects. He'd seen his share of spiders, too, but never one like this.

It skittered to the edge of its fly-dotted web, as if daring them to enter.

Brooke backed up as far as the railing would allow. "My cell phone is in my purse. On your front seat. Do you have yours with you?"

"It's on the dash," he said without taking his eyes from the spider. "Why? Who you gonna call, Web Busters?"

"I was thinking of taking its picture and sending it to the Guinness people."

"To the…" He stifled a laugh. "Seriously?"

If her indignant expression was any indicator, she was.

"The thing is huge, but I've seen bigger. Not that it matters. It won't live long enough to pose for a photograph."

She gave an indifferent shrug. "I know there's a broom in the kitchen, but to get it we have to go through *that*." Brooke pointed at the huge web.

"I keep one in the truck. For sweeping up saw-dust and whatnot." He started down the stairs. "If it moves—"

"—we'll find out if I can fly."

Grinning despite his foul mood, he headed for

the pickup, and while he jostled packing boxes and trash bags stuffed with clothes and toys, peripheral vision told him she hadn't budged. A minute later he was at her side again, holding the broom like a rapier. "Maybe you should wait downstairs. In case I miss."

"That would hardly be fair. You're only here because—"

"Because I want to be." And because her eyes flashed guardedly, he tacked on, "For Connor." He stabbed at the web, which clung to the broom's bristles.

And so did the spider.

It dashed up the handle, stopping a few inches shy of his fingers. In a blink, Brooke squashed it with her bare hand.

"I can't believe you just did that," he said, giving her his handkerchief.

"I'll get you a new one," she said, grimacing as she tossed it into the trash can on the landing. "Because I am *not* washing that with the rest of my laundry."

Why did she always have to even the score?

"Don't bother. I have dozens." He used the broom to knock down the remnants of the web. And once the doorway was clear, Hunter added, "Now that you've slain the eight-legged dragon, I guess we can get busy."

They heard Connor shrieking like a banshee in the backseat of the pickup.

"I'd better get him over to Deidre's," she said, "before he shatters the windows in your truck."

He watched as she raced down the stairs to free Connor from his car seat and continued watching as she balanced him on one hip. From this distance, he couldn't hear what she was saying, but whatever it was inspired a full-blown smile on the baby's face. And a hug.

"I won't be long," she called up to him. "At least, I hope not."

"Take your time. I have plenty to keep me busy."

He watched her walk up the flagstone path, stopping now and then to jump or blow kisses into the crook of Connor's neck or spin in a dizzying circle that made him giggle until he was breathless. It was such a happy, hopeful sound that it brought tears to Hunter's eyes. He loved that kid like his own, and it hurt like hell when the formerly cheerful toddler turned into an ill-tempered mess.

The baby's laughter faded as Brooke carried him deeper into the house. It seemed as though Dr. Rosen had been right. He hadn't voiced his opinion, but at the start, he'd been suspicious of the direction Dr. Rosen wanted to take Connor. Maybe she wasn't a quack after all, prescribing a slow approach to the baby's problems. Clearly showering him with love, affection and plenty of attention was working. And Brooke had doled out more of all three than he and Deidre put together. The result? Connor's behavior was improving, hour by hour.

Hunter felt grateful...but wary. Harry had warned, "It often takes longer to adopt a child than to have one by natural means," the lawyer said, "especially in cases like yours. Are you sure you want to move forward with these proceedings?" Hunter hadn't needed help decoding the question: if he was going to do this, he had to do it soon and push the paperwork through the system as quickly as possible. Because in another nine months, Connor's attachment to Brooke would be as strong as it had been to Beth. It wouldn't matter that from the age of two months, Connor had spent two or three days a week at Hunter's house. Moving him yet again might send him into another downward spiral, and this time, the boy might not find his way out.

By the time Brooke returned, Hunter had moved all of the boxes into the apartment. "Good grief," she said, looking around the living room, "did you leave anything for me to do?"

An aluminum bucket dangled from the fingertips of her left hand and the handle of a sponge mop rested on her right shoulder, making her look more like a girl on her way to the fishing hole than a nearly thirty-one-year-old woman. Hunter caught himself gawking and stood up straighter.

"I left plenty," he said. "Wait until you see the inside of that refrigerator. And the bathroom." He expelled a two-note whistle. "Hope there are some powerful cleaning supplies in that pail." Her shoulders sagged. But only a little. And only for a moment. Grudging admiration made him question Kent's opinion of her *and* his motives. Again. On occasion, when the guy went on a Brooke rant, Hunter had had a notion to dig deeper, find out what was really behind the surly attitude. But it had been easier to shrug it off as typical in-law rivalry, like the kind that caused hard feelings between his brothers' wives from time to time. Besides, much as he hated to admit being so petty, it felt good hearing Kent tear down the woman who consistently questioned his own basic decency.

Brooke lined the counter with furniture polish, dish soap and an array of other cleaning supplies. "Gram usually pays a service to get an apartment ready for a new tenant. She said giving me the tools to do the job is cheaper than hiring someone," she explained, filling the bucket with hot water. "Lucky me, huh?"

Maybe he was losing it. Not five minutes ago, he'd finessed his plan to take Connor from her. Now here he stood, feeling bad for all she'd been through lately. Admiring her pluck.

He slapped a hand to the back of his neck. "I have no idea where to start."

"You've already done more than enough. You must be exhausted."

"I'm fine," he said, "and I'm here." He spread his arms wide and grinned.

One look at her "I can handle it alone" expression was enough to tell him she was gearing up to reject his offer. But he couldn't let her. She was Connor's main caretaker. Yes, she'd handled things pretty well these past few weeks, but according to Beth, she had a definite breaking point. Hunter didn't know how much more it would take to expose it, but he knew this: he didn't want Connor around when it happened.

He reached up, stuck his finger into a cobweb. "And I'm staying," he said, wiping it on the back pocket of his jeans. "So what's the plan?"

"I'll start here in the kitchen," she said. "After I load the dishwasher with as much as it'll hold, I'll scrub the cabinets and the appliances. By the time the dishes have gone through the dry cycle, I should have the bathroom under control, too." She squirted something green into the bucket, then emptied the contents of the silverware and serving-utensils drawers into it.

"I'm fine," she said, quoting him. "Really. You don't need to stay."

"You won't be fine for long if you keep going

at this pace. Leaving Richmond, losing Beth, the prospect of starting a new job, moving in here, all while dealing with a kid whose emotions are out of whack?" He shook his head. "I'm not going anywhere. Accept it."

Brooke stacked plates, cups and tumblers into the dishwasher as he added, "Look at it this way. The sooner we're finished, the sooner you can get rid of me."

"Well," she said, grinning, "when you put it that way...."

What's going on here? he wondered. If he didn't know better, Hunter would have to say Brooke actually *liked* him.

"I hate to vacuum," she admitted. "And if it doesn't offend your male ego, maybe you could dust the furniture afterward?"

He couldn't afford to go soft now.

He vacuumed the living room rug, then rearranged and polished the furniture. Next he set up Connor's crib and gave the bureau a scrubbing that would have earned a thumbs up from his hard-to-please drill sergeant.

In the mirror above Connor's dresser, he saw Brooke across the hall, spritzing glass cleaner onto the bathroom faucet. The way she worked reminded him of a favorite childhood cartoon character. Only instead of the chaos and destruction created by the Tasmanian whirlwind, Brooke left orderly calm in her wake. He caught sight of his own reflection then, and decided it was good that she had her back to him, because if Brooke had seen the dopey look on his face, she'd know what he'd tried so hard to deny until that moment: He was falling, and falling hard.

For the next two hours, Hunter did his best to avoid her. Polishing bookshelves, knocking down cobwebs, wiping months of grime from the mini-blinds and sweeping grit from the tiny front porch kept him busy, but couldn't distract him from the whorl of confusion and indecision spinning in his brain.

He was at the sink washing his hands when Brooke asked, "Are you as exhausted as I am?"

Actually, he was dog tired, but because he suspected her question was rhetorical, he let it go unanswered. As he turned to toss his paper towel into the trash can, Hunter saw her sprawled on the couch.

She lay on her stomach, left hand under her cheek, right knee pointing into the room, reddish-brown curls splayed across the sofa arm. The sight froze the breath in his throat, because that was almost exactly how her mother had landed that night in the convenience store. He took note of his damp palms and pounding pulse.

He needed air, and needed it now. "The, ah, the

cooler is still in the truck," he stammered, one hand on the doorknob.

"I hope there's something cold to drink in it."

Hunter nodded dumbly. "Bottled water. Couple of sodas, I think." *Get out of here, you bonehead,* he thought, *before you say something you'll regret.*

Brooke levered herself onto one elbow and studied his face. Probably wondering what had come over him all of a sudden.

Hunter couldn't get out the door and down the stairs fast enough. He walked around the truck a few times, muttering, cursing under his breath, punching right fist into left palm. He looked up at the apartment she'd call home for the next few months. He'd been happy to help her make the place livable, but after seeing her on the sofa that way...

She had no way of knowing how often a simple gesture, a well-chosen word, a look could remind him of that night. Part of him didn't want to go back to the apartment and take the chance that he'd see her lying there.

"You're an idiot," he growled, grabbing the cooler's handles.

Lately, as he watched her, listened to her, interacted with her, the "Brooke's Positives and Negatives" list he'd been tallying in his head had grown considerably plus-heavy. No wonder he'd been having such crazy thoughts. No wonder he'd begun to doubt his decision to adopt Connor.

It had to stop. He needed to harden his heart. Needed to get tough.

The funerals were over. Soon, she'd start her new job. Connor had a safe place to live. It was time they all got back to square one. He'd spent half a lifetime searching for ways to earn her forgiveness. Hunter wasn't happy about it, but he knew himself well. Knew the signs, too. If he didn't back off, *way* off, he'd end up wanting a whole lot more than forgiveness.

CHAPTER FIFTEEN

DEIDRE'S YARD HADN'T seen a crowd this big since her retirement gala ten years earlier. Everywhere Brooke looked, people laughed and talked, some balancing plates piled high with picnic foods, others sipping iced tea or lemonade from frosted glass mugs, all while children batted at colorful balloons and crepe-paper streamers tied to the porch railings.

But Deidre wasn't fooling Brooke. This so-called birthday bash was, in fact, a fund-raiser where her grandmother hoped to target friends with deep pockets to fund her latest pet project.

Brooke had just poured herself a glass of lemonade when a woman stepped up beside her.

"Brooke? Brooke O'Toole? How lovely to see you!"

It had been years, but Brooke recognized her right away. "Good to see you, too, Mrs. Stone."

"Please, call me Constance." She leaned back slightly. "You just get prettier and prettier."

Brooke smiled, remembering that she'd met Hunter's mom only once, at one of Beth and Kent's backyard get-togethers. She searched for a topic of conversation that wouldn't involve Hunter. When none materialized, she said, "May I freshen your drink?"

"Just a splash," she said. And as Brooke added lemonade to her glass, Constance pointed at Deidre. "Your grandmother is an inspiration. I hope I have half her energy when I'm her age."

Brooke laughed. "I wish I had half her energy now!"

"I took the liberty of inviting my ladies' club today." She leaned in close to whisper, "I'm sure they'll contribute to her theater fund. We all think it's wonderful that she hopes to introduce under-privileged children to the arts."

"Yes," Brooke said, handing her the glass, "wonderful."

Connor toddled up just then and, whimpering, threw his arms around Brooke's legs.

"Aw, what's wrong, sweetie?" she said, putting down her glass to pick him up. "You look all tuck-ered out. You ready for a nap?"

He rested his head on her shoulder. "No nap. No nap!"

"Sorry," Brooke said over his shoulder. "He still hasn't fully adjusted to life without…"

Constance tilted her head and sent Brooke a sympathetic smile. "I can't tell you how much I admire what you're doing for this adorable little

fellow. You're so young and lovely—and single—
so I'm sure it hasn't been easy putting your whole
life on hold to take care of a child who's too young
to understand that he's grieving."

"Anyone would do the same in my position."

"No, they most certainly would not. But I suppose it is a little easier for you…with Hunter at
your beck and call, willing to help any way he
can."

At her beck and call? Yes, he'd stopped by to
see Connor every evening since she'd moved, but
Hunter had barely said three words to her directly.
Besides, she hadn't asked for his help. Not once.
Ever. Where had Constance gotten such an im-
pression?

"Hunter couldn't love that boy more," Constance continued, smiling at the baby, "and I know
he's grateful that Connor is in such good hands."

Brooke scanned the yard, and when she spotted Hunter, squinting one eye as he lined up his
horseshoe with the stake across the way, her heart
skipped a beat. The reaction made no sense given
their history. He stood taller than the other men
and, despite their various-size bellies, probably
outweighed them by twenty pounds of pure muscle.

Constance was looking at him, too, Brooke noticed.

"It's so good to see him smile," she said. "Really

smile. He's been a mess since, well, you know...."
The woman sighed. "Can't sleep, nightmares,
afraid to commit to a woman for fear he's destined
to let her down the way he let his partner down,
the way he let y—" She cleared her throat and
blinked back tears. "Breaks my mother's heart,
I tell you, watching him punish himself all these
years for something that wasn't even his fault, that
could have happened to anyone."

Where had she heard *that* before? Brooke
thought, glancing at Deidre.

Constance gave her forearm a gentle squeeze.
"You probably have no idea what a huge weight
you've lifted from his shoulders by...just by being
nice to him. I can't thank you enough." Smiling
sadly, she traced the contour of Connor's jaw. "But
I'm sure you understand exactly how I feel now
that you're a mommy."

A mommy. She watched as Constance joined
her friends, thinking that under the circumstances,
a mommy is exactly what she was. *And Hunter is
his part-time daddy,* she thought, glancing toward
the horseshoe pit. He must have sensed her watching, and when he looked at her, the sixty-plus-foot
distance separating them shrank to mere inches.

"Cake?" Connor said, pointing.

Grateful for the legitimate excuse to break the
intense eye contact, she kissed the baby's cheek.
"How about a cookie instead?" She carried Con-

nor to the dessert table and chose the smallest treat. "Pretty soon," she said, handing it to him, "Gram will light the candles on her cake, and we'll all sing 'Happy Birthday,' and *then* you can have a slice, with a big fat frosting flower on—"

"Whoa. What's this? Miss I Hate Sugar giving the okay to eat a cookie *and* cake?"

"I don't hate sugar," she defended, "in reasonable doses."

Hunter chucked Connor's chin. "Hear that? I'm your witness, buddy." Facing Brooke, he said, "So you and my mom are pals now?"

She hadn't said or done anything to rile him—at least, not that she knew of—so why did he seem so *angry?*

"Your mother is lovely, and so was our conversation." Until the woman pointed out that Brooke had caused—and eased—Hunter's grief. "But I'd hardly call us pals."

He responded with a dismissive shrug. "Think Deidre will squeeze enough money out of her guests to get her theater program up and running?"

Brooke shifted Connor to her other hip, putting herself between him and Hunter. "I think you knew the answer to that even before you asked the question." She forced a smile. "When my grandmother sets her cap for something, she doesn't give up until she gets it."

He leveled her with a steady gaze. "The way she coerced poor old Percy into marrying her?"

Not a hint of humor on his face, she noted, nor in his voice.

"Hope that isn't part of the O'Toole genes."

Even if trickery *was* in her family's DNA, she failed to see how it concerned him, since they'd never be more than… Brooke didn't know how to define their relationship, so she didn't even try.

"Connor's sippy cup is empty," she said. "I should get him a refill."

Hunter relieved her of it, unscrewed the top and looked inside. "Instant lemonade? I'm surprised you're okay with him drinking this stuff," he said, filling the cup. "It's loaded with preservatives."

"And I'm a little surprised that you're still beating that dead horse. Will you let the 'natural foods' thing go, already!"

When Hunter laughed, heads turned. And Brooke blushed.

He poured himself a glass and brought it to his lips. "So what sort of family secrets did my mother reveal?"

He looked a little sexy—and a whole lot dangerous—staring at her that way over the glass's rim.

"No secrets." Brooke tried to sound as bored as possible. "She just reiterated what everyone else has been saying…that Gram is a saint for trying to help underprivileged kids, and I'm a saint for taking Connor in when not everyone would."

His eyes narrowed. "*I* would. In a heartbeat."

Five words, each sounding more like a threat than the last. For the hundredth time, she wished that Beth and Kent had left a will.

He sipped his drink, then nodded at Connor. "How did he sleep last night?"

"Better. Two three-hour stretches, with a one-hour cry-fest in between."

"Me, too." He chuckled. "Except for the cry-fest. Well, that isn't entirely true. I blubbered a little thinking about that big fat check I wrote to your grandmother." His eyes widened as Brooke stiffened. "What, she didn't tell you?"

"Gram still sees me as a little girl who needs protection from any discussion involving money. Not that it's any of my business who contributes and who doesn't. But no, she didn't tell me about your donation."

"Secrets, huh? Another O'Toole trait?" A humorless chuckle punctuated his comment. "Then I guess it's safe to say she doesn't know about your nest egg."

Secretive and manipulative. Was that how he saw her? "She knows I paid cash for my town house and that when I sold it, I invested half and put the rest in the bank. But Gram being Gram, there's no telling what Broadway thing was on her mind when we had that discussion."

Hunter had roused countless negative emotions in her over the years, all related to what *he'd* done. But these past few weeks, it seemed that his very presence was enough to underscore her unattractive traits. *Who's the traitor—and the hypocrite—now?* she asked herself.

"I need to get Connor upstairs," she said. "He needs a nap."

Connor squirmed in her arms. "No nap," he said again. "No nap!"

"I hate to interfere, but you promised he could watch them light the candles and sing the birthday song *and* eat a big fat frosting flower." He nodded toward the dessert table. "Doesn't seem fair to put him to bed just as they're about to cut the cake."

It seemed more and more as if he was intent on inciting a verbal sparring match. Brooke dodged the comment, because she had no intention of throwing the first punch.

"You're absolutely right," she admitted. And to Connor, "You've been a really good boy today. You deserve a treat!"

Hunter held out his arms, and Connor willingly fell into them, leaving Brooke no choice but to tag along as he walked toward the cake. Brooke stood back slightly, listening as his distinctive baritone blended with Connor's sweet voice, singing the birthday song.

Deidre was beaming when she said, "Help that sweet baby blow out the candles, Hunter!"

He leaned over the cake and showed Connor what to do, and when the job was done, the baby squealed with glee. "Blow!" he told Brooke. "Blow all gone!"

"Yes, sweetie," she said as Deidre began cutting the cake, "the candlelight is all gone."

Brooke grabbed a slice and a plastic spoon and, one hand on Hunter's forearm, led him away from the dessert table. He didn't say a word—and neither did Connor—as bite by bite the slice got smaller. When it was gone, Brooke wrapped a paper napkin around her condensation-dampened glass.

"There," she said, using it to wipe crumbs and icing from her nephew's face, "Connor is all clean and shiny."

She stepped away just long enough to dispose of the napkin, spoon and plate. "I'm sure he'll sleep like a rock," she said, taking Connor from Hunter's arms. And walking away, Brooke added, "It's been quite a day, hasn't it, sweet boy?"

She'd gone only a few steps when Hunter called, "Brooke. Wait up. There's something I need you to see."

Was it the grim set of his jaw or his no-nonsense

voice that made her slow her pace? "Whatever it is," she said when he caught up with her at the bottom of the stairs, "will have to wait until this little guy is asleep."

He relieved her of the apartment keys and followed her up the stairs. "I'm in no hurry," he said, unlocking the door.

Brooke was in no hurry, either. She took her time changing Connor into a comfy lightweight jumpsuit, then rocking him to sleep, because out there, pacing in her tiny temporary living room was the living, breathing reminder of the most painful event of her life *and* the reason she and Connor had to move into the apartment in the first place.

Exhaustion, frustration and confusion sapped the last of her energy, and she leaned into the rocker's headrest and closed her eyes. She hadn't been in the store that awful night, but that didn't stop her from imagining what had probably happened. As drowsiness overtook her, the grisly pictures that so often startled her awake materialized: her mom, smiling as she shopped for vanilla ice cream and chocolate sauce. Smiling as she stood at the counter, waiting her turn to pay for the treat her girls' straight As had earned. Smiling until a masked robber burst into the store waving a pistol, demanding money from the cash drawer, from the customers and the cop who stood in line as his partner snoozed in the squad car, mere feet from the register....

Connor sighed and squirmed slightly, bringing her back to the here and now. Thankfully, she'd had the good sense to pull down the window shade earlier, because if he saw tears on her cheeks, he'd cry, too.

He yawned, stretched. "Bed," he mumbled. "Conner go to bed."

Brooke kissed his temple, then eased him into his crib. "Sweet dreams," she whispered. "I love you." He was asleep before she pulled his door shut.

In the hall, she summoned the strength to walk into the living room and the self-control to keep Hunter from seeing that the terrible nightmare had unleashed her tears.

Brooke headed straight for the kitchen and turned on the flame under the teakettle.

Suddenly, he was behind her. "That didn't take as long as I thought it would," he said. "Think it means he's finally coming around?"

Brooke shrugged. "We can hope."

He pulled out two kitchen chairs. "So about this thing I want to show you...."

She kept her back to him, putting tea bags and spoons into two mugs, taking the sugar bowl from the cabinet, thinking how ridiculous brewing hot tea seemed, since outside, people were sipping icy beverages.

"This pot heats up pretty fast," she said, "so—"

"This won't take long."

She tried to shake the dream-image of him leaning back in the seat, his cop hat's visor hiding his snoring face while—

"By the time it whistles, I'll be gone."

—while her mother lay dying.

"Unless you insist on waiting for the inevitable." *The watched pot that never boils?*

"All right." She sat across from him. "So what's this mysterious thing that just can't wait?"

He had turned his chair around and now sat with one muscled forearm atop the other on the chair's back. Hunter slid a folded envelope from his shirt pocket and placed it on the table.

Brooke couldn't imagine what might be inside. A moment passed before he moved it a half inch closer.

"Well, are you going to open it, or do I have to do it for you?"

Brooke's hands shook as she picked it up, opened it and leafed through the pages inside.

Surely she hadn't read correctly. Brooke looked up from the materials list, building permits, a 9 x 12 blueprint—everything he'd need to rehab Beth's house—and the zero balance on the last page.

"You're crazy if you think I'd let you pay for all of this."

His brow furrowed slightly. "I told you. Everything I'll need is in my shop, taking up space."

"Yes, I remember. But the permits…they weren't just lying around gathering dust. And people don't make up blueprints for free. And unless I'm mistaken, you have to pay your crew, and there's a fee for every outlet and switch and—"

"Why don't you just let me worry about all of that?" His frown deepened. "I'm doing this so Connor will be safe when he's over there."

"When he's over there?" she echoed. "You make it sound like he'll only be visiting. Occasionally. And we both know that's just…just silly." A nervous laugh punctuated her statement.

But he ignored it.

"Seems there were perks to working for an insurance agency," he said. "Kent wrote himself a killer homeowner's policy." He nodded at the envelope. "Trouble is, it doesn't cover wiring. Or plumbing. If he hadn't written his own policy, the place never would have passed inspection. Never would have qualified for a mortgage. I'm sure he had every good intention of making repairs, but… you know Kent."

Unfortunately, she did. "His credo was 'Never do today what you can put off till tomorrow. Or the next day.'" She stared into Hunter's eyes. "What I don't know is…how you got a copy of the policy?"

Hunter lowered his head, clasped his hands. Oh, to know what was going on in that stubborn, handsome head!

"The only thing that should matter," he said quietly, "is that I'm going to bring the place up to code. From basement to attic, inside and out. When I'm finished, Connor—and you—will be safe."

"Is that your polite way of saying that unless I blindly go along with your plans, I'm not interested in Connor's safety?"

He stared her down. "I didn't say that."

"Then…what *are* you saying?"

Hunter's hazel eyes darkened and his lips thinned. "I'm saying that Kent bent the rules knowing full well that his wife and baby boy would have to live in that fire trap."

"To be fair, they didn't have Connor when they bought the house."

"Doesn't change the facts. They lived in it for more than seven years. I had my suspicions and never should have looked the other way. I should have nagged him. Helped him." He grimaced. "Something."

Brooke couldn't escape the fact that if Hunter hadn't stumbled on the wiring problem, she and Connor would still be living in that fire trap.

She put the paperwork back into the envelope. "I appreciate what you're proposing," she began, "but I can afford to take care of Connor and the house he lives in. I have my savings and some investment income. And my new job. Plus there's some money left from my grandfather's estate. I don't need your charity."

"Charity?" he growled. "You're impossible!"

He got to his feet, and as she stood, Brooke shoved the envelope nearer the edge of the table.

"Keep it," he said, facing the door. "I have copies."

The teapot whistled, and she used it as an excuse to turn away from his accusatory glare.

"None for me," he said as she filled her mug. But she poured him a cup anyway.

He was half in, half out the door when he said, "So you need some recommendations, then?"

"Recommendations…?"

He looked at the ceiling, as if the answer to her question were written up there.

"Other contractors. Guys who'll do the job without ripping you off."

"I…I never said I didn't want you to do the work." She placed both mugs on the table. "I only said I can't let you do it for free."

He was staring right at her, so why did Brooke get the feeling he wasn't seeing her?

"I didn't notice a signature page," she said,

pointing at the envelope. "What do I need to sign? To get things under way, I mean."

He was looking at the toes of his shoes when he said, "You don't need to sign anything. I trust you." Hunter exhaled a frustrated sigh, then met her eyes. "I'll get a crew over there tomorrow. We'll start by tearing down the plaster walls so I can see what's behind them."

It dawned on her that Deidre's house—and every outbuilding on the property—was on the registry of historic homes. How could she be sure that this apartment was any safer than Beth and Kent's house? She voiced her concerns to Hunter.

"When your grandmother turned this place into a boarding house years back, I redid the wiring and plumbing. Installed new windows and doors, new insulation, new roof," he said, thumb pointing upward, "here in the apartment and on the big house, too. So don't worry. You're safe. Besides, you'll only be here for a couple of months."

"Tomorrow, after you have a better idea what's involved, maybe we can discuss a payment plan."

"For the luvva Pete, Brooke, will you quit being so mule-headed? I'm doing the job. No strings attached. Because I love that kid. Because I—" One hand slapped the back of his neck, the other formed the Boy Scout salute. "You've got my word on it."

"I can count on one hand," she said, more to

herself than to Hunter, "the number of people I can take at their word."

"You can take this to the bank. I'm one of them."

He held her gaze for half a second, then left without another word.

Staring at the closed door, Brooke absentmindedly stirred sugar into her tea. She shouldn't trust him so completely, and yet, she did.

CHAPTER SIXTEEN

"Listen to him back there," Deidre said, "chattering like a chipmunk."

Brooke glanced into the rearview mirror. "I'm almost afraid to say it out loud, for fear of jinxing things, but it's good to hear something other than whining out of him for a change, isn't it?"

"I'll say!" And when Brooke turned onto Route 40, she said, "Where are you taking us?"

"It's a surprise."

"You know I hate surprises…."

"Yeah, right. And I hate chocolate."

They shared a moment of quiet laughter that even Connor joined in on. But Brooke knew Deidre: if she didn't change the subject soon, the woman would start talking about the play. Or the theater project. And the whole point of this Saturday outing was to get her mind *off* work.

Now, how to steer the conversation from anything related to the stage….

"I had the best week at the hospital. I think maybe I am cut out for this job."

"I never should have said you weren't."

It was as close to an apology as she'd ever get from her grandmother, and Brooke smiled.

Deidre leaned forward as far as the seat belt would allow and peered through the windshield. "Where *are* you taking me, anyway?"

"You'll find out soon enough. Just sit back and enjoy the ride."

Deidre's crazy schedule had forced her to cancel two lunch dates with her sorority sisters. So when Brooke ran into one of the ladies—a volunteer at the hospital gift shop—she'd decided to make sure her grandmother didn't miss another. And while the ladies were at lunch, Brooke would run a few errands—including a stop at the post office to see if the guardianship papers had arrived.

"You're awfully quiet for a girl who's supposedly tickled pink about her new job. What has your brain in such a knot?"

"My brain isn't in a knot," she said, grinning.

"Oh. Really. They maybe you can tell me why you look like the Cheshire cat."

"Gosh, aren't *you* good for a girl's ego!"

"Hey. I calls 'em as I sees 'em." She reached across the console and patted Brooke's hand. "Seriously, honey, you're beginning to worry me. Judging by those dark circles under your eyes, you haven't slept a wink since my birthday party."

Brooke rolled her eyes. "Listen to the pot calling the kettle black. You've been running around like a chicken without a head for weeks."

"Apples and oranges, O Mistress of Clichés. I'm not the one with a brand-new job and an active toddler to take care of."

"I'm fine," Brooke said. "Honest."

"You might as well tell me what's bugging you...."

"In other words, 'Talk, or I'll nag you till you cry uncle.'"

Deidre chuckled. "Something like that."

"It's no big deal, really. Except...it's been two weeks since I filled out those forms."

"If memory serves, that nice young woman from Child Protective Services told you it could take three or four weeks. Right?"

"I sent them two weeks ago yesterday."

Deidre groaned, and when Connor mimicked her, the women laughed.

"Brooke, don't you know by now that nothing happens fast when government red tape is involved? It took nearly two years, if you'll recall, to get my second husband's name deleted from my accounts." She tapped her chin. "What *was* the old runaway's name...?"

"As if you could forget." Brooke shook her head. "Malcolm. His name was Malcolm Hooper." The poor guy hadn't run away. Deidre had driven him away with her insults and surly attitude.

The thought reminded her of something Hunter had said, when he'd wondered if she'd inherited some of her grandmother's not-so-stellar qualities. Shame reddened her cheeks, because the things Deidre had said to Malcolm? She'd thought them all—and then some—about Hunter.

"Well, we're here," she said, parking alongside the curb. "But we're early."

"Early? Early for what?" Deidre read the restaurant's sign aloud. "Duesenberg's Café." She turned to Brooke. "What's going on?"

"How about while I park the car, you ask the hostess to seat you at a table for four. I'll explain when I get inside."

"Four?" Deidre got out of the car, then leaned into the front seat. "You'd better not be playing matchmaker, young lady!" she said, and slammed the passenger door.

"Gram thinks it's a blind date," she said, laughing to herself. "Priceless!"

While she parked in the lot across the street, Connor did his best to repeat the word. And when they entered the café, Brooke politely turned down the hostess's offer of a high chair. "We're just here to keep my grandmother company until her friends arrive," she explained.

She hadn't even situated herself when Deidre demanded, "All right, out with it. Tell me all about this old dude so I'll know what to expect. I'd hate to lose my lunch even before I order it!"

"Gram," Brooke whispered, "I think sometimes you forget how far your voice carries."

"Fiddlesticks. Without proper projection, you're doomed as a stage actress!" Deidre fluffed her gleaming white curls and struck a pose.

"But you're not on stage." Brooke drew her grandmother's attention to the stares of diners seated nearby.

"Pish posh," Deidre said with a dismissive wave. "They're probably just trying to decide whether they remember me from *Cabaret* or *Camelot*. Or *Bye Bye Birdie!*"

Connor pointed at a tall dark-haired man across the way. "Uncle Hunter?"

"No, sweetie, not Uncle Hunter."

"Speaking of whom, I haven't seen the man in days. You didn't hurt his feelings again, I hope."

"No, Gram. I haven't hurt your precious Hunter's feelings."

"Is that why you're in such a sour mood? Hunter has been making himself scarce?"

If not for those brief daily visits with the baby, she wouldn't have seen him, either. "For your information, I see him nearly every day. When he comes to see Connor."

"Then you'd better put those documents out of your mind. They'll get here when they get here, and worrying won't make them get here any faster."

"But...but what if something awful happens to me while I'm waiting? What'll become of Connor?"

"Why, Hunter will take him, of course."

Deidre had said it so quickly, so matter-of-factly, that it almost seemed rehearsed.

"Uncle Hunter," Connor said, pointing at the stranger again.

Brooke handed him the stuffed car she'd tucked into his diaper bag.

"Well, as I live and breathe," Deidre said, "it's Maureen and Rachel!" She waved them over. "And Susan, too?" She smiled at Brooke. "Is this why you brought me here?"

Brooke didn't have time to answer, because the women were already exchanging hugs and hellos. They fussed over Connor, told Brooke that she looked just like her grandmother had at her age, and promised to get her home safely.

"Lovely offer, girls, but I'm not going home after lunch," Deidre said. "I need to stop by the theater. Rehearsal starts today, you know." She returned Brooke's hug, then walked with her to the door. "I'll probably get in late, so don't sit up watching for headlights to come up the drive."

"Conner go home?" her nephew said.

Home. Last time Brooke had one, she was sixteen. Gram and Gramps had welcomed her and Beth with open arms after their dad's suicide, but their house had never quite felt like home. Although she'd redecorated every room in her Richmond condo, it fell short of the mark, too. Following the Donald fiasco, she'd left Virginia and moved into Deidre's guest room, and then it was on to Beth and Kent's to babysit Connor while they were away. And despite everything she'd done to turn the apartment into a cozy home for Connor, *it* didn't feel that way, either.

"Are you sure you don't need me to pick you up after rehearsal?"

"No, but thanks, honey. Felix will be there since he's in the show. And it isn't like he has far to go after dropping me off!"

Even her grandmother's grizzled handyman had a home…in the three-room guesthouse at the rear of Deidre's property.

"He's playing the part of Mitch in our rendition of *Streetcar,*" Deidre said. "Some might say he's a little long in the tooth for the role, but with good makeup and lighting, the audience will never notice." She gave Connor a sideways hug. "Now scoot. Looks like this little man could use a nice long nap."

"No nap," Connor said, pouting. "No nap!"

Deidre frowned slightly. "He never used to fight

bedtime. Do you suppose he dreams about them, and that's why he fights sleep?"

"Good question. I'll ask Dr. Rosen during our next session."

"And how's that going?"

She glanced over Deidre's shoulder, where her sorority sisters sat, sipping tea and pointing at their menus. "I'll tell you all about it tomorrow. Now *you* scoot. And have fun!"

"Scoot," Connor echoed. "Have fun!"

"It never ceases to amaze me how well he talks," Deidre said, kissing a pudgy finger. "You make your old Gram look like a big fat fibber, because your big fat vocabulary makes it hard for people to believe you're only eighteen months old!"

Brooke smiled. "Let's go, li'l Einstein."

"While you're at the post office, check my box, will you?" Deidre asked, walking away. "And if it isn't too much trouble, could you put my mail on the kitchen table?"

Brooke and Connor spent the next hour picking up groceries, then stopped at the post office on the way back to the apartment.

"How frustrating," she muttered, tucking Deidre's mail into an outer pocket of Connor's diaper bag. "Gram gets this huge stack and I get two lousy catalogs?"

The baby grabbed at one of the colorful sales

brochures. "Mine," he said, wrinkling the cover. "Mine."

"All right," she said, heading for the car, "enjoy them while you can." *Because the minute you're belted in, they're going straight into the trash.*

His stuffed car didn't do the trick of distracting him this time, so Brooke handed him a teething toy shaped like a key ring.

After unloading the groceries, she and Connor walked hand in hand to Deidre's to deliver her mail.

"Blink-blink," Connor said, pointing at the answering machine's red light. "Blink-blink."

She balanced him on one hip and grabbed paper and pencil, then leaned in to let the baby push the message button.

"Hey, Deidre. It's me, Hunter. Hate to bug you, but Brooke must have turned off her cell phone. Again." He chuckled. "When you see her, ask her to give me a call, will you? I need to ask her something about the kitchen over here. Thanks."

Strange, Brooke thought, because she'd already listened to the two messages he'd left on her cell phone explaining that he needed her help choosing the floor and countertop materials. Connor's face puckered. "Uncle Hunter…"

"Aw, don't cry, sweetie." Brooke hugged him tighter and, pointing, said, "Look, your favorite, toy. Gram's rocking horse!"

He wailed for a full minute, and then as quickly as his tears had started, they stopped.

"Down?" he said, reaching for the wooden horse.

Brooke sat cross-legged on the floor, arms extended to catch him in case he lost his balance.

A week ago, when Hunter had delivered the plans and paperwork, his officious attitude had touched a raw nerve. To prove that she didn't need his charity—and that he couldn't control her—she'd gone to the bank first thing Monday morning and cashed in one of her grandfather's bonds. Not a fortune, but more than enough to defray the cost of printing blueprints and filing for permits. His parting comment asking her to trust him was the main reason she hadn't called before now. Once Connor was down for his nap, she'd get it over with.

But she'd brought files home from work, and read one of four patient advocate handbooks her mentor had loaned her. Washed three loads of laundry and tidied the apartment. And before she knew it, the afternoon sun was high in the sky.

When Connor woke up, she took him outside for some fresh air, and as they made their way to Deidre's house, Connor noticed an early-blooming butterfly bush, covered with swallowtails, monarchs and Angelwings. "Look, Connor...a Baltimore Checkerspot," she said. "See the pretty butterflies?"

One flew near his head, and he giggled. "Butterfly," he said, swatting at it.

Deidre joined them on the flagstone path beside the flower bed. "You were about Connor's age when a butterfly landed on the back of your hand. Gramps and I cringed, worrying you'd crush it." Smiling, she met Brooke's eyes. "But you were gentle as a lamb, even then."

Gentle. That was what Donald had called her... right before he announced that he'd been seeing someone else.

"I think your kindness is responsible for every one of your breakups," her grandmother continued. "It makes you too eager to please, too quick to give everyone the benefit of the doubt. Everyone except for Hunter, of course." Deidre shook her head. "If you'd shown them a tenth the vitriol you've hammered Hunter with over the years, those fellows might have treated you with a modicum of respect."

Brooke took a deep breath, let it out slowly.

Deidre plucked a flower from the shrub and handed it to Connor. "Not in your mouth, now, or Gram will take it away...."

Whew, Brooke thought, *saved by the blossom.*

"I should have taught you and Beth to have more respect for yourselves. Maybe then you'd both have been more discriminating and wouldn't have been so quick to settle. Then again…"

Connor had tired of watching the butterflies flit from bloom to bud. "Down," he said, folding himself in half. "Conner down."

The instant his feet hit the ground, he filled his hands with newly mown grass and pulled. "Rain!" he said, tossing both handfuls into the air. "Rain, rain, rain!"

Brooke laughed. "Why is it I never have my camera when he does adorable things like that!"

"You can't change the subject that easily, you sly girl, you." Deidre wiggled her eyebrows. "If you ask me, you need a man like Hunter. And before you start in with your tired old 'he killed my mother' spiel, let me remind you all he's done for us lately, despite the despicable way you've treated him all these years. He has proven himself to me."

He'd proven himself to Brooke, too. She just wasn't ready to admit it out loud. Yet.

"He isn't always thinking of himself, doesn't spend every waking moment trying to think up ways to take advantage of someone's good heart, the way your so-called boyfriends did. Hunter is a good man with a big heart and a generous nature. Why else would he put so much time and energy into opening Last Chance, that school for troubled boys?"

"What? I never heard anything about that."

"Doesn't surprise me. When would he have had time to tell you about it, when you keep him so busy fending off your ill-timed attacks?"

"Hunter and I have been getting along fine… lately."

"Because he's bending over backward to help us out. More proof of how generous and thoughtful he is. Not just with us, mind you. Last I heard, he was working with the county executive, who's trying to help him finalize a deal that will let him buy that abandoned canning factory down on Main Street. Hunter wants to turn it into a technical school where he can teach kids the trades, like plumbing, electricity, welding, carpentry, so that when they graduate—or quit school, as so many do these days—they'll have some practical knowledge and skills to fall back on."

"How noble of him."

"I'd stake my life—and yours and Connor's—on this, he'd never hurt you like Donald and the rest of those bozos did."

"He already hurt me. Fifteen years ago."

Deidre's hard stare softened. "You worry me, honey. These black moods you get into, the way you've held on to this grudge all these years? I'm so afraid you'll end up like your father."

That was a low blow, but Brooke chose not to respond to it.

Connor ambled up to her. "All gone," he said,

tossing the wilted flower to the ground. Before Brooke or Deidre could stop him, he plucked a new one. "Mine, mine, mine!"

Brooke scooped him up. "I can hardly wait until those papers get here," she said, kissing his cheeks, his chin, his forehead, "so you'll be mine, mine, mine!"

"Your aunt is the master of distractions, Connor," Deidre said, fanning herself with one hand. "It's too hot out here for me. I'm going inside for a refreshing glass of iced tea." Halfway down the walk she stopped and faced Brooke. "You coming, honey?"

"I'd love to, but this poor kid needs an N-A-P," she spelled.

Deidre shrugged and muttered something unintelligible. "I'll just say one more thing, and then the subject is closed."

For how long? Brooke wondered. *A minute? Five?*

"Mark my words. Someday, you'll regret your spiteful attitude."

Spiteful? For putting the blame where it belonged?

Connor yawned, and Brooke seized the opportunity. "Maybe we'll pop over after he wakes up?"

"We'll sit out back and watch the sun set."

"I'd love that. And I love *you,* you opinionated old woman," she teased.

"Ditto, you pigheaded whippersnapper."

It was a private joke that they'd shared for years, and Deidre was still laughing as the screen door closed behind her.

An hour later, while Connor snoozed in the playpen, Brooke opened the closet door and stared at the battered box positioned between the vacuum cleaner and the broom. She'd found it in Beth's front hall closet and brought it to the apartment, hoping if she didn't unpack it, it might serve as a good-luck charm of sorts that would get her and Connor back into the house sooner. Since Hunter made it clear that repairs could take months, she decided it was time to find out what her sister stored in the carton labeled Keepsakes.

Under a stack of how-to manuals and recipes torn from magazines, she found two cookbooks and miscellaneous photographs. Beneath that, Beth's high school diploma, Kent's college yearbook, a dog-eared paperback copy of *White Fang,* Beth's favorite novel.

Her cell phone buzzed, interrupting the search.

Hunter, calling with more bad news about the house, no doubt. Brooke let the call go to voice mail because she needed time to process Deidre's warning. *Mark my words,* Deidre had said, *someday you'll regret your spiteful attitude.*

Brooke removed a big yellow envelope from the box, and, tucking it under one arm, checked on Connor. *Oh, to conk out that way when I climb into bed,* she thought, settling onto the sofa.

Brooke pried open the envelope's metal clasp and peeked inside. A fat pink diary—its tiny key secured to the cover with an X of clear tape—lay atop Beth's graduation photo. Why would her sister have kept *two* journals?

She peeled back the tape and inserted the key into the minuscule lock and thumbed through the book: Kent surprised Beth with a candlelit dinner; Beth finally finished sewing new curtains for the kitchen; Deidre's laryngitis kept her from singing in the dinner-theater production of *Phantom;* Brooke was coming home for good…punctuated by six exclamation points; then an entire page filled with Beth's girlish script.…

Poor Kent worries so about our finances. If only I could help out by putting my teaching degree to use. If only we could afford the cost of recertification. *If*…the biggest little word in the English language!

And a few pages later, "Why do I feel so helpless and inept when Connor gets sick?"

Three quarters of the way through the book, more of the same.

Or so she thought.

I can hardly wait to walk hand in hand on those white-sand beaches with the love of my life. I'll always be grateful to Brooke for putting her move on hold to watch over my sweet Connor.

The date—two days prior to their departure for the islands—hit Brooke like a blow to the jaw.

Anger surged through her. Why hadn't Beth talked Kent into drafting a will to protect Connor? Surely her sister had been aware of the defective wiring; how could she have tolerated Kent's foot-dragging knowing it might pose a danger to her precious boy?

But her ire vanished as quickly as the wisp of smoke from a spent match, and in its place, raw, unbridled grief. The tears came fast and hot, and with them, rib-racking silent sobs. Why such an extreme reaction, she wondered, to a few simple words!

The answer hit like a second punch: because every rounded *a,* each curlicued *g*—whether penned in blue or red, black or green—served as a harsh reminder that the diary was all Brooke had left of her little sister.

Connor stirred, and she willed herself to stop crying. Something the preacher had said at Beth and Kent's funeral chimed in her memory: *One day at a time, one step at a time, our heartaches will heal and our mourning will lessen. We never forget those we've lost, who touched our lives in innumerable, immeasurable ways, for they will live in our hearts and minds forever.*

She forced a cheery smile and walked over to the playpen. "Hey, little guy, did you have a good nap?"

His empty expression concerned her far more than his tantrums and pouting. "You poor little thing," she said, scooping him up. "You don't know how to feel, do you?"

He snuggled close and exhaled a big sigh.

"One day at a time," she whispered, "one step at a time."

She carried him into the kitchen, and as she clicked the high chair's safety belt into place, Brooke admitted that if not for Connor, the ache of her loneliness might be overwhelming.

Her cell phone buzzed again as she sprinkled Cheerios onto the tray. She couldn't avoid him forever.

"Hey," she said.

"Hey, yourself. What's up?"

"Just feeding Connor an after-nap snack."

"Let me guess. Cheerios."

She heard the smile in his voice, and it inspired one of her own.

"Mind if I stop by for a few minutes?"

"We'll be here all afternoon."

"Great," he said, and hung up.

He hadn't said why he wanted to come over. Didn't say how long he'd stay. Maybe if she could keep Connor occupied, she'd write Hunter a check and explain yet again why she needed to…why he needed to let her.

Connor offered her a damp O.

"Why, thank you, sweet boy. You are the most adorable kid in diapers."

"Kid," he echoed.

She leaned both elbows on the tray. "Soon as you're finished, we'll change you into an outfit that's as cute as you are," she said, sticking a wet Cheerio to his cheek, "so you'll look handsome for your—"

Three soft raps at the door drew Connor's attention.

He must have been in the driveway when he called. "Come in, Uncle Hunter," she said. "It's open."

Connor squealed and bounced up and down in the chair as Hunter strode into the room.

"Thanks, Aunt Brooke," he said, shoving a brown paper bag into the freezer. Bending at the waist, he kissed the top of Connor's head. "How's my buddy?"

He sat beside the high chair and let Connor feed him a Cheerio. "Man, it's good to see you, kiddo."

"Guess it's true what they say—time flies when you're having fun."

His eyebrows rose slightly. "Meaning...?"

"Meaning one minute you're on the phone, and the next you're here."

His lips slanted in a half smile. "I was just around the corner when I called."

"There's iced tea. And the coffee's hot...."

"Tea sounds good."

She'd barely delivered it when Connor fused his gaze to hers, and then, gripping the arms of his high chair, he looked frantically around the room. "Mama?" Straining against the safety belt, he said it again. "Mama?"

Brooke's heart clenched as she remembered what Dr. Rosen had told her to say. "Mama is gone," she said around the lump in her throat.

He sat quiet and motionless for several seconds, no doubt processing the information.

"Mama all gone?"

"Yes, sweetie. Mama's all gone."

He picked up a Cheerio and looked at Hunter. "Daddy?"

"Daddy's gone, too, kiddo."

Eyebrows drawn together in a frown, he stared at his cereal-littered tray, then heaved a heavy sigh.

"Uncle Hunter?"

"Yep. That's me. Uncle Hunter."

He pointed at Brooke. "Aunt Brooke."

She kissed the chubby fingertip. "Yes, sweetie. Aunt Brooke."

Nodding, he filled both hands with cereal, tossed it into the air and grinned slightly as Os rained down around him. Giggling, he did it again.

"First time he's asked about Beth and Kent?" Hunter asked quietly.

"Yes. And I have to admit, your timing is perfect."

"Why?"

"Because I don't know how well I would have handled...that...without backup."

It had been surprisingly easy to admit. Brooke was searching her mind for ways to rationalize it when Hunter gently plucked an O from her hair. Not knowing what else to do, she reached for the broom.

"Told you weeks ago. That mess isn't going anywhere," he said, taking it from her, "and neither am I."

CHAPTER SEVENTEEN

Dr. ROSEN SCRIBBLED something on the top page of Connor's file, then put down her pen. "I have to hand it to you two," she said, nodding approvingly. "He's come a long way in just two months."

Hunter leaned forward, rested his elbows on his knees. "I'd originally thought about making major changes to the house," he said, clasping his hands in the space between, "since it's all torn up anyway. You know, to better reflect Brooke's tastes."

He cut a glance in her direction, but she was too busy watching Connor through the floor-to-ceiling window between Rosen's office and the playroom to notice.

"But she dug in her heels. Wants me to put it back exactly the way it was before. Or get as close as I can, anyway. Less for Connor to adjust to. What's your take on it, Doc?"

"I guess that depends on how drastic your changes would be."

He shrugged. "Beth was big into bright colors and bold designs, and Brooke's tastes are more… subdued."

She looked at Brooke and smiled. "Then I'm inclined to agree. At least for the time being. As we've discussed before, the fewer drastic changes, the better. He's already coped with moving into the apartment, so…"

Hunter had a feeling that's what Rosen would say. But he'd also sensed that Brooke wasn't one hundred percent comfortable with her decision. Now, with the doctor's opinion on the table, he hoped she could relax.

Dr. Rosen leaned back in her chair and, balancing the file on her lap, clicked her ballpoint. "So tell me a little more about these 'mom and dad are gone' discussions Connor has been initiating. Has he pressed you for more detailed explanations yet?"

Brooke was quick to answer. "No, the few times he's called out for them, he seems satisfied with simple answers."

"Good." The doctor removed her glasses and looked directly at Hunter. "Have you spent any time alone with him since the crash?"

"Well, ah, sure. A little." Fact was, Brooke had Connor pretty well locked up. Except for the few occasions when he'd stepped in so she could attend meetings with patients' families or her boss, she'd always been present when he and Connor were together.

"Could you be a little more specific?"

From the corner of his eye, he saw Brooke sit up taller and cross her legs away from him. He understood enough about body language to know what that meant: she didn't trust him to answer in her favor.

"Brooke chose a job that lets her work part-time," he began, "so naturally, she's with him more. I'm over there every chance I get, though."

Spectacles back in place, the doctor added that bit of information to the file. But where would his response take her next?

"I envy you, Brooke," Rosen said. "You must have the most understanding boss on the planet." She tapped her pen on the desk. "I hope you won't take this the wrong way, but I have to ask. How are you doing financially? The reason I ask… being cash-strapped can be a major stressor. And you're under enough pressure maintaining an 'everything's fine' environment for Connor, all while adapting to a new job *and* managing your own grief."

Brooke scooted to the edge of her chair and planted both feet flat on the floor. "I'm fine. Really. I have money in the bank, some from the sale of my town house, some inherited from my grandfather, and some investment income. I'm not making as much as a patient advocate as I did as a trauma nurse, but it's enough. And the hours are flexible."

Rosen jotted that down, too.

"How are you sleeping?" She looked at Brooke, then at Hunter.

A shudder passed through Brooke. It lasted all of a nanosecond, but he wondered if Rosen had noticed, too.

"I'm fine. Eating, sleeping, working, spending every spare minute with Connor. Speaking of whom…correct me if I'm wrong, Doctor, but aren't these sessions supposed to center around *him?*"

Rosen smiled. "Yes. They are. And to keep the focus on him, you know why I need to look closely at anything—and anyone—who has a direct impact on his life." She glanced from Brooke to Hunter and back again. "If you two are a mess, naturally, it'll spill onto Connor."

He heard Brooke's soft sigh of frustration. Knowing her, she was probably wondering why the doctor had decided to zero in on her instead of him. "I also have to understand your relationship better."

"Oh, Connor and I are very close."

"I was referring to you two." Rosen used her pen to draw a line between Hunter and Brooke. "Are you a couple? Good friends? Help me understand."

He read the terror in Brooke's eyes. Hopefully,

he didn't have the proverbial "deer in the headlights" look, too.

"Brooke and I have known one another for
years," he began, sitting up straight. "Slightly
more than fifteen years, to be precise. Her sister
and brother-in-law were like family to me."

"Interesting." Rosen wrote on her pad and without looking up said, "I sense there's a whole lot
more here, and a certain hesitancy to get into it
today. So we'll table it for now and address the
details at a later date."

She let her challenge hang like a mallet in search
of a nail to pound.

Hunter tensed, wondering if Brooke would fill
the silence by telling Rosen how—and why—
they'd met.

Brooke cleared her throat. "You're right. There
are—were—issues." Lifting her chin a notch, she
added, "But for Connor's benefit, we've set them
aside."

"Temporarily?"

"For as long as Connor needs us to present a
united front."

He would have said "good answer" if not for
that DVD.

Rosen tapped the pen against her chin. "And
this was a mutual decision?"

Together Brooke and Hunter nodded. "Yes."

They exchanged a quick glance.

"You seem surprised," the doctor observed, "to be in agreement on that."

Now Hunter and Brooke sat quietly, staring straight ahead. After a moment, Rosen asked, "Tell me. Were these…issues…set aside as in avoided? Or as in resolved?"

Brooke looked up, as if the answer were written on the pocked ceiling tiles.

"Avoided, I suppose." She crossed her legs, this time toward Hunter. "For the time being, anyway."

"Seems pretty normal to me," Hunter said, "for two people who've known one another as Brooke and I have to have a few unresolved issues."

Dr. Rosen folded her hands on the desk blotter. "I agree." Then she checked her watch. "Well, we have about five minutes. Is there anything more you'd like to address today?"

"Thanks," Brooke said, getting to her feet, "but I think we're through."

Hunter couldn't think of anything more he wanted to say, but it irked him that Brooke had ended the session without even checking to see if he had more questions or concerns.

The doctor walked around her desk and stopped beside his chair.

"How much time would you say you spent with Connor before the accident, Hunter?"

Why did he get the feeling it was a loaded question?

His grandfather had taught him that to win at chess a player needed to think three, four, even five moves ahead: if he told Rosen that as owner of Stone Contracting, he set his own hours and could spend all day with Connor if he wanted to, she might deem him cocky. If he told her that Brooke was the one making all the rules, he'd sound uncooperative. Or worse, confrontational. And he couldn't afford to rile the woman who might be called as a witness in the adoption hearing.

"It's important that you spend as much time with him now as you did before." She gave Brooke a stern look, then faced Hunter again. "One. On. One."

"Will do," he said. "Anything for that kid."

Rosen rewarded him with her best therapist's smile. "I believe you." She walked with them to the door. "You know how to reach me if anything comes to mind." She shook his hand. And, shaking Brooke's, she said, "Same time next week?"

"I'll have to get back to you. My schedule is flexible, but the hours change week to week, depending on patients' needs." She went on to explain that her grandmother had agreed to keep Connor afternoons and that Deidre's friend Felix would take the morning shift. "But if you have evening hours, or better yet, Saturday, we can put something on the calendar right now."

Hunter was thunderstruck by the revelation.

Deidre? And *Felix?* He would gladly have taken care of Connor anytime for as long as she needed...if only she'd asked him.

Rosen flipped through her appointment book. "How's Wednesday, seven o'clock?" She looked to Hunter for an answer.

"I'm not the one with the inflexible schedule," he said, then turned to Brooke. "Does Wednesday evening work for you?"

She grabbed her purse from the hall tree. "I'll make it work."

But she hadn't met his eyes to say it, he noticed.

At the door, she asked, "Is it all right if I take Connor home now?"

She'd excluded him. Again. Why wasn't Rosen scribbling *that* in the file?

Because with Brooke being next of kin, even the doctor thinks she's a shoo-in to raise Connor.

"Sure. I'll talk with my assistant and watch the tapes later. If anything stands out as troublesome, I'll let you know. Otherwise, I'll see you next week."

As they exchanged thank-yous and goodbyes, Hunter made up his mind: he needed to stop finding excuses to put it off. First chance he got, he'd call Harry, find out where he stood with the courts, whether or not he'd need to subpoena the doctor's file on Connor, or Rosen herself.

During the drive home, Brooke seemed more

fidgety than normal. Her voice shook a little, too, when she admitted that she couldn't wait to curl up on the sofa with a good book and a cup of herbal tea as soon as Connor had a snack and a bath, and she'd tucked him in for the night.

Snack, bath, bed. Three more Connor-related decisions she'd made without asking his help or his input.

Hunter made his mind up about something else: he'd hang around while Connor had something to eat. Then *he'd* carry the boy to the apartment. Bathe him. Put him to bed. Then he'd find out what made her think she got to call all the shots. She'd been in Richmond for most of Connor's life, spent a couple of hours with him during her monthly visits, while he'd been an almost daily part of the boy's life. By that measure, shouldn't it be the other way around?

"Good news, bad news," he said once they were inside. "Which do you want first?"

She eyed him warily. "Might as well get the bad news out of the way."

He eased Connor into his high chair and said, "I'm not going home yet."

A guarded grin prefaced her response. "Oka-a-ay. And the good news?"

"You are hereby relieved of bed-and-bath duty."

Brooke continued cubing cheese and slicing apples for Connor's snack. "Is that so?"

"It is." He took some leftover ham out of the fridge. "You said yourself that you're exhausted." He slapped the meat onto a paper plate. "There's no shame in asking for help." *I sure will, when I'm in charge of the kid.*

"So what's going on at Beth's house?"

"Now that the walls are down and the floorboards are up, we'll rip out all the old wiring and pipes."

She put a few cheese cubes and apple slices on the high-chair tray. "Any closer to knowing how long—"

"Apple," Connor said, and stuffed a slice into his mouth.

"Yes," they said together, "apple."

The whole scene seemed way too domestic, considering her attitude...and his plans. Twice in the span of an hour, they'd said the same thing at the same time twice. He could count on one hand—and have fingers left over—the number of times they'd seen eye to eye on anything. What was going on here?

"I'm guessing rewiring will take three, maybe four days. Same goes for the plumbing and carpentry, unless we run into problems."

"Problems?"

"Like tree roots clogging the main drain. Rotting support beams. Damaged sills. Termites. Any one of a hundred things could be wrong in a place that old."

She sighed, and he continued.

"But I've never encountered a problem that didn't have a solution. If we run into a setback, we'll fix it. Then it's on to drywall. Reinstalling and refinishing the hardwood." He glanced at the ham spinning round and round inside the microwave. "You know what's gonna be tough? Trying to match stain and paint colors. I might need some help with that. But why am I boring you with all this? It's all listed on your production schedule."

"Nothing that gets us back into that house is boring," she said, handing Connor a sippy cup of milk.

"Choc'late?" the baby asked.

"No, sweetie. It's too close to bedtime for—"

The microwave dinged, and when Hunter reached inside to retrieve the ham, the paper plate collapsed, splashing hot juice onto his hand. Not wanting to startle Connor, he stifled a yelp.

"Good grief," Brooke said, leading him to the sink. "It's red already." She turned on the faucet. "How long did you set the timer for?"

"Only ten minutes," he said through clenched teeth.

She thrust his hand under the water. The cold spray felt good, but not nearly as good as having her so close beside him. Maybe instead of calling his lawyer, he should talk with a doctor, check out the possibility that he had some psychological disorder.

"*Only* ten minutes? For one half-inch slice of ham?"

"Hey," he said, "I do hammers and miter saws, not kitchen appliances."

"Maybe that explains why a successful guy like you isn't married."

Oh, you don't want to go there, Brooke. You really don't want to go—

"If it doesn't blister up after a minute or two, you're out of the woods." She reached into a kitchen drawer and withdrew a first-aid kit.

"And if it does?"

Brooke daubed ointment on the burn. "You'll elicit a lot of sympathy from your crew tomorrow," she said, "when you show up for work sporting a big fat white bandage."

Hunter inspected the hand. "Looks good," he said, "but I heal fast. Trust me. This thing won't be there in the morning."

She leaned against the counter. "So what did you make of Dr. Rosen's attitude today?"

"She talked and acted like a shrink, same as always." He did his best psychiatrist impersonation: "'Interesting.' And 'how did *that* make you feel?'" He looked up from his burn to see if the tension in her voice was evident on her face, too. "Why do you ask?"

"I don't know." She shook her head. "Maybe after reading Beth's journals, I'm overreacting. But it seemed she was digging. Trying to unearth something that isn't there."

"Like…?"

"Like that nonsense about a relationship between you and me, for starters." She crossed both arms over her chest. "And what's with all that talk about my finances? As long as her bill gets paid, what does she care about my savings account balance?"

He'd barely heard the last part of her comment because his brain was stuck on the first part: whether she wanted to admit it or not, they had a relationship. Just because neither of them knew how to define it didn't make it untrue. It bugged him that she'd sloughed it off, that she'd done it without giving any thought to his opinion. Again.

Brooke grabbed his wrist, adjusted the gauze. She was close enough that he could see blond strands shimmering in her dark hair. And as the faint scent of her shampoo wafted into his nostrils, he tried to figure out why it mattered whether it was lilacs or lavender. The top of her head barely reached his shoulder, and he doubted she weighed a hundred and ten pounds. Appearances could sure be deceiving, because to the casual observer,

Brooke might seem fragile and weak. He'd learned through hard experience how off beam that assessment was.

"Does it sting a lot?"

Not nearly as much as the way you always shut me out. "I'll live."

"Good."

He hoped she meant it.

"Goodness, Connor. You've finished your snack already?"

"A-a-all gone," the baby said. "More?"

Grinning, she gave him the last few slices of cheese and apple.

Hunter inspected his hand. He'd seen plenty of bandages in his line of work. Some wrapped by his guys, others by E.R. nurses. But none had ever looked more precise.

"What's wrong? Is it too tight?"

"It's perfect," he admitted.

"I'll have you know I earned straight As in How to Bandage a Carpenter class."

"But I wanted to give Connor his bath tonight."

She shrugged. "Nope. Not tonight. Sorry."

Just like that. Leave it to her to turn a warm moment cold. He hoped she was enjoying every minute of riding her high horse, because if things went as he hoped they would, she'd be out of the saddle soon.

Brooke leaned against the counter again. "Do you mind telling me something?"

"Depends…"

She stared at the toes of her shoes. "I've been thinking about Kent a lot lately. I guess because Beth wrote so much about him in her journals. I know he resented me for trying to talk her out of the marriage, for encouraging her to leave every time he got drunk and made threats. But from what I read, he flat-out hated me."

Brooke looked up then, directly into his eyes.

"You two were close," she continued, "so I was wondering…did he ever say anything that will help me understand why? Not that I'm letting myself off the hook, mind you, because certainly I didn't go out of my way to ease tensions between us. I only ask because the better I understand it, the better parent I can be for Connor."

Parent. Right.

"You can tell me the truth. I can take it."

He didn't want to tip his hand, but it couldn't hurt to drop a hint or two. "Just so you know, I don't agree with most of this," he said.

"Okay…" She'd already crossed her arms over her chest. Now she crossed her ankles, too.

"He said you were the wrong guardian for Connor, and…"

"And?"

"And I wish you hadn't opened this can of worms."

Brooke inhaled a ragged breath, let it out slowly.

"He wasn't an easy guy to understand."

"So you've said."

She dampened a paper towel and cleaned the high-chair tray. Connor yawned as she wiped his face. "You know what, cutie pie? I think maybe that bath can wait until morning."

The baby must have noticed that something was bothering her, because he hadn't taken his eyes from her face since she picked him up.

Brooke walked right up to Hunter. "Tell your uncle Hunter good-night," she said.

Connor held out his arms. "Up?"

And so Hunter took him, heart thumping with an undercurrent of trepidation. "G'night, buddy," he said, kissing both plump cheeks. "Happy dreams."

The baby started to fuss when Brooke retrieved him, but he quieted as she carried him down the hall. "Go straight to sleep," Hunter said, "and I'll see you tomorrow."

The last thing he saw before she rounded the corner was Connor's sad-eyed face, his tiny dimpled hands reaching for him. His heart told him, *Get in there, pack up the boy's stuff and take him out of here now.* But his brain reminded him that patience was the better part of valor. Yeah, Brooke confused him, annoyed him, hurt his feelings. But this was about Connor, not him.

Hunter threw away the overcooked ham, and as he sopped up the drippy mess on the counter and floor, he couldn't help but wonder…

If his skim-the-surface answers to her questions about Kent had the power to send her into a near tailspin, how much more would it shake her watching the man's scorn…in living color?

CHAPTER EIGHTEEN

WHEN BROOKE TIPTOED from Connor's room, the last thing she expected to see was Hunter in the easy chair reading the newspaper, socked feet propped on the footstool, sneakers on the floor beside it...like a husband relaxing at home after a long, hard day at work.

Standing quietly in the hall, she tried to make sense of the conflicting emotions the scene provoked. Brooke decided to concentrate on their cease-fire, designed and tolerated to provide a peaceful, loving environment for Connor. Because, to quote Hunter, she'd do anything for that kid.

Hunter didn't look up as she padded into the kitchen or as she held the teakettle under the faucet. Brooke tried to come up with a polite way to tell him to hit the road, that unless Connor was awake, he had no valid reason to be in her house.

You're such a hypocrite, she thought, adjusting the flame beneath the kettle. It seemed beyond wrong to accept his help—with moving, repairs on Beth's house, Connor's care, letting him drive her just about everywhere—when it made life easier, yet want to boot him out the door when it didn't.

Even when there had been a man in her life, Brooke spent most of her off-duty hours alone. Since the plane crash, she'd had precious little time to herself, and she yearned for some solitude, to accept her losses and count her blessings and make sense of the impractical, affectionate thoughts she'd been having about Hunter. How could she resent his interference one minute and miss his quiet strength the next?

Brooke brewed them both a cup of tea.

"Oh, thanks," he said, barely looking up when she sat his mug on the table beside the chair.

"Welcome." Sitting on the love seat across from him, she picked up a magazine, hoping it would distract her from Kent's hatred, which appeared in so many passages of Beth's journal. Something told her Hunter knew more, that he'd held back to keep from hurting her, and she added it to the growing list of reasons to like and admire him. Maybe Beth and Deidre had been right about him. Maybe...

When the magazine's recipes and decorating tips failed to hold her attention, she tossed it aside and grabbed the diary, turned to an unread page. Surely that would get her mind back on track.

Kent and I intend to make the most of this vacation since it's probably the last we'll take for a long, long time. Six months from now, our precious little boy will have a baby sister. I can hardly wait to see my sister's face when I tell her we're naming our little girl after our mom.

Eyes closed, Brooke held her breath and pressed a palm to her chest. She'd barely accepted the fact that her sister was gone, and now this?

She heard the newspaper rattle and opened her eyes as Hunter got up.

"What's wrong?" He sat beside her, leaned in close and read Beth's words over her shoulder.

Brooke tensed. If he said, *Oh yeah, I heard about that,* it would break her heart, knowing that Beth had shared something that intimate with him but not with her.

He ran a hand through his hair. "I had no idea." He took the journal from her. "You okay?"

"I'm fine. Shocked, but fine."

His hands shook slightly as he closed the book and placed it on the coffee table. His voice trembled, too, when he said, "I can't...I can't believe it." He sat back, looked deep into her eyes. "How far along do you think she was?"

Brooke had only read the passage once, but she'd never forget what it said.

"Three and a half months?"

"Wonder why she didn't tell anyone."

"The miscarriage," Brooke whispered, remembering how brokenhearted Beth had been, telling her about the baby she'd lost just eight months ago.

"She didn't tell me about that, either."

So much for her theory that Hunter and Beth were as close as siblings.

"Well, you know how superstitious she was," Hunter said. "Beth probably convinced herself that if she talked about the pregnancy too soon…" His expression said what words needn't. "Still…" After a long, somber silence, he added, "Y'just had to love the girl, quirks and all."

"You can say that again." Brooke frowned. "What you can't say is that I was a good sister," she said, mostly to herself. "Stubborn, judgmental, critical…and now that she's gone, I can't apologize. Can't make things right or tell her how much she meant to me."

Brooke hid behind her hands. "I've done a lot of stupid things in my life, but nothing that made me ashamed of myself. But I'm ashamed of the way I treated Beth."

He took her hand, and Brooke didn't fight him.

"Aw, c'mon. You were a great sister. She said so all the time." He gave her fingers a little squeeze. "This will sound corny, but I believe she's up there," he said, aiming a thumb at the ceiling, "watching everything you're doing for her little boy."

Brooke didn't know if she believed in heaven, but if it existed, her sister—who'd never done a cruel or selfish thing in her life—certainly deserved to spend eternity there.

"She knew you loved Connor. That you loved her, too."

"I don't know if I believe that, but it's nice of you to say. Thanks." And then she yawned.

He cupped her chin in one hand and, squinting, turned her face left, then right. "I don't see anything here that a good night's sleep won't fix."

Well, she thought, staring into his blazing brown eyes, *it finally happened—you've completely lost your sanity. Would a sane, rational woman want to press her lips to his just because he was close enough to kiss?*

Hunter blinked as a furrow formed between his dark brows. He licked his lips and moved forward a fraction of an inch, froze, then abruptly stood. Had he read her mind?

He crossed the room and, one hand on the doorknob, said, "I'm just a phone call away, remember, if you want to talk…"

He'd said the same thing on the night Donald made his surprise visit.

"I'm a habitual insomniac, so don't worry about waking me."

She had a pretty good idea why he had trouble

sleeping. *Small consolation,* she thought, *but tonight you'll have company.*

"Lock up good and tight now, hear?"

"Mmm-hmm."

"I'll stop by on my way home tomorrow, give you a report on the house. Spend a little time with Connor."

"Okay."

Pocketing one hand, he leaned on the doorjamb. "I'm having a hard time leaving."

I noticed, she thought, swatting at a moth, lured through the open door by the living room lamps.

One shoulder lifted in a slow shrug. "I hate leaving you this way."

"What way?"

"Looking like you're gonna burst into tears any second."

"I'm not. I won't." *At least not while you're here.* "I'm fine. Honest. Now close the door, will you, or I'll be up all night, whacking moths."

"Remember, if you want anything—anything..."

"Well, I've always wanted a red convertible," she said. "Stick shift, white leather interior, chrome hubcaps...."

His expression of concern became amusement.

Now it was Brooke's turn to look puzzled... as he closed the interior door and returned to the easy chair.

"Didn't finish my tea," he said, lifting the mug.

Hunter put the cup back onto its coaster. "Tell me," he began. "Why did you choose nursing over following in your grandmother's footsteps?"

"Me? An actress?" Brooke laughed. "Thanks, but no thanks." The June breeze wafted through the screen door that led to the deck, and tousled his sandy-brown curls. Brooke didn't know why, but she had to fight the urge to finger-comb them from his forehead.

"I got my fill of the stage at the tender age of fourteen," she said, tucking her fingertips under her knees. "Gram talked me into playing Wendy in her little-theater production of *Peter Pan*."

The inexperienced director, she told him, put her into an ill-fitting harness that broke loose from the Kirby wire as she soared high above the stage. "The fall caused compound fractures," she said, patting her left thigh. "Beth called me Humpty Dumpty because it took four surgeries to put me back together again."

Hunter winced. "Sorry I revived that memory."

"Don't be. The accident was destiny, in more ways than one."

He glanced at her shorts-clad legs. "Guess I never noticed because you don't limp."

"That's what four weeks of rehab will do for a girl. The only lasting effects are weather related." She patted the thigh again. "This baby is a better forecaster than that guy on Channel 13's morning show."

"Marty Bass?"

"Yeah. Him."

"I'm surprised you don't know the name by heart. He's been with the station for as long as I can remember."

"Gram is a Channel 2 girl. Always has been. And I spent five years in Richmond, don't forget."

Why was she encouraging conversation when she wanted him to leave?

"So tell me...why 'destiny, in more ways than one'?"

"I'm sure Gram has told you all about her single-girl days, when she worked with the likes of Ethel Merman and Carol Channing, Pearl Bailey..."

"Only a couple hundred times," he said, grinning.

"Well, before anyone knew who Kathleen Nolan was, she played Wendy in the Mary Martin version of *Peter Pan,* and Gram was her understudy. So she'd done it all by the time she tried her hand at directing...and got the harebrained idea that I might follow in her footsteps. After the fall, she never put *Brooke* and *acting* in the same sentence again."

Chuckling when she yawned again, Hunter got to his feet. Again. And headed for the door. Again.

"Remember, call if you need me."

She nodded as he closed the door behind him, wondering where she'd find the inner strength, as sleep eluded her tonight, *not* to dial his number.

CHAPTER NINETEEN

"But Honey," Constance insisted, "you just have to come. We're all talking about how it seems you've been avoiding us lately, and we miss you!"

Hunter couldn't help but grin. His mom—who loved telling anyone who'd listen that she was still tiny enough to fit into her size-four wedding gown—referring to herself as *we*. She knew as well as he did that he and his brothers touched base at least once a week, even if only for a minute or two. He knew they were fine, and they knew the same about him. So he'd already heard about Rafe's not-so-surprise party.

"Surely you can spare an hour to celebrate your brother's fortieth."

Had she paused to give him time to remember that Rafe's wife had recently sewn sergeant stripes onto her husband's sleeve, or that the department had just awarded him the Medal of Honor? Only way a cop earned that one, a lifetime around policemen taught him, was by risking his life in the line of duty.

"You don't want to be the only Stone who isn't here, do you?"

He clutched the handset tighter. "Don't worry, Mom. I'll be there." And to change the subject, he added, "Maureen asked me to pick up Rafe's cake on the way over. Need anything else?"

"Aren't you a sweetheart to ask! Do you have a pen?"

He should have known her list—ice, sodas, chips—would include something that would take him out of his way. Hunter was about to find out just how far....

"Would you call Deidre for me? You know how that woman loves to talk. Normally I wouldn't mind hearing about her theater project or her latest play or some star she used to work with or how adorable her handyman is. But with everything else I need to do to get the house ready for the party..."

Hunter listened as she recited another list, this time of all the chores and errands that would fill her hours between now and Sunday afternoon.

"Mom, I'll never understand why you go to all that bother before a party. You know better than I do that what you do will be undone by the kids. Besides, the party is for family. Nobody cares if there are dust bunnies under the guest room bed."

"*I* care," she countered.

Shouldn't have wasted your breath.

"So you'll call Deidre for me?"

"No problem."

"And Brooke?"

Just what he needed as his brothers and uncles discussed cop awards. Brooke, watching and listening as they did their best to avoid any mention of his most shameful moment.

"Why? Deidre and Brooke aren't family." Never would be, he thought, if Brooke had anything to say about it.

"Because we think a party will be good for them. Especially that darling little boy."

"We?"

"Your sisters-in-law and me, of course." Constance sighed resignedly. "All right. Fine. I'll call them myself." She clucked her tongue. "But really, Hunter, if you ask me, this…this grudge match between you and Brooke is ridiculous. It isn't healthy for either of you. Or for Connor."

He could have said the obvious: *You'd think after all these years, you'd know I'm not the one holding the grudge.* But why bother? It wasn't as though his mom asked a lot of him. Besides, it would be good for Connor to spend time with Stone aunts and uncles, cousins and Constance herself, who'd become his grandmother once Harry worked his magic in court.

"All right," he said, "I'll call them."

The minute he hung up with his mom, Hunter

drove to the nearest toy shop and bought a colorful plastic train set for Connor. Because how would it look if he dropped in just to deliver the invitation?

Brooke was on the phone when he showed up, and she waved him inside. She didn't say hello or invite him to sit down, ask how he was doing or if he'd like something to drink. Must have been something work-related to put that serious look on her face.

As she stepped out of the room to complete the call, Hunter got onto the floor and showed Connor how the train cars connected to one another, how they rolled around on the shiny black track. The baby was doing his best to emulate the chug of an engine when Brooke returned carrying a basket of freshly laundered towels. She put it on the couch and joined them on the floor.

"It's so cute," she said, connecting two cars. "Wherever did you find it?"

"There's a little toy shop on Main Street," he told her. "Mumbles and Squeaks. Ever been there?"

She got up and sat beside the basket. "Can't say that I have. But I need to check it out. I like things that are safe and unusual." Perched on a sofa cushion now, she flapped a hand towel. "It was really sweet of you to pick it up. I packed up most of his toys when we moved over here."

Yeah. He remembered, because he'd been the one who carried the boxes into Beth's basement.

"It's nearly suppertime. Have you eaten yet?"

Levering himself onto one elbow, he grinned. "What is it with you and food?"

She'd already made a tidy stack of hand towels and washcloths and started a new pile of bath towels. "Me and food? What do you mean?"

"I'm not complaining, mind you, but I've probably gained five pounds since…" Reminding her of the crash didn't seem smart, so he finished with "Since you moved back to Baltimore. Keep this up, and I'll need a whole new wardrobe."

"Sounds like a complaint to me." Brooke smoothed the top towel. "And it isn't like you're a Christmas goose—no one is force-feeding you."

She was smiling, but he wasn't sure how to respond.

He helped Connor sit in the circle of train tracks. "You'd think the animal activists would have put a stop to fattening birds up just to sell them for a few cents more per pound."

"You'd think."

Had enough time passed so she wouldn't think he'd stopped by solely to invite her to the party? Only one way to find out….

"So I was talking to my mom earlier. She and my sisters-in-law are throwing my brother Rafe a surprise party for his fortieth this Sunday."

"Rafe is you oldest brother, right?"

"Yeah, and Mom wants you and Deidre to come."

She grabbed the last towel from the basket. "Connor had a lot of fun playing with your nieces and nephews at Deidre's party."

How was he supposed to interpret that? As an acceptance or a polite rejection?

"What time should we be there?"

"I, ah… Four o'clock, I think."

"Perfect. Connor will have had a nap."

"What's that?" Connor asked, pointing.

Hunter picked up the end car. "It's a caboose, buddy."

"Cah-*boose*," he echoed, then picked up the car and inspected it. He pointed to the platform and met Hunter's eyes. "Porch?"

"Close enough," he said. "And this—" Hunter touched the raised portion of the roof "—is a cupola."

Connor put the car back on the track and fussed when it didn't instantly connect to the boxcar in front of it.

"Hold on a sec, kiddo. Let your ol' uncle Hunter help you get back on track."

As he realigned the car, Brooke groaned at his joke. "Were you into trains as a kid?"

"You could say that. I still have the engineer's hat I got on a field trip to the B&O Railroad Museum. Mom can tell you, that outing was a curse and a blessing. I added to my collection every year. I ended up selling half the stuff, but I still have enough to set up a bona fide train garden in the basement."

"Do you run tracks around your Christmas tree?"

"Never had a tree of my own. Unless you count that little ceramic job I found at a flea market. Only reason I bought it was so Connor would have *something* Christmassy when he spent time at my place."

"No tree of your own? Why not?"

"Too much time and trouble considering how little time I spend at the house. Besides, Mom always does her place up to the nines. When I want a taste of the holiday, I just go over there."

Connor started gnawing on the little blue engine.

"Uh-oh," Hunter said, "teething, eh, big guy?"

Brooke placed the neatly folded towels into the laundry basket. Standing, she balanced it on one hip. "He's been drooling and chewing everything in sight lately," she said, heading for the hall. "Would you mind putting him in the high chair and getting him a couple of teething biscuits? They're in the cabinet above the coffeepot."

He did as she asked, and helped himself to a biscuit. "Blah," he said, grimacing. "Tastes like

cardboard. How do you eat these things, kid?"
Breaking it in half, he tossed the bitten end into
the trash as Brooke entered the room.

"I think I'll bring cone cakes to the party."

"Cone cakes?"

"Like cupcakes, only you pour the batter into
ice-cream cones. Kids love 'em, and so do moms.
No messy papers to throw away."

"Sounds good, but you don't need to go to all
that bother. Mom says she and the girls have everything under contr—"

"Of course she did. That's what women always
say."

"They do? Why?"

She shrugged. "So the men in our lives won't
see us as needy, whiny females?"

The men in our lives. Did that mean—

"If we get to your mom's early, you can help me
carry them inside."

We? So…not only did she want to go to the
party, she wanted to go with him?

"Then maybe if you'll keep an eye on Connor,
I can help your mom and sisters-in-law with the
last-minute setup."

No maybe about it. *Your assignment—whether
you choose to accept it or not—is to mind Connor while she infiltrates your family.*

But why would she want to, considering their
history?

And why did she automatically assume he was okay with it?

Better question: Why was he standing here nodding like the fuzzy brown dog that once sat in the rear window of his grandfather's Oldsmobile?

Hunter knew that if he didn't hit the road soon, he might just break out that DVD and let her have it with a firm *Your "I'm the boss of you and Connor" days are O-V-E-R, Brooke O'Toole!*

But it was too soon for that. He needed to schedule a sit-down with his lawyer. Needed to plan a strategy.

"Better hit the road," he said, getting to his feet.

"So you're not staying for supper? I made tuna salad and macaroni and cheese. All I have to do is heat up the noodles and toast the bread for sandwiches. There's more than enough."

Had his mother told Brooke that tuna salad was one of his favorite sandwich fixings? "I, ah, I'd better not. Payroll to take care of and bills to pay." He opened the door. "See you Sunday."

"What's best for you? Three o'clock?"

"Better make it two-thirty. Mom gave me a list of things to pick up on the way to her place."

Smiling and nodding, she said, "We'll be ready."

"Right. Ready. See you then." And he left so fast that he forgot to hug Connor, didn't tell her goodbye.

THREE DAYS HAD passed since that afternoon, and as he and his brothers congratulated Rafe, Hunter could hear Brooke and his sisters-in-law swapping "It isn't easy balancing work and chores and kids" stories. He heard Connor, too, giggling at the antics of his nieces and nephews. Nice change from the depression-induced whining, he thought.

During their last session, Dr. Rosen said that the baby's cranky behavior could continue indefinitely or, because kids his age were remarkably resilient, he could just as easily wake up one day and behave as if his parents' deaths had never happened.

The boy squealed with glee at a silly noise one of Hunter's nephews had made, and he'd been just as happy when he delivered the little train days ago. If this behavior continued...

Connor's calm, content demeanor gave Hunter hope that moving permanently into his house wouldn't cause psychological damage, now or down the road. But what if a judge decided to give Brooke full credit for the baby's adjustment?

Part of him agreed, and part did not. She'd started out on shaky ground, running from Baltimore to Richmond to escape romance-related problems, then running back again for the same reason. She got rattled way too easily, in his opinion, and since starting this new job, Brooke seemed more frazzled than ever. Oh, she'd tried to hide dark circles under makeup, but he'd noticed them.

Hunter wondered if Harry charged double for Sunday-evening consults. Not that it mattered. He'd second-mortgage his house, use the equity in Stone Contracting to finance the adoption if he had to. He needed to get on the ball. Because with every passing day, Brooke was racking up more "good parent" credits.

"Come and get it!" his mom called.

As the family crowded around the long dining room table, something else became obvious: connor looked right at home with the Stone family. Yet another reason to make things legal sooner rather than later.

He glanced at Brooke, who looked anything but exhausted today. Maybe it was the pink of her shirt. The earrings that dangled from her lobes. The matching stone-and-bead necklace that enhanced the warm brown of her big eyes. Funny, but she looked right at home with his family, too. How much simpler would everything be if she'd just let go of the past and marry him.

Hunter nearly laughed out loud at the absurdity of the thought. And yet...

"I'm almost afraid to ask what that sly grin is all about," his mother said, sitting beside him.

She'd made Rafe's favorite, lasagna and meatballs, and as the baking dishes moved up and down the table, she leaned close and whispered, "I don't blame you for staring. Brooke is such a lovely girl."

He could have kicked himself for not being more careful. If his mother had caught him staring, maybe others had, too.

Hunter took a bold chance and looked at her, and he breathed a sigh of relief when he saw that she was too busy laughing at something Gabe had said to notice. Yeah, she was lovely, all right. Lovely, and then some.

"Admit it," his mom was saying, "you could do worse." Laughing, Constance elbowed his ribs. "You've already done worse! If you're smart, you'll snap her up before some other guy realizes what a treasure she is."

"I would if I thought for a second that she'd have me."

Had he actually said that out loud? And if he had, had his mother heard it?

"I expect grandchildren from you, too," she continued, "and you're not getting any younger, you know."

He winced.

"Now, now, I didn't mean to hurt your feelings." Constance squeezed his hand. "You always were my sensitive one, weren't you. Maybe that's why you couldn't make it as a policeman like every other man in the Stone family."

In a two-minute time span, she'd reminded him of his poor choices in women, told him he was getting old and underscored what she saw as the reason he'd failed as a cop.

"Ouch," Hunter said. "When did you enroll in the Don Rickles Insult-a-Minute class?"

His brother Gabe looked up. "What's this? Mom's gone back to school?"

Constance waved the question away. "Oh, don't pay any attention to him. He's just upset because I said he should snap up—"

"Mom," Hunter broke in, "pass the Parmesan, please?"

She handed him the cheese shaker and took a breath. And Hunter knew it meant she intended to finish her sentence. "And how about some meatballs?"

He could tell even before she let go of the bowl that his mom would spill the beans…if he let her.…

"Delicious," he said around a bite of lasagna. "Did you do something different to the sauce?"

Gabe laughed. "Oh, you're good, kid. Real good."

Hunter didn't have to ask what his older brother meant. The smirk, the teasing glint in his eyes, that sly tone of voice told him that Gabe had overheard most, if not all, of his conversation with their mother and knew exactly what Hunter was up to.

"But as the youngest—and the last man standing in this house—you oughta know better than the rest of us that she has a one-track mind."

"She's stubborn," Jesse agreed.

"An immovable object," his wife added.

Gabe's wife chimed in with, "Mom isn't easily sidetracked, that's for sure."

"The girls are right," Gabe confirmed. "Nothing short of a bulldozer plowing through the dining room will distract her."

"Good grief," Constance said, feigning a frown. "Listen to the bunch of you!"

Had they all been eavesdropping? Hunter wondered.

"So if I'm the sensitive one," he said, grinning, "which of your boys is the tactful one?"

From the opposite end of the table, Rafe said, "Hey. I turned forty today. There shouldn't be any laughter or lightheartedness. This is a solemn occasion."

"Age is only a number, old man," Gabe said. "Turn off your hearing aids and enjoy your lasagna."

"My plate is clean," he said. "How 'bout the bunch of you do the same so we can get to the main course, cake!"

By now everyone at the table—including the kids—had joined in the laughter.

"Leave it to you, Constance," Deidre said as

Hunter's cell phone rang, "to throw a simple family dinner…and have a wild party break out!"

He pretended not to notice his mother's scolding expression and excused himself to take the call. Last Chance, said the caller ID. "Hey, Mitch," he said, stepping into the foyer, "haven't heard from you in months. Those hooligans eating up all your free time?"

The young counselor laughed. "No more than usual."

"How many kids in your care now?"

"Sixteen. And they're the reason I'm calling. They're going stir-crazy now that school's out, so I was wondering…could you use a few helpers, you know, to fetch tools, haul drywall, sweep up sawdust, the way they did last summer? Can't have 'em lying around here all day watching TV and playing 'Monster Hunter' on the Wii."

"I swear. If I live to be a hundred, I'll never understand what teenagers get out of those video games."

"I'm in favor of anything that keeps 'em off the streets—" Mitch chuckled "—and each other's backs. But they need fresh air and exercise, too, along with practical lessons that could give them some direction in life."

Hunter turned in time to see Brooke nodding and looking somber at something his mother was saying. *God help you, Mom, if you're repeating that "why don't you snap her up?" nonsense....*

He turned his back to the table. "As it happens," he said to Mitch, "I just started a whole-house rehab." Hunter pictured the Sheridans' house. "How many of the kids are old enough to work?"

"Five."

"Well, you know the drill, send them in their rattiest jeans and T-shirts because they'll get good and grimy. I'll supply safety glasses, work gloves and hard hats. You supply the transportation." He paused. "And work boots, 'cause sneakers won't cut it on a construction site."

"Right. I'd almost forgotten about that. Got a donor's check in the mail today, so I'll take them shopping tonight."

Hunter gave Mitch the Sheridans' address and told him to drop the boys off at six-thirty. "That'll give me twenty minutes or so to give them a quick tour of the place—and run down the rules—before the rest of the guys get there."

"Can I hang around, listen to your 'How Boys Become Men' speech?"

Hunter laughed. "Only if you bring coffee. Large. Black."

Of the seven kids Mitch had sent him last summer, three returned to high school in the fall, two moved on to college and one—still employed by Stone Contracting—was racking up the hours required to earn journeyman status. The seventh had been taken from the job site by ambulance after overdosing on crystal meth, and last Hunter heard, the boy was still in rehab.

"Any problems I should know about?"

"Not this year," Mitch said. "At least, none I'm aware of. Yet."

"That's good, for your sake and mine *and* the kids'. See you at six-thirty."

Last thing he heard before dropping the phone into his pocket was Mitch groaning, "Six-thirty."

"We thought you'd never hang up," Deidre scolded when he returned to the table. "What was so important that it couldn't wait until after your brother's party?"

She had never approved of his work with the once-troubled boys who called the Last Chance home. But gratitude—that she'd forgiven him and treated him like a grandson—had inspired his long-standing decision to keep his involvement to himself. "Just lining things up for work tomorrow."

He glanced at Brooke. "I'll have a full crew at the house first thing in the morning, so we'll probably make some serious progress by day's end."

"Good," she said. "I'm glad."

She sure didn't sound it. Didn't look it, either. Maybe it had hit her, finally, that she was stuck in this house, surrounded by people she barely knew, people directly related to *him*.

"Well, kids," Constance said, gathering her grandchildren close, "what do you say? Is it time?"

His nieces and nephews squealed happily and followed their grandmother into the kitchen. When the last child rounded the corner, a ripple of envy coursed through him at the affection shining in his sisters-in-law's eyes, the unadulterated pride beaming from his brothers' faces. Hunter wanted that. Wanted it so much that he ached inside. But unless he found a way to put his guilt to rest, he'd spend the rest of his life feeling unworthy of a life like theirs.

Connor, wide-eyed and quiet, was drinking it all in, too. Seeing that, Hunter's ache dimmed; he might never have everything his brothers had, but soon he'd have a slice of it. *Don't worry,* li'l guy, Hunter thought. *You won't feel like an outsider for much longer.*

Constance entered the room, barely visible behind the halo of forty candles flickering atop Rafe's cake. "I think I know what the Pied Piper felt like," she joked as five eager grandchildren trailed behind her. "Everybody back to their chairs now," she told them, "so we can sing to the birthday boy and let him open his presents."

Connor pointed. "Cake," he said, looking at Hunter. "Conner have cake?"

He was about to say of course when Gabe's wife, seated beside him, beat him to it. "You can have a great big slice, cutie," she said, ruffling his hair. She shot a guilty look Brooke's way. "If it's all right with your mommy, that is."

Connor looked at Brooke, too. "Mommy," he said, pointing again. "Mommy."

Only moments ago Hunter had reiterated the importance of not letting too much time pass before making his move. As Brooke basked in the glow of her new title, fear clutched his heart: Was it already too late?

CHAPTER TWENTY

She'd been friendly during the party, chatted amiably as they drove Deidre home. But after they'd dropped her grandmother off, and as he helped her carry Connor, his diaper bag and leftover lasagna and cake to the apartment, Brooke barely said a word. And when he left, she barely said goodbye.

Hunter tried everything from watching black-and-white Hitchcock flicks to reading Grisham novels to get Brooke out of his head, and when that failed, he started pacing the length of his living room…

…until he stubbed his toe on a table leg.

He started a pot of coffee at 3:05. By 3:15 he was at his desk, sipping the strong black brew while flipping through suppliers' catalogs in search of a faucet for Mrs. Carter. But not even trying to please his most difficult client took his mind off Brooke. If he didn't get a grip, a throbbing toe could be the least of his troubles.

At 4:00 he settled into his La-Z-Boy and opened his laptop and fell asleep surfing the Net. How long would he have slept if the trash truck hadn't lumbered down the road? Well, at least he didn't need to make coffee. Hunter nuked a cup and showered, hoping to clear the no-sleep buzz from his brain before heading to the Sheridans' to meet Mitch and the kids. When he arrived at 6:15, he found his foreman already setting things up for the day's work.

Sam took one look at him and commented, "Another nightmare night, eh, boss?"

What night wasn't? But rather than dwell on the disturbing images that plagued his sleep, Hunter grumbled about the impossible faucet lady, who owed Stone Contracting nearly fifteen grand... and pretended discontent with materials and subcontractors was reason enough to hold on to that money. He grumbled about plumbers and electricians who didn't show up on time and suppliers who delivered the wrong materials—or the right ones in the wrong quantities.

His foreman plugged in the Sawzall. "Don't bellyache to me," he said, adjusting his safety glasses. "I've already told you how you could solve most of those problems."

The blade bit into a 2 x 6 upright, spewing an arc of sawdust behind it. Hunter winced, not at the noise but because he knew exactly what Sam would say the minute that board hit the floor: "Long workweeks are the price you pay...when you're a control freak."

Hunter agreed. Hiring a project coordinator to help with estimates and orders or a secretary to handle the phones and filing would definitely save time. If he had the time to place an ad and interview candidates. If he found someone, how was he supposed to fit the employee—and an additional desk—into his already-overstuffed home office? And if he did manage to squeeze them in somehow, when would he find the time to teach them things specific to Stone Contracting, like which subcontractors consistently performed well, which supply houses stocked affordable quality merchandise, and how to finesse customers who expected ten-million-dollar results from ten-thousand-dollar contracts? Facing all of that, it made more sense to do things himself.

As it turned out, Sam's impatience with his decision was the least of Hunter's problems. The minute the walls came down at the Sheridans', it became clear that what should have been a simple rewiring project would require a full-scale interior rebuild. In addition to using inferior wire throughout the house, the previous owners had also slapped inferior shingles over the originals without patching leaks. So for decades, rainwater and melting snow had been seeping between the exterior brick and the interior plaster, building a layer of mold that had gnawed into every board and beam. Now it was up to him to make things right without bankrupting himself, all while setting the adoption process in motion. Good thing he'd learned to get by on three hours' sleep, he thought as his cell phone rang.

When he saw that it was Deidre, Hunter groaned under his breath. The woman could be sweeter than rocky candy when she put her mind to it... especially if there was a leaky faucet to fix or a squeaky hinge that needed oil. He left the Last Chance boys in Sam's capable hands and headed outside to find out what Brooke's grandmother needed this time.

"Hey, lady. What's up?"

"I just got home from signing the papers to make the little theater mine, all mine!" she announced.

The excitement in her voice was rivaled by his own surprise. He hadn't heard that the place was for sale, let alone that she'd been interested in buying it. Evidently, keeping secrets and making decisions without consulting anyone really was an O'Toole family trait.

"I was hoping you could meet me over there later today," she said, "and since you have an inspector's license, I thought maybe you could have a look around, see if you think I got my money's worth."

"Deidre. Are you kidding? Why didn't you have the place inspected before you bought it?"

"Calm down, Mr. Worrywart. The price was so good I couldn't pass it up for fear someone might come along and buy it right out from under me! Besides," she said, laughing, "if there's anything wrong with that gorgeous old building, I have a handsome young contractor friend who can fix her up good as new."

So she'd made that decision, too, without running it past him.

"If today isn't good," she said, "we can do it tomorrow...."

Hunter visualized this week's to-do list: estimates to prepare, inspections to schedule—and inspectors to meet on site—materials and equipment to order, teaching Mitch's kids the difference between a wrench and pliers, finding time to see Connor....

"Things have been crazy at work lately," he said. "Best I can do on such short notice is to meet you over there first thing tomorrow."

"So exactly what does a fine-looking he-man like you mean when he says 'first thing in the morning'?"

He summoned the self-control to keep from saying, *Flattery might work on the egomaniac actors you surround yourself with, but it won't work on me.*

"Six."

Hunter heard her exasperated sigh and hoped

the early-morning hour would get him off the hook; he kept a short list of home inspectors in his cell phone and would gladly recommend one who'd be straight with her.

"Well, that's going to be a wasted day," she complained. "Up at dawn, over to the theater with you, then back here to babysit Connor. Will I ever learn to say no?"

"If you do, teach me how to do it, will you?"

Deidre must not have heard him, because she continued with "If I had a dollar for all the no's I should have said…"

The O'Toole women would be the death of him…if they didn't drive him crazy first.

Hunter's call waiting punctuated the thought. "Somebody's on the other line," he said. "See you at six."

He pressed Talk and barked, "Stone Contracting…"

"Goodness," Brooke said. "I'm almost afraid to ask how things are going over there."

Oh, great. He'd barely uttered two words, and already she'd taken him to task for his abrupt tone. He might as well dump the bad news on her. At least then she'd have something legitimate to complain about for a change.

"I was talking with your grandmother when you beeped in."

"Well, that explains why you sound like your

shoes are on fire. I hope you didn't let her talk you into another fix-it project."

"'Fraid so," he admitted. Hunter gave her a rundown of the conversation and found himself mildly surprised that Deidre hadn't mentioned the theater purchase to Brooke, either.

"For a self-professed savvy old lady," she said, "that wasn't very smart, was it?"

If Brooke thought he planned to get in the middle of a family squabble, she had another think coming.

"The fact that Gram made a decision that important without consulting anyone tells me one of two things," Brooke said. "One…she knew I'd try to talk her out of making such a huge commitment at her age, or two, it's on the verge of collapse."

Hunter grinned. "You're probably right, on both counts. But at least she's smart enough to know she needs some honest input now."

"What do you bet when you get over there, you'll find a "Condemned" poster hidden away somewhere?"

Hunter chuckled, because the Sheridans' house wasn't in much better shape.

"So how are the boys from the Last Chance working out?"

He sensed that she was working up the nerve to ask for a production report, but he saw no point in delivering one until he knew the full extent of the damage.

He heard two hollow pings in the background and said, "The kids are doing great."

Two more pings preceded a nasal announcement: "Dr. Modesto, call on line three. Dr. Modesto, line three…"

Brooke was calling from the hospital?

"Who's with Connor?"

"Felix."

She said it as if he should have known…and approved. Well, he didn't.

"Don't get me wrong," Hunter began. "I like the guy, but he's a bit long in the tooth to be minding a kid Connor's age, don't you think?"

"Are you kidding? He's strong as an ox. Besides, Connor is a great kid. Easy to take care of."

"Sometimes. And sometimes he can whip himself into a frenzy. I've never seen Felix under pressure. Think he can handle a full-fledged tantrum?"

A tense moment passed before she said, "I would never leave him with someone who isn't capable. And trustworthy."

Amazing, he thought, how quickly she'd reverted to her cool detached tone. Hunter could almost see her, back ramrod straight and chin up as she paced the hospital corridor.

"Are things going as planned at Beth's?" she asked.

"For the most part. But you probably should come over here first chance you get. We uncovered a few problems that could impact the completion date."

"I'm off at two today. Then I'll need to swing by the apartment and get Connor. Will you still be there between three and three-thirty?"

"Not sure it's a great idea to bring him down here. Place is a wreck. Too dangerous for a kid his age, so you won't be able to put him down. He's not gonna like that."

"You could be right, but we won't be there long."

He chose to ignore the "could be right" comment. "So how are things going with the new job?"

"We lost two patients, and I had to tell both families. One right after the other." She exhaled a ragged sigh. "I need to learn how to distance myself."

"Why?"

"Well, when they get teary eyed, I do, too. And that's the last thing they need at a time like that."

He'd never forget the look on his mom's face that rainy afternoon when a stiff-lipped nurse blurted, "Dr. Naik sent me to tell you that your husband is dead." Her voice had held less emotion than if she'd just told them visiting hours were over. Hunter shared the experience with Brooke, adding, "Getting bad news from someone who cares is exactly what families need at a time like that."

"I don't know about that. I think what they need is someone strong and calm and—"

"Who fed you that load of baloney?"

"It's… That's the impression I get watching the woman who's training me. She's considerate but in an arm's-length, no-nonsense way."

Hunter snorted. "In other words, her way makes things easier for *her*. If you ask me, it's a blessing for everyone concerned that she's leaving. Bad news—especially that kind of bad news—is a whole lot easier to hear if it's delivered by someone who's kind and empathetic, not some stone-cold clinician."

Brooke was quiet for so long that he took the phone away from his ear to see if he still had bars and battery power.

"I'm sorry losing your dad was so hard for you and your family, Hunter."

It made him wonder how she'd been told about her own parents' deaths and the words the deputy chose to deliver the news about Beth and Kent.

"Millions of people have lost parents," he said. "But for now, I hope you'll forget everything that heartless broad taught you and remember this, you can't go wrong if you're honest with people." He thought of all the Connor-related decisions she'd made without including him. "And if you don't hold back important information."

"Right. Well, it's something to think about, anyway." She paused as the call went out for Dr. Modesto again.

"So I'll see you around three, then?"

Hunter checked his watch. He had just under four hours to give the boys some pointers, visit his other job sites and get back here in time to write up the list of unexpected repairs—and extra time—the Sheridans' house would require.

"Sounds good," he said.

As he hung up, Sam tossed a waterlogged two-by-four onto the trash pile. "Who was that?"

"Connor's aunt. She's the homeowner here, sort of." It would have been good to see the debris mound growing if it weren't symptomatic of all that was wrong with the place.

"How does somebody sort of own a house?"

"Connor's mom and dad didn't leave a will, so everything they had automatically becomes his. But since he's not even two, his aunt will probably act as his guardian." *For now,* Hunter thought.

"Probably?"

"Brooke—I mean Connor's aunt—is the only blood kin capable of handling the legal stuff on his behalf."

Sam chucked another two-by-four onto the pile. "Uh-huh."

Hunter added a board, too. "Uh-huh what?"

"Sounds like somebody's been talking to a lawyer."

"What makes you say that?"

"Oh, no reason." Sam shrugged and kicked a nail aside. "Except maybe that you're spewing legalese like a fountain."

Close, Sam, he thought. Maybe too close.

"All I can say is, this aunt of Connor's must be one heck of a shrew." Another board slammed into the pile. "'Cause you usually reserve that kind of snarling for deadbeats and suppliers who don't supply."

If he'd sounded that angry to Sam, who was used to the way he talked to people who didn't hold up their end of things, how had he sounded to Brooke?

Hunter smacked sawdust from his palms. "I have to check out the Fox and Nakamura jobs," he said. "I should be back around two." He pointed toward the kitchen. "Put the boys to work taking down the kitchen and bathroom cabinets." He handed Sam a business card. "And when they're finished, call Mitch to come pick them up. Tell him I'll pay them for a full day."

"Uh-oh," Sam said, tucking the card into his shirt pocket. "Firing the lot of 'em already?"

"No. From what I've seen, they did great...for their first day. I just don't want them here when

I'm breaking the bad news about this dump. Tell them to get a good night's sleep and be back here tomorrow, seven sharp."

"Yes, sir, Mr. Generosity," Sam joked.

He'd been anything but generous when telling Brooke how he felt about her job.

"If Connor's aunt gets here before I do, don't say anything."

"Don't worry, Prince Charming." Sam winked. "I'll bring a chair up from the basement and steal a bottle of that water you bought for the boys. You can break the bad news and then come to her rescue when she keels over."

Rescue? The only reason Sam could say a thing like that was because he knew very little about Hunter's past.

If only he could say the same about Brooke.

CHAPTER TWENTY-ONE

BROOKE USED A blue-plaid tablecloth to hide the knicks and scratches on the claw-foot table and filled a blue delft vase with black-eyed Susans. White stoneware bowls sat on red plates, each with a bright yellow bread-and-butter plate at ten o'clock. White napkins cushioned pistol-handled forks to the left and matching dinner knives and spoons to the right. Big goblets for water and small ones for wine held the two o'clock spot.

She stood back to inspect her handiwork and, realizing she'd forgotten the pewter trivet to hold the Crock-Pot, placed it beside the centerpiece. "Take that, Martha Stewart!" she said.

Tonight, things had to be perfect, because Beth would have turned twenty-seven today, and Brooke decided it was time to celebrate her sister's life, not her death. From now on she'd embrace Beth's memory, not run from it.

And because tonight she'd confront Hunter.

Hopefully, the confrontation would bring things back into focus....

Brooke had needed someone to blame for the

violent, senseless way her mother had been taken from her, and Hunter had been the easiest target. The bitterness had been with her so long that it felt like an angry old friend, and the new emotions born of his thoughtful gestures and acts of kindness seemed unsettling and scary because Brooke knew she hadn't earned any of it.

Like this afternoon, when he'd been patient to the point of long-suffering, explaining everything that was wrong with the house. And though he'd nodded agreeably as she pressed a check into his hand, Brooke had got the distinct impression he'd never cash it...or any of the others she'd written.

His behavior was both remarkable and confusing and left her feeling off balance...especially in light of what Deidre had told her about his plans to help underprivileged kids.

So Brooke had invited him to supper. "Just a Crock-Pot roast," she'd said. "Way too much for Connor and me." Then she'd steeled herself for a rejection, because why would anyone accept such an off-the-cuff invitation? Instead, Hunter had thrown her further off balance by asking what time he should be there.

"I don't get it. I just. Don't. Get it."

Connor stood in the playpen and held out his arms.

"Why has he been so nice lately?" she wondered, picking him up. "I understand why he's good to *you*. The guy loves you as much as if you were his own little boy." Hugging him tight, she kissed one cheek, then the other. "And who can blame him!"

Brooke carried him to the window.

"But why is he being so good to *me* after the abysmal way I've treated him all these years?"

"Car," Connor said, pointing at Deidre's big black sedan. Facing Brooke, he added, "Bye-bye?"

She kissed his fingertip. "Not tonight, sweetie."

He pointed again, this time at the big house. "Gram house."

"That's right," she said, looking across the yard at the grand old mansion. As executor of her grandmother's will, she knew that one day it would be hers. But unless she had Connor to share it with, it would never feel like home.

Connor sniffled and rubbed his nose with a chubby fist.

According to Felix, the baby had taken a three-hour nap today, waking just a few minutes before she got home from work. But if that was true, why did he look so sleepy?

"I hope you aren't coming down with a summer cold."

Brooke deposited him in the high chair and buckled him in.

"This should hold you," she said, sprinkling

a handful of Cheerios onto the tray, "until your uncle gets here."

"Uncle," he said, nodding. "Uncle Hunter."

He didn't say it with his usual enthusiasm, but he seemed content enough, building and toppling a cereal tower. Dr. Rosen had warned her not to celebrate this apparent return to his former always-happy demeanor, because it could very well be short-lived...a precursor of deeper depression.

She crouched beside the chair. "That isn't going to happen, right? You're happy and adjusting and you're going to stay that way, aren't you!"

He allowed her to sprinkle his face with kisses... for a second or two. Grinning, Brooke straightened. "Well, thanks for indulging me, however briefly."

She stepped into the powder room for a last check of her hair and makeup. She could see him in the mirror, giggling as handfuls of tiny Os pecked the linoleum. Then a flash of silver caught her attention—light reflecting from the silver wolf earrings Beth had given her last year for Christmas. Clutching the matching pendant in her fist, she remembered the way her silly sister had wrapped everything in separate boxes and stacked each, one inside the other. *I miss you.*

"You. Will. Not. Cry. Not on Beth's birthday!"

Brooke took a deep breath and straightened the collar of her sleeveless blouse. *Wouldn't have killed you to take an iron to it,* she thought, frowning at her reflection. But what difference did a few wrinkles make? Men didn't notice such things. Hunter wouldn't notice her wide belt—same shade of pink as the swirls in her paisley broomstick skirt—or the strappy white sandals she'd chosen, either. A good thing, since stereotypical male obliviousness would add believability to the last-minute "sound" of her invitation.

She flicked off the powder room light and, standing in the middle of the living room, asked, "Is it just me, or is it way too quiet in here?"

Connor answered with a silly laugh as another handful of cereal rained to the floor. Brooke pecked the keys of her iPhone and, after turning up the volume, hoisted the baby from his high chair. "The Eagles were your mommy's favorite group," she said, "so let's do a birthday dance in her honor!"

He squealed happily as she whirled around the room, and when she dipped him, he giggled until he was breathless. "Oh-oh-oh-oh, sweet darlin'," she sang at the top of her lungs.

"Oh-oh-oh-oh…" Connor copied. And then he pointed at the door.

There almost wasn't time to feel embarrassed. Almost.

"How long have you been out here?" she asked, opening it.

"Exactly long enough." Hunter rapped on a frosted pane in the door. "Long enough to decide that next chance I get, I'm replacing these with clear glass."

He was a contractor. Had he noticed a defect that she hadn't? "Why? What's wrong with them?"

"Nothing, except your little show would have been a whole lot more entertaining if I could have seen it clearly." The grocery bags he carried crinkled when he leaned in to kiss Connor's forehead. "Is it my imagination, or does he feel a little warm?"

She pressed her lips to the baby's forehead. "It's probably just all that laughing and dancing. But just to be sure, I'll take his temperature when I change his diaper in a few—" The look on his face stopped her. "What?"

"You read temperatures…with your lips?"

Brooke led the way into the kitchen. "It's more effective than a thermometer."

Grinning, he winked. "Aren't you medical pros all about science and instruments instead of old wives' tales and superstition?"

Now, really. How did he expect her to respond to that!

"Hope you don't mind," he said, putting a half gallon of Neapolitan into the freezer and an apple pie on the counter. "I brought dessert. And some teething biscuits for Short Stuff over there."

Except for holiday dinners and special occasions, Brooke wasn't big on dessert. And she would have told him that before he went shopping…if he'd asked.

He slid Connor's cookies into the cabinet above the coffeepot. "Do we have time for a little nephew-uncle tomfoolery before we eat?"

Tomfoolery. Instantly, her ire dimmed. Who but Hunter could make the outdated word sound like everyday English?

"Supper should be on the table in, oh, fifteen minutes or so."

He held Connor above the high chair and gave him a gentle shake. "You were hiding enough cereal in your lap for another snack," he said, laughing as Cheerios rained onto the seat. He popped one into his mouth. "First bite I've had since last night."

"You skipped breakfast *and* lunch? Why?"

He put Connor on the living room floor and upended the toy box. "Lots on my agenda today," he said, stretching out beside the baby. "Tell her, sport, how your uncle Hunter works like a dog, and how he never would have made it here by five if he'd taken time out for doughnuts and coffee or a burger and fries." He looked at Brooke and added, "I'm a busy guy!"

"Busy," Connor said, grabbing a plastic key chain.

Brooke watched as the pair shared quiet laughter. Nose to nose that way, they could have been father and son. Same wavy hair. Same long-lashed eyes. Same quick smile....

Although Beth had put on a good show for outsiders, she'd been miserable after their dad's death...until Kent came along. She might have been happier still if Brooke had ignored his flaws and treated him more like family for no reason other than he'd brought so much joy into her sister's life.

A strange melancholy settled over her admitting that, because if there had been even a glimmer of truth in what Deidre had overheard...

Hunter must have read her shaky sigh to mean she wasn't pleased about the pile of stuffed animals, rubber balls and tiny trucks strewn across the floor.

"Don't worry," he said. "I'll clean it up before I leave."

She wasn't worried. In fact, Brooke rather liked the way the two of them looked surrounded by a mess of little-boy toys.

Nodding, she forced a smile and got busy opening and closing cupboard doors. How would she answer if he asked what she was looking for?

What she ought to be looking for was the reason she'd done a complete about-face when it came to Hunter. Or the best way to begin her unrehearsed speech now that she'd started seeing him as something other than the enemy.

"Table looks great," he said, standing behind her.

"Good grief! You scared me half to death!"

"Sorry." He shifted Connor to his other hip and touched a forefinger to the baby's nose. "How come you never told me that your aunt Brooke is related to…" Facing her, he said, "What's the woman's name? Who wrote all the etiquette books?"

Brooke grabbed the loaf of French bread. "Amy Vanderbilt? Emily Post?" She dug around in the utensil drawer. "There are dozens of etiquette books, all written by different manners experts. Now, where is that bread knife?"

He used his chin to indicate the drainboard. "Is that the one you're looking for?"

Grabbing it, she exhaled a breath of annoyance.

"What can I do to help?" he asked, raising his voice slightly to outtalk Connor's cheerful babble.

You could leave right now and spare me the agony of baring my soul once Connor is asleep.

"How 'bout if I move Connor's high chair into the dining room, and if you think of anything else I can do, say the word."

Nodding again, she silently admitted that since the place crash, their hard-won civility had taken on a softer, sweeter edge. Would that still be true after she'd put the baby to bed…and said her piece? A girl can wish, she thought, because Connor needed them working as a team.

She arranged the salad bowl and tongs, water pitcher, bread and butter on a wooden serving tray, and in the midst of Connor's happy squeals, a frightful thought flitted through her mind: What if, instead of clearing the air, what she planned to tell Hunter took them back to pre-plane crash days?

Was it worth the risk?

Brooke set the tray down with a clunk that made the ice clank against the ceramic pitcher. She'd waited this long to tell him. What could it hurt to wait until Connor was completely back to normal?

"You sure you don't need a hand with anything?"

Brooke unplugged the Crock-Pot and put it beside the tray.

"I'm fine. Why do you keep asking that?"

"Because you look a little, ah, out of sorts."

"I haven't cooked a real meal in so long, I'm worried I've forgotten something, that's all.

Something between relief and contentment beamed from his face as he settled Connor at the table.

"Smells fantastic," he said, watching as she spooned a braised potato, one carrot, some green beans and a small chunk of meat onto Connor's plate. She diced them into bite-size pieces, then held the plate under his nose.

"Blow," she said, "just like Goldilocks!"

Connor's lips puckered, and so did Hunter's. Then the baby inhaled a big breath and let it out with a whoosh...

...spattering beef broth onto Brooke's blouse.

"Uh-oh," Connor said, eyebrows high. Wrinkling his nose, he added, "Uh-oh. Brooke *dirty.*"

Brooke was the first to laugh, and when Hunter and Connor joined in, she laughed harder still. It was nervous laughter, she knew, brought on by lack of sleep, feeling lost at work and concern that her speech might set unalterable events in motion.

"Help yourself," she said, handing Hunter the big serving spoon. "I'll be right back."

She caught sight of his worried, confused face as she closed the powder room door. Caught sight of her reflection in the mirror, too. Despite all the makeup she'd applied earlier, she looked washed-out. Plucking a tissue from the dispenser on the vanity, she dampened it, held it to her temples. Deidre and Beth had often accused her of living life by the "shoot first, ask questions later" rule. That might have been true a year ago, but it wasn't true now. Since the accident, she hadn't made a decision, even one as small as what to fix for supper, without considering its impact on Connor.

Connor....

She could hear him out there, laughing at something Hunter had said.

"You can't risk it," she whispered. Perched on the edge of the tub, she closed her eyes and replayed the conversation with Deidre, whose worried voice alone had stiffened her spine and made every muscle tighten. She'd held her breath, too, when Deidre said the unthinkable:

"When he was at the theater, he took a call. I heard him talking to his lawyer. About adopting Connor."

But that was crazy, Brooke had told her. No judge would hand Connor over to a workaholic bachelor when he had a loving aunt ready and willing to raise him as her own!

Deidre admitted that since she'd been privy to just one side of the conversation, she might have misunderstood the part about Kent giving Hunter a DVD with instructions about Connor's future. "Sounded to me," Deidre whispered, "like the movie version of a written will."

He'd been so patient and kind walking her through Beth's house, pointing out faulty plumbing and moldy wood, explaining the solutions to each problem. Could he really behave that thoughtfully while plotting to take Connor from her? What better way to find out, she'd thought, than by calmly plying him with questions as she fed him a satisfying meal?

She'd been sure the scheme would work, until she saw him on the floor with Connor and realized that the easy rapport between those two had started long before the plane crash. Much as it pained her to admit it, Hunter was the most stable presence in Connor's life right now. And she couldn't—wouldn't—break that bond. Not even if it gave him more time to put his plan into action.

She needed time. Time to find out if Deidre had been mistaken. To hire an expert who'd protect her if Deidre had heard correctly. Time to figure out how she'd cope with her growing affection for Hunter if everything her grandmother suspected was true.

Brooke squirted a drop of redness reliever into each eye and touched up her mascara, took a deep breath and returned to the dining room, where Hunter had just fed Connor another bite of juicy roast beef. Her Connor.

"You okay?" he asked, frowning slightly as she sat down.

"Of course." She laid a napkin across her lap and hoped her smile wouldn't look as strained as it felt. "Why wouldn't I be?"

"No reason. I suppose."

Why the hesitation? she wondered, as thunder rumbled and lightning sizzled outside. A heavenly warning about what happens to people who lie?

Hunter helped himself to a second portion of

roast and vegetables, and as Brooke nibbled from her own plate, he talked about the weather. The latest hike in gas prices. The governor's dream project—a casino in Baltimore's Inner Harbor. She hoped he wouldn't run out of newsy tidbits before Connor went to bed. Hoped that once the baby was tucked in for the night, he'd go home so she could get online and search for attorneys who specialized in family law.

Hunter's cell phone rang, startling her.

"Better not be somebody trying to sell me aluminum siding," he said, snapping it open. "Hunter Stone…" Seconds into the conversation, he slapped a palm over his eyes. "No way. Are you sure? When? Be there in ten."

Then, nodding, he pressed the phone's mouthpiece to his chest. "That was one of the Last Chance kids," he explained, "calling to let me know that Mitch has been in an accident. From the sound of things, it's pretty bad. Hate to eat and run, but I need to get to the hospital, see what I can do to help."

"Of course," she said, meaning it.

On the landing, he hesitated. "You planning to turn in once you get that li'l monkey tucked in?"

"No." *Because I have some important research to do.*

It seemed he needed to hear more, so Brooke

added, "Call me when you know something. Doesn't matter what time."

Relief softened his features. Why did it feel so good knowing that her simple promise eased his mind? Well, she'd have all night to come up with an answer to that one, because something told her that whether or not he called, she wouldn't get much sleep.

"You sure? Could be late…"

"I'm sure," she said.

Even more confusing, she was sure…though she had no rational reason to be.

CHAPTER TWENTY-TWO

HUNTER ROUNDED UP the boys, and over slices of pepperoni and mushroom at their favorite pizza joint, told them what the doctors had said: Mitch made it through surgery just fine, and so had the elderly man who'd fallen asleep at the wheel, crossed the center line on Route 40 and broadsided Mitch's Harley. Mitch would need a few days of bed rest when he got out of the hospital. And after that, weeks of physical therapy to help rebuild muscle in his broken leg.

"You know what that means," he said, looking at each in turn.

"Laundry," said one.

"Vacuuming," offered another.

A third piped up with "Mow the lawn?"

"Nobody has a driver's license," said the first. "How we s'posed to get to the grocery store, and back and forth to work for you?"

Inside, Hunter's nerves were jangling, but he couldn't let the kids see it.

"Let me worry about that," he told them.

And during the drive from the hospital to Last

Chance, Hunter formulated a plan: at six-thirty, either he or Sam would pick up the boys who'd work at the Sheridans'. Those who wanted to come along to watch and learn were more than welcome…provided they wore hard hats and steel-toed boots.

Then, when he dropped them off, Hunter asked for pen and paper, wrote up a list of daily chores and taped it to the fridge. "Anyone not interested in hanging around the construction site can stay here," he told them, "working on this stuff."

The emotional stress of seeing their surrogate dad laid up had hit them hard, and they were all out for the count by midnight. Hunter decided to stretch out on the sofa until Mitch's assistant, Lyle, showed up. A perfect chance to make good on his promise to call and update Brooke. But he dozed off the minute his head hit the cushions. It took a flock of screeching crows to bring him round again at five.

Too early to call Brooke. He'd give her the details when he asked her opinion on hardwood stains. She didn't know Mitch, after all. Had never even heard the name until the call about the motorcycle accident interrupted their meal.

Still, it felt good that she'd offered to be his sounding board. It put him in such an upbeat mood that he decided to fix breakfast for the boys. When the scent of sizzling bacon and biscuits roused them, they joined him in the kitchen and sat yawning around the table.

Kenny poured himself a glass of juice. "Heard from Mitch this morning?"

Hunter buttered a slice of toast. "Talked to him an hour or so ago. He's in some pain but doing pretty well, all things considered."

"Well, *that's* a miracle," Darren said, "'cause he looked horrible in the hospital."

Trevor shuddered. "You'll never catch me on a motorcycle again. No way. No sir. Not after last night."

The rest of the boys agreed, and as Hunter put the food on the table, Kenny asked, "So what will we be doing at the Sheridans' house today, Mr. Stone?"

"I'll have to talk with Sam, find out where he needs you. And call me Hunter, okay?"

As the stack of bacon and biscuits dwindled, Hunter remembered what Sam had called Mitch earlier. "Doggone hooligan," he'd grumbled, "calling at the last minute to tell me that clown nearly killed himself doing all sorts of foolishness. Would've expected that from the kids. But Mitch? He should have known better, set a better example."

Hunter chuckled to himself. He'd bet his next job that Mitch had been called a lot of things over the years…except a hooligan.

"If Sam gets busy on another job, I could run the Sheridan job for a while," Darren said. "Been working for you more than a year now, so I know how you like things done." He hesitated. "Did I ever tell you that I worked construction with my dad before he ended up in the slammer?"

Hunter did his best not to wince.

"If you were over twenty-one, I'd say yes. But the county has a slew of rules and regulations. One toe over the line—and putting a minor in charge of a job site would be way over—could cost me my business license."

Frustrated groans and "we're not stupid" complaints floated around the room until Hunter silenced them with another serving of bacon and biscuits. When he was their age, his mother eased a lot of disappointments with food...and the quiet conversations that took place as it disappeared. "Teachable moments," she called them. If these kids had grown up under the steady influence of parents like that, they might never have ended up in a place like Last Chance. But there was every reason to hope that when they left here for good, they'd likely stay on the straight and narrow thanks to Mitch and his odd assortment of teachers and mentors.

Thoughts of their parents and his made him wonder how Brooke had slept last night. She'd seemed agitated and preoccupied at dinner. Hunter didn't want her to become a casualty in his Adopt Connor mission—he'd already caused her enough grief—but this wasn't about Brooke. It was about doing what was best for that terrific kid. Period.

Mitch's assistant burst into the kitchen. "What stinks?" he asked, grinning.

One by one, the boys recited breakfast sides.

Lyle hung his backpack on the doorknob. "You guys sound like a talking menu," he said, grabbing a plate. "Think it'll taste better than it smells after I nuke it?"

The lighthearted banter continued while Lyle shared what he'd just learned at the hospital. When he finished, Hunter told them he had to grab a change of clothes before heading to the Sheridans'.

"Anyone coming with me," he said, "better put on his work boots. The truck leaves in five. If you're staying here, pick up cleaning rags and buckets."

A chorus of groans filled the air as half of the boys got busy clearing the table and the other half piled into Hunter's pickup. A pecking order of sorts had formed as the older, more experienced boys decided what the newcomers would do. Grinning, Hunter let them have their fun, knowing that Sam would set them straight soon enough.

He left the kids in Sam's capable hands and headed back to Deidre's theater. A few things he'd seen during yesterday's inspection had raised concerns. Nothing major, but still, he felt obliged to take a closer look. On the way over, he dialed Deidre's number to let her know he was on his way, but she didn't answer. Hunter left a message, hoping the back window that had been ajar yesterday would still be open today. He was more than a little surprised to find her there, wearing a baseball cap and rubber gloves as she scraped old paint from the double-wide entry doors.

"How long have you been here?" he asked, glancing at his watch. "It's barely nine."

"Long enough," Deidre said, tucking the putty knife into her apron pocket. Eyes narrowed, she folded bony arms across her chest. "Better question is, what are *you* doing here?"

She sounded angry. But why? And with whom?

"Saw a couple of things that could be problematic when I was over here yesterday. Just thought I'd give 'em a quick once-over, make sure it's safe for you to be here." He raised an eyebrow. "Especially if you're going to make a habit of being here alone."

He headed inside, stopping long enough to run a fingertip over the newly exposed mahogany her scouring had revealed. "Nice job, by the way."

She answered with a one-shouldered shrug and, scowling, went back to work. The only other time he'd seen her look that way was in the O.R. waiting room fifteen years ago, when she'd hugged Beth as Brooke lit into him with everything she had.

Hunter made his way to the orchestra pit, where he'd spotted what appeared to be a bare wire.

Deidre had been a little quieter than usual when he left yesterday. But then, not even Deidre could talk nonstop. At least, that was what he'd told himself as he drove away.

Kneeling in front of the questionable outlet, he slid the Maglite from his tool belt and aimed its beam, trying to remember if he'd said or done something to offend her. "Nothing," he muttered. And the outlet looked fine, too.

It dawned on him that Deidre's attitude yesterday, and today, as well, echoed the way Brooke had behaved last night. But how to describe it? Angry? Resentful?

Suspicious. Yes. The word fit very well.

Brooke had never fully trusted him. But Deidre? Deidre considered him a friend. And on a couple dozen occasions introduced him to her friends and associates as "the grandson I wish had." What had happened to change her feelings toward him?

He walked deeper into the building. It was huge and dark and smelled like his grandmother's attic. No surprise there. In a few short years, the place would qualify for historic status.

Deidre whipped open a curtain, freeing a cas-

cade of dust motes that danced on a sunbeam…
and scared him half to death.

"So did you find the problem?"

In the bright light, she looked more annoyed
than before. And impatient to boot.

"Not yet. I want to have a look at the roof," he
said, "and the basement. And check the support
beams for rot, just to—"

"To make sure I'm safe. Uh-huh. Right."

He reholstered the flashlight and, leaning on a
doorframe, said, "Okay, let me have it."

"Careful what you ask for…"

The upper half of her face was shaded now by
the baseball cap's brim. "If I did something to offend you," he said, bending in an attempt to make
eye contact, "I'm sorry."

"I'm not the one who deserves an apology," she
said, then turned on her heel.

That left Brooke, he thought, following her back
to the entry door.

"Brooke was fine when I left the apartment last
night."

"If you say so."

Admittedly, Brooke had been out of sorts, staring off into space while he blathered on about
Orioles scores and weather forecasts, disappear-
ing into the bathroom halfway through the meal,
barely touching her food. He'd chalked it up to ev-

erything coming to a head—the accident, the new job, the house falling apart... Had he been wrong?

At the rate Deidre was scraping, she'd need a half cup of putty to fill the gouge. But he wasn't about to tell her that.

"Look. Deidre. I've never been any good at word games. Maybe if you tell me why you're so fired up, I can—"

"I'm busy, Hunter."

He stood staring for a moment. "So I'm dismissed." He lifted his arms, let them fall to his sides with a quiet slap. "Just like that."

"You weren't summoned," she said dully, "so you needn't be dismissed." Deidre paused but didn't turn around. "I understand you have Beth's house completely torn up."

"That's right."

"Then I suggest you get over there and put it back together as fast as you can."

He could almost see the tension rippling from her hat to her sneakers. Hunter held his breath, wondering what had happened between yesterday and today. Wondering what she'd say next, and how he'd keep a civil tongue in his head.

She spared him by stomping to her car to dig through a box in her trunk.

"You O'Toole women will drive me crazy one day," he muttered, passing her on the way to his truck.

"If we don't kill you first."

His footsteps slowed, but only slightly. Hunter refused to stop. Wouldn't give her the satisfaction of knowing how much her anger hurt, particularly when he had no idea what had caused it.

But she'd made one valid point. He needed to finish Beth's house, and the theater, too. Partly because he'd given his word to do the work, but mostly because his soon-to-be son would spend a lot of time in both places, and he couldn't in good conscience allow that unless he knew for certain Connor would be safe.

Brooke and Deidre didn't know it—and they'd probably fight him if they did—but he had their backs. Always had. Always would…

…for Connor's sake.

Period.

CHAPTER TWENTY-THREE

THE MINUTE SHE walked in the door, Brooke noticed the blinking red light of her answering machine. She put Connor in his playpen and hit the play button.

"I need to talk with you, honey," Deidre said. "It's important, so come on up to the house when you get this message. Don't worry about supper. I made meat loaf, so bring an appetite!"

Deidre had mastered half a dozen recipes in her lifetime, but meat loaf wasn't one of them. She didn't know it, though, because between her age and her outspokenness, no one had ever mustered the courage to tell her.

"Well, sweetie," Brooke said, hefting Connor from the playpen, "you're a little young to learn the 'suffer in silence' code, but I'll make it up to you later." She kissed his cheek. "Promise."

His big eyes twinkled as he studied her face.

"You don't have a clue what I'm talking about, do you?"

He pointed. "Ball?"

Normally, she didn't let him haul toys to

Deidre's, but tonight she'd make an exception. "It's the least I can do," she said, shoving trucks, teddy bears and stacking rings aside to grab his favorite ball, "considering what's about to happen to your poor innocent taste buds."

She handed it to him and hung the straps of his diaper bag over one shoulder. "Ready to pay Gram a little visit?"

"Gram," he said, clutching the ball. "Gram house?"

Half an hour later, with the bland meal behind them and Connor dozing in his crib upstairs, Brooke offered to clear the table, more to hide the food still on her plate and Connor's than because Deidre needed the help.

"So now that our boy's asleep, what did you get me over here to talk about?" she asked, scraping meat loaf and drippy mashed potatoes into the trash.

"Hunter stopped by the theater today."

Brooke tensed, wondering what Deidre had overheard this time.

"Again? Why? To give the place two thumbs up?"

"Not yet. He said he saw a few things that raised red flags yesterday, and he wanted to check them out."

She remembered what his little investigation had revealed at Beth's house.

"And you're upset because of what he found?"

"No. As a contractor, there's no one better. It's… Other things are bugging me." Deidre had been uncharacteristically quiet during supper, but Brooke hadn't made too much of it. The poor thing had been under a lot of stress lately, balancing her directorial duties at the Corner Theater while working on her theater. And asking her to mind Connor for a few hours a week had added to her burdens.

She sat at the table and took her grandmother's hands in her own.

"Hey. Lady. What's up?"

Imitating comedian Jerry Lewis had been a joke they'd shared since Brooke was a girl. When Deidre barely cracked a smile at her sad impersonation, Brooke's concern heightened.

"Gram, you're beginning to worry me. What's wrong?"

"I think I messed up today."

"This isn't about that adoption nonsense again, I hope."

Deidre shrugged. "I'm not sure. Could be. I was just so…so *mad* that Hunter wants to take Connor from you that I might have inadvertently tipped your hand."

She pressed her forehead to Deidre's. "Until I hire a lawyer to find out if Hunter has already started proceedings, I don't have a hand," Brooke admitted. She sat back and met her grandmother's eyes. "So you couldn't have tipped it. Relax, okay? There's nothing to worry about." Brooke hoped it was true.

"He was pretty riled up when he left."

"If he said anything to hurt you, I'll—"

"No-no-no, he'd never do anything to hurt me. Not deliberately, anyway. It's just, well, he's been like family for so long that I can tell when he's upset."

"You can? How?" The information might be useful down the road.

"Oh, little things like the way he stands. Hand gestures. Facial expressions."

Well, that's not much help, Brooke thought.

"Hunter probably has no idea you overheard that phone call. So don't give it another thought."

"Easy for you to say. You keep things so close to the vest there isn't room for another thought. But I'm not like you."

She could react to the sideways insult and invite a lecture—or pretend she hadn't heard it.

"So what did he say about the theater? Will the renovations be time-consuming and expensive?"

"If I only knew!" Deidre threw her hands into the air. "He can't write up an estimate until the inspection is complete, and he can't finish the inspection until later in the week." She sighed. "But the way we left things today, he might never come back."

"That doesn't sound like the Hunter we both know and love."

Deidre's eyebrows rose, and Brooke held her breath. She couldn't believe she'd said such a thing, either.

"What I mean," Brooke continued, "is…aren't you always telling me that he's a man of his word? Good and decent, with a heart of gold?"

"Yes," she said dully.

"I trust your instincts. If he told you he'd do the job, he will. Right?"

Deidre sighed again. "I guess."

Brooke realized it also meant if he said he'd fight for Connor, he would. And knowing how self-absorbed her grandmother could be when she wanted something as badly as she wanted the theater project to succeed, Brooke had to ask herself if anything Deidre had overheard was accurate.

"I know you told me already," she said, sliding an arm across Deidre's shoulders, "but humor me. Tell me again what you think Hunter said?"

Deidre all but glared at her. "I don't think anything. I know what I heard! He was talking to a lawyer. I could tell from all the legal mumbo jumbo. Words like *petitions* and *pleadings* and *subpoenas*. And some confounded DVD that Kent gave him."

Almost word for word what she'd said yesterday. But it didn't mean she'd interpreted Hunter's side of the conversation correctly.

"Did he say anything about the house?"

"No, but I did. I told him in no uncertain terms that if he was going to put me off like some ordinary customer, it had better be to work on Beth's house."

That inspired a grin, because Brooke could almost see her fiery seventy-six-year-old grandmother giving Hunter the full-blown O'Toole what-for.

"We can't afford to alienate him right now," Deidre was saying, "so I'll have to find a way to explain my rude behavior today. Then we'll keep him busy fixing up the theater and Beth's house. Hopefully, too busy to continue with this adoption nonsense." She leaned forward and whispered, "And while he's distracted, we'll find our own lawyer. A real shark. The best shyster money can buy. And when Hunter least expects it—" she fist-pumped the air "—pow! Right in the kisser!"

Brooke couldn't help but laugh. "Stone Contracting isn't the only remodeling firm in town, you know. We could hire someone else to do the work, at the house and at the theater."

"Why on earth would we do that? Hunter may have flaws, but his work sure doesn't. And as we've already established, he's a man of his word."

"You realize, of course, that you sound a little disingenuous."

"Oh. Really."

Brooke held out one hand. "You say he's a big jerk who can't be trusted." She held out the other. "Yet he's a man of his word?" Brooke linked her fingers together. "You know him a whole lot better than I do, so help me understand. For Connor's sake, I need to know. Is he a jerk or a good guy?"

"I never called him a jerk," Deidre huffed. "I hate it when people put words in my mouth. I'm not senile, you know. I remember what I said." She crossed both arms over her chest. "And to answer your question, he didn't lie to either of us. He kept something from us. Two very different things. Besides, he's a man, isn't he?"

Brooke frowned. "Meaning…"

"Meaning sometimes he's a jerk, and sometimes he isn't. Sometimes he'll be genuine, sometimes he won't."

The conversation had upset her grandmother, so Brooke chose a subject Deidre would happily discuss. "So how are rehearsals at the Corner Theater going?"

Deidre's entire deportment changed. "Fantastic! And you know what? One of our understudies works for the County Executive. She's met Hunter, and thanks to me, she thinks he and I are as close as kin." Smirking, Deidre added, "She told me to congratulate him."

"For…?"

"For being this close to opening his vo-tech school."

"I don't get it," Brooke admitted. "What he wants to do for those kids is a good thing. Why keep it a secret?"

Deidre only shrugged.

And Brooke laughed. "Look who I'm asking—the woman who bought a dilapidated theater without telling a soul."

"You have no room to talk, Miss 'I'm in Love with the Jerk but Can't Admit It.'"

Brooke couldn't have been more shocked if Deidre had thrown a bucket of ice water onto her head.

"Okay. I can take a hint. Your feelings for Hunter are off-limits."

What feelings? Brooke wondered.

"I'm glad we had this little talk, honey," she said, patting Brooke's clasped hands. "I'll sleep better tonight, thanks to you."

The image of an adoption document hovered in her mind.

At least one of us will, she thought, blinking it away.

CHAPTER TWENTY-FOUR

DEIDRE WAVED BROOKE CLOSER. "What would you say about having a backyard barbecue on the Fourth of July?"

Brooke perched on the footrest of Deidre's wicker lounge chair.

"Nothing big. Just my sorority sisters, maybe some people from the play." She toed off her flip-flops.

"Sounds good to me," Brooke said as Connor plucked petunias from the flower garden, "but I won't be able to help much."

"Oh, I know, I know. You're *so* busy learning the new job and taking care of Connor and choosing kitchen faucets and bathroom tiles." She sighed exaggeratedly. "Well, it might interest you to know that I'm busy, too. Hip-deep, in fact, in paint samples and curtain swatches at my theater, and even with the help of those brown-nosers, the work just isn't getting done fast enough to suit me."

"Brown-nosers?"

"Would-be actors who keep trying to butter me up so I'll give them a juicy part in the next production or introduce them to Bette Midler or Tom Selleck. But they aren't fooling me."

She'd always been a name-dropper, but as far as Brooke knew, Deidre had met Bette Midler only in passing and didn't know Tom Selleck at all. "And exactly how did you get the juicy parts back in your day?"

"Good point, I suppose," Deidre said. "But that doesn't change things. They need to work harder. Faster. Sometimes I think the place will never be finished!"

"I know how you feel," Brooke said. "I'm beginning to think Connor and I will never get back into Beth's house."

"You really need to quit calling it that. It's your house, chimney to cellar. You're the one paying the mortgage, and don't think I'm not aware of all the unpaid bills Beth and Kent racked up—and left you to deal with."

Deidre wiggled her eyebrows. "Don't ask how I know," she said, right hand raised traffic cop–style. "Friends in high places are like little birdies, and sometimes they peep things I'm actually interested in!"

The peeper was probably that stuffed-shirt manager at Deidre's bank who considered himself special because Deidre had included him in her social circle. How dare he leak private financial matters to anyone, even someone he considered a "star!"

"Will you be able to take off part of the day?" Brooke asked. "Go to the parade or the fireworks with us?"

"What kind of American would I be if I missed our country's birthday?" One eyebrow rose slowly. "But who, exactly, is *us?*"

"You, Connor, me and, since we're trying to butter him up, Hunter. I'm sure he gives his employees the day off on the Fourth."

"He does. He spent the whole day with us last year, remember?"

Yes, she most certainly did. She could still see him laughing and talking with some of Beth's other neighbors. She'd tried not to stare, had done her best not to admit how handsome he looked in his crisp white shirt and snug blue jeans.

Deidre sighed heavily. "Hard to believe it's been almost five months since the crash, isn't it."

The thick, odd sound in Deidre's voice made Brooke look more closely at her grandmother. It wasn't often that she allowed anyone to witness her tears…unless she was onstage.

Brooke patted her hand. "It's odd, don't you think, how our feelings change from day to day. Sometimes it seems like forever ago that we lost her. And other times it seems like yesterday."

For a long while, they simply watched Connor, chasing a rabbit around the yard. The critter had just disappeared into a blooming azalea shrub when Deidre broke the silence.

"It isn't easy outliving your children, your husbands, even your grandchildren. I often wonder why the Man Upstairs took all of them and left an ornery old broad like me behind."

"You aren't an old broad."

"So you're saying I'm ornery."

Brooke laughed. "No, you said it, remember?" A yellow swallowtail landed on her wrist. "And life goes on," she whispered as it fluttered away, "as if nothing happened."

"If it didn't, we'd spend the rest of *our* lives wallowing in self-pity. That isn't good for anybody. And doesn't honor the people we've lost, either."

Brooke was about to ask if that was a line from one of Deidre's plays when her cell phone rang.

"May I speak with Brooke O'Toole, please?"

Instantly, she recognized the crisp no-nonsense voice of the clerk of the court. "Mrs. Damian. Hello."

Deidre cupped a hand beside her mouth. "Don't let her push you around," she whispered. "Make her tell you when those papers will be delivered!"

"Just returning your call," the woman said. "I have your file right here in front of me, and it seems we're missing a few things."

She couldn't imagine what. Brooke had researched the process thoroughly and fulfilled every obligation step by step. She'd started with an appearance at the clerk's office of the circuit court, where she'd explained in painful detail how her sister and brother-in-law had died…and hadn't left a will. She'd filled out the forms and, as directed by the clerk, quickly returned them to the court. A week later Brooke had received copies of the documents, and now she was waiting for the official notice of the hearing date. In anticipation of the order to appear with someone who could substantiate that Beth and Kent had indeed perished in the crash, Brooke had asked Beth's neighbor to attend the hearing. Deidre would come along, too, to verify that Brooke was the only relative who was eager, able and fit to raise Connor and that the relationship between Brooke and Connor was deep and strong. She'd made a file that contained death certificates, the obituary, copies of everything Brooke had done on behalf of Connor—putting his name on Beth and Kent's bank accounts—and proof that she was in the process of having his name added to the deed, as well, all in the hope that at the conclusion of the hearing, the judge would make her Connor's legal guardian. Without that, she couldn't start the adoption process.

On her feet now, she walked from one end of Deidre's covered porch to the other. "As you know, Mrs. Damian, I pay my taxes in full and on time.

Why, there isn't so much as a parking ticket in my record, so I don't understand what could possibly be missing from my paperwork."

"I realize that, Miss O'Toole, but—"

"You have reports in that file. Written by a specialist in child psychology. You sent social workers to my home unannounced, and they interviewed me. Took notes as Connor and I interacted. Interviewed my boss and coworkers. I hate to sound impatient, but if you'll just tell me what exactly is missing, I'll do everything I can to see that you get it, quickly."

"I'm sorry, Miss O'Toole, but it seems I have another call. I'll touch base with you again in a few days," she said…

…and hung up.

Brooke stared at the silent phone for a moment, then hung her head.

"Please tell me that my temper tantrum didn't just cost me everything."

"From what I could hear, you were far more patient than I would have been," Deidre admitted.

"I have an idea. I'll get in touch with that nice social worker who visited us. She told me to call anytime with questions."

She found the woman's number in her contacts list. Heart pounding, head aching, Brooke brought the young woman up to date.

"I'm looking at your file now, and I think I

know what put a stop to Mrs. Damian's questions. Correct me if I'm wrong, but didn't you mention notations in your sister's journal that describe how beautifully you and Connor get along?"

"Yes."

"And it's accessible?"

"Well, some of the pages were loose. I was afraid they might get lost during construction, so I stored them in a shoe box with recipes and craft ideas Beth had torn from her favorite magazines." Brooke hesitated, thinking she knew where the social worker was going with this line of questioning. "None are dated, though."

"But they're in Beth's handwriting?"

Brooke pictured the tidy teenage-girl penmanship. "Yes. All of them."

"I suggest you go through them and single out pages that detail your relationship with Connor. And if you find one or two that mention you as the person she'd prefer taking care of him in the event anything happened to her and your brother-in-law, so much the better."

"How soon would you need them?"

The woman laughed. "How soon can you get them to me?"

Brooke asked her to hang on, then calculated the time in her head: ten minutes from Gram's to Beth's house, five more to find the shoe box in the basement, another fifteen to drive from the Oella neighborhood to the social worker's office. She muted the phone and faced Deidre. "Can I leave Connor with you, just for an hour or so? It's time for a nap, so I'll put him down before I leave."

"Of course, honey. Knowing him, he'll sleep the whole time you're gone anyway. Go. Do what you need to. We'll be fine."

Brooke unmuted the phone. "I can be there in forty-five minutes or less, if that works with your schedule."

The social worker rattled off her address and suite number, and Brooke wrote both in the dust on the porch floor. "I know you're not usually a praying woman, Gram," she said, transferring the numbers to her cell phone, "but while I'm gone, I need you to have a little chat with the Big Guy."

"Anything for you and that sweet kid," Deidre promised.

It took longer than expected to get Connor changed and into his crib at her grandmother's house. Took longer than usual for him to fall asleep, too. Brooke blamed his uncanny ability to read and react to her moods.

As she raced toward her car, Brooke called out, "I won't be long. Wish me luck!"

"You don't need luck," Deidre called back, "when you have *right* on your side. Drive carefully, now, hear?"

She hoped what her grandmother said was true.

Because according to her research, Connor could end up in foster care if the judge didn't grant her guardianship. And in his fragile emotional state, that might destroy him.

It surprised her when she turned onto Beth's street to find no pickup trucks and vans in the driveway. She couldn't imagine why all of Hunter's men would be away at the same time. Still, she parked out front to give them easy access if they arrived while she was in the basement.

Brooke had just stepped out of the car when she remembered that the box wasn't in the basement, but on the top shelf of the dining room's built-in china cupboard.

If she'd been thinking straight when Hunter helped her pack up to move to the apartment, she thought, selecting the house key from her key ring, she would have taken those loose pages with her instead of mixing them in with random recipes and craft projects. Why was it so hot and dark inside? she wondered, stepping into the foyer. And then she saw the boarded-up windows. She wished she'd had time to clear everything out of the house before Hunter and his men tore down the walls and ceilings. She couldn't quite figure out how he was going to manage it around furniture, but she saw that he'd covered everything in tarps.

Brooke left her purse beside the front door and

surveyed the stacks of lumber and coils of wire lining the walls.

Two-by-fours supported the thick ceiling beam that separated the dining room from the kitchen. Hunter had told her about the rotting wood that compromised the second story. But seeing was believing.

What she needed was tucked safely in the black-and-white shoe box she'd put on the top cupboard shelf.

"You'd think a bunch of construction workers would have a ladder," she grumbled, squinting into the gritty gloom. "Or at the very least, a step stool."

She spotted a cardboard box marked Brackets. It took a few minutes of pushing and shoving to get it close enough to the built-in hutch, and when finally it was in place, she stepped onto it. From there she climbed onto the countertop.

The box was mere inches out of reach.

"Whatever possessed you to put this thing on the top shelf?" she muttered, stretching. "It isn't like you're six feet—"

The box caved in under her weight, throwing her off balance. Brooke grabbed for the nearest thing to steady herself…one of the two-by-fours supporting the second floor. The board shifted. Not much. But enough to start a shower of soot that blinded her.

Just as well, because if she'd been able to see what caused that eerie groaning from above, Brooke might have fainted right there, with one knee on the countertop and one foot on the misshapen box as the ceiling crashed down around her.

Seconds later all was silent, save the quiet pecking of sawdust raining down onto the floor. She tried to get up but couldn't. Her head ached. Her leg ached more. And no wonder, the way it bent at an odd, awkward angle.

Nauseous and afraid, she clenched her jaw. She knew that if she vomited in this position—on her back, head tilted back—she'd choke to death.

Stay calm. Think. Breathe in. Breathe out.

Deep breaths were a bad idea, she decided when dust clogged her throat, started a coughing fit that sent waves of agony throughout her body. She was trapped, alone, with no way to call for help because, like an idiot, she'd left her cell phone in her purse and put her purse beside the front door.

No one had ever accused her of being a hysterical female, but if being buried alive wasn't an excuse to panic, Brooke didn't know what was.

Hot tears stung the scrape on her cheek, and the room began to spin. She closed her eyes as the room spun, grew dark, darker...

...and slipped slowly into unconsciousness.

CHAPTER TWENTY-FIVE

HUNTER LIKED IT a whole lot better when Brooke and Connor lived two doors down. Driving to Deidre's sent him in the opposite direction from most of his other jobs. Soon, he thought, the mess at the Sheridans' wouldn't be a mess anymore, and they could move back in.

And he could stop by every day, the way he did when Beth and Kent were alive.

He decided to head home early, catch a quick shower and walk over to the Sheridans' to make sure the granite countertops and glass backsplash tiles had been delivered. Yesterday when he'd gone over to inspect the day's work, he'd noticed one of Connor's stuffed animals wedged between the back of the sofa and the wall. He should have rented a storage unit, instead of tarping the furniture. It would have spared the guys having to lift and slide the pieces from one side of the room to the other as they worked, saving time and effort. He'd meant to grab Connor's lop-eared rabbit, but got distracted by a question from one of the boys. That excuse wouldn't work today, since they had the afternoon off. But delivering the toy would provide the perfect excuse to visit Brooke. *And Connor.* He smiled.

It surprised him to see her car parked out front.

Just inside the door, the toe of his work boot collided with her purse. "Brooke?" he called. "You'd better not be upstairs. The floors up there aren't stable."

Looking up, he noticed the gaping hole directly above the dining room. "What the...?"

He'd recognize that dainty white sandal anywhere. His boots felt weighted down as he closed the gap between the foyer and the huge mound of debris up ahead.

He attempted to lift the main support from her torso and failed. She was jammed in there, and he knew better than to move anything. He did a quick initial assessment: blood—lots of it—on her forehead, across her cheek and forearm, and oozing from the jagged gash in her thigh. Hands trembling, he opened his phone.

"911," answered a female dispatcher. "What is your emergency?"

From that point on, things were a blur, with Hunter describing what little he could see between bricks and boards and feeding the woman information about Brooke's condition. Her pulse was thready. She had a compound fracture of the femur. There was a large cut on her forehead. No response when he called her name. He felt like a fool admitting that he didn't know if she had allergies to medications or health conditions the paramedics needed to be aware of. Felt more so when he had to guess her height and weight. How could he have known her all these years without really *knowing* her?

He heard the sirens getting louder and closer as the 911 dispatcher said, "Stay with her, and stay on the line with me, sir, until the paramedics arrive." Was she out of her ever-loving mind? It would take an army to get him to leave Brooke's side.

Two lean men, one burly guy and a husky woman burst through the door, toting big rectangular cases into the room. "Step aside, sir," said the woman. "We've got it from here."

Her radio hissed, startling him as he backpedaled. Then it hit him that if Brooke was here, Connor must be with Deidre. He needed to call her grandmother, but not until he knew more.

"Hey. Buddy," said the biggest man, "give us a hand, will you?"

It took every ounce of their strength to heave the beam aside. From the corner of his eye, Hunter saw the woman toss a chair, a basket, a couple of mismatched sneakers from Brooke's motionless body. Again he wished he'd been more insistent about renting a storage facility, clearing the place of knick-knacks and furniture.

Now the the foursome got to work inserting needles, attaching tubes, hoisting up fat clear bags that would deliver antibiotics and glucose into Brooke's veins.

One guy fetched a gurney while another secured her fractured leg to a board. Standing two on Brooke's left, two on her right, they lifted her onto the cart.

"I'm going with her," Hunter said, running alongside them.

"No, sir, you are not," the woman countered.

"But…but she's…she's my fiancée.

The woman smiled, but only slightly. "You can follow us and meet us over at Howard County General."

His mom had told him the EMTs had said the same thing the day his dad was rushed to the hospital. He'd said it himself during his brief long-ago police career. He had to obey the "no riders" rule, but he didn't have to like it.

Two EMTs got into the ambo's cab, and the big guy and the woman climbed into the back. "Drive safely, you hear?" she said, and slammed the rear doors. And off they went, lights flashing and siren screaming.

Hunter stood alone in the driveway, vaguely aware of neighbors peering from their windows as he remembered how Brooke had looked right before they loaded her up. Tiny, pale, bruised and broken, like the porcelain ballerina his little niece had brought to him last Christmas. "Fix her, Uncle Hunter," she'd wailed, handing him the pieces. "She's my favorite…"

The quaint neighborhood had fallen silent, save the occasional tweet of a bird or distant bark of a dog. It surprised him that Mrs. Sinnik hadn't shuffled across the street in her flowered muumuu and threadbare flip-flops. The woman spent every waking hour in the recliner near her bay window. Probably a good number of her nights, too. He climbed into the cab of his pickup. Later he'd call her daughter, make sure the woman was okay.

He was climbing into his truck when a woman's voice stopped him.

"Hunter," Ivy asked, "what happened?"

He gave her a quick rundown. "Can't stay," he added. "Gotta get to the hospital."

She wrung her hands. "If there's anything I can do…make phone calls or whatever…let me know, okay?"

"Check on Mrs. Sinnik, will you? It isn't like her not to show up for something like this."

Ivy looked like she was about to cry. Weird, he thought, considering she barely knew Brooke.

"So much tragedy," she said. "How much more can one family take?"

Hunter nodded as she asked, "Will you call me when you know something?"

"Sure. Of course," he said, shifting into Reverse.

At the traffic light on Frederick Road, he dialed his mother's number. She rarely said hello when she picked up the phone, and today was no exception.

"I hope you're not calling me from the road, because that's against the law in Maryland, you know."

He didn't have time to apologize or explain. Didn't have time to sugarcoat things, and thankfully, she didn't interrupt as he told her what happened to Brooke. He wrapped things up with "Do me a favor, will you, and see if Deidre needs help with Connor? She's a tough old bird, but he can be a handful when he puts his mind to it." And when Brooke didn't come home tonight as expected, he might just put his mind to it.

"Of course," Constance said. "I'll call the girls, too. They adore that boy, and so do the kids. I'm sure they'll all be happy to help any way they can."

His brothers' wives could sometimes drive him to distraction, but they were also the type who'd show up to help, any time, no questions asked. When Brooke came to, she'd be relieved to hear that Connor was in good hands.

When he pulled into the parking lot, he saw Brooke's ambulance at the E.R. entrance. Good. That meant she was inside the facility now affiliated with Johns Hopkins, one of the best hospitals in the world.

Inside, he walked through the waiting room, past a mother comforting a little boy, a guy holding an ice pack to his eye and a hodgepodge of people who showed no outward symptoms.

"They just brought a young woman in here," he told the woman at the check-in counter. "Brooke O'Toole. Where did they take her?"

She looked away from her computer monitor long enough to say, "Sorry, family only back there."

Hunter cursed under his breath. Some rules, he thought, were just plain stupid. "She's my fiancée." It was easier telling the lie this time.

The woman looked back at the screen. "She's in triage."

Nodding, he pushed through the E.R. doors. Triage. Such an intimidating name.

Two of the paramedics who'd brought Brooke in stepped out of a cubicle. When they saw him, the looks on their faces were enough to make Hunter's knees go weak.

"How is she?" he asked, falling into step beside them.

"Too early to tell."

The second EMT softened the news with, "But she couldn't be in better hands."

He'd told the "shc's my fiancée" lie back at the

house, too. If only he knew the right questions to ask.

The men exchanged a tired glance. "You should get in there," his partner said. "They're at the sixty-four questions stage of the exam. You could help with that." Then they went to join the other two EMTs, already in the ambulance.

Sixty-four questions, he repeated, walking into Brooke's cubicle. He hadn't been able to ask *one* that made sense just now. Hadn't said one useful thing during the 911 call, either.

A nurse with a clipboard pulled him aside. "You the fiancé?"

He nodded.

"Doc ordered a CAT scan, followed by surgery."

He'd barely had time to repeat it in his mind when two guys in scrubs pushed her on a gurney past him. How was it possible for her to look smaller and weaker than when she'd been in the ambulance?

"Surgery?" he choked out. "For what?"

The nurse glanced at him. "To rule out internal bleeding."

Everything she said after that assumed a faraway underwater quality: Brooke's spleen or liver could have been nicked, and if that was the case, blood might have leaked into the peritoneum. Broken ribs could have punctured a lung—or worse, her heart—and with a head injury that severe, there were concerns about swelling in her brain.

"And the leg?" he asked, staring down the long empty hall.

"Right now that's the least of her worries." She tapped her pen against the clipboard. "Now, let's get this out of the way, shall we, so we can get you to the O.R. waiting room."

ONE BY ONE, members of the Stone family filled the waiting room's short-backed chairs. As the hours ticked slowly by, the number of half-empty disposable cups, doughnut wrappers and lunch-size potato-chip bags littering the tables grew.

Rafe snored softly in the chair nearest the soda machine, and when Jesse's can dropped into the bin, he lurched...but went right back to snoring.

Gabe sat to Hunter's right, pretending to read a raggedy issue of *Ladies' Home Journal*. Yawning, he pointed at a glossy color photograph of grilled chicken. "Think I'll try this next time we have a barbecue." He yawned. "I'm tired of burgers and dogs, aren't you?"

"Yeah," Hunter said. "Tired."

He appreciated their support, especially when all three had wives and kids at home and schedules far crazier than his own. He'd learned the hard way what exhaustion could do to a cop.

"You guys should get out of here," he said.

"There isn't a thing you can do but sit and look at the four walls."

"Beats looking at the little woman's too-long to-do list," Gabe said, tearing the chicken recipe from the magazine.

"And *Ladies' Home Journal*," Jesse said, pointing at the magazine.

Gabe rolled it up and smacked Jesse with it. "Give a guy a break. There's an acre of shin-deep grass waiting for me at home." He tucked the recipe into his pocket. "And lucky me. The riding mower is on the fritz."

"Waa-waa-waa," Rafe said, opening one eye. "I'm only here 'cause it's quieter than it is at home—least it *was* till the three of you started clucking like a bunch of old hens." He shifted in the chair and closed his eyes again.

Grinning slightly at his brothers' attempts to joke around and lighten the situation, Hunter nodded. "Thanks, guys."

Gabe punched his right arm. "Don't mention it."

And Jesse punched the left. "Don't mention it to anyone, or you'll ruin our 'coldhearted cop' reputations."

"Seriously, dudes, can't a guy catch a few *z's?*" Rafe said.

Jesse and Gabe exchanged looks, and Gabe used the rolled-up magazine as a pointer. "Are you thinking what I'm thinking?"

Jesse picked up a tired old issue of *Sports Illustrated* and the pair marched toward Rafe.

"Do it," he said without moving, "and they'll be checking *you* in for surgery, to remove my boot from—"

The doors to the surgical suite whooshed open, and all four brothers stood at attention as a gowned, masked nurse stepped into the waiting room.

"Mr. Stone?" she said, pulling the mask under her chin.

Together, the men said, "Yes?"

She looked confused until Hunter stepped forward. "I'm Brooke's…" His brothers hadn't heard the lie yet. "Fiancé…"

He could feel their eyes drilling holes into his back in reaction to the statement.

"How is she?" Hunter asked. In the recovery room by now, he hoped, because it had been nearly six hours since they'd wheeled her into the O.R.

"It'll be another half hour or so," she said. "Dr. Norris will be out to update you just as soon as he can."

But she hadn't answered his question, and that worried him. He stepped closer. "So how's she doing?"

"So far, so good," she said, and hit the button that opened the doors. "She's critical, but that's to be expected."

While he stood there wondering what that meant, the doors closed behind her.

"That was smart," Rafe said, "saying you two are engaged."

"Yeah," Jesse agreed, "sometimes that whole 'next of kin only' thing is stupid."

Gabe didn't say anything, and when Hunter met his gaze, it was clear he understood that there was more truth than lie to the "I'm her fiancé" statement.

"So now that the real waiting is about to begin," Rafe said, stretching, "I think I'll head on home."

"Same here." Jesse gave Hunter a hug. "Hang in there, okay? I'm just a phone call away."

"You coming, Gabe?" they asked, walking toward the elevators.

"Nah," he said, tucking his fingertips into his jeans pockets. "Think I'll hang around until they let Hunter go in to see her."

As Jesse and Rafe left the hospital, Hunter prepared himself for a few brotherly wisecracks. Only...they never came. Instead, Gabe grabbed the nearest chair. "You'd think they'd have the decency to turn the volume up," he said, glaring at the silent TV hanging from the ceiling. "Kinda makes me wish I hadn't ditched school the day they taught lip reading." For the next hour and a half, the slowly turning pages in Gabe's magazine were the only sound in the room.

Except for the beating of Hunter's heart.

CHAPTER TWENTY-SIX

HUNTER HADN'T BEEN in the picture when Deidre buried her first husband or when her only son committed suicide, but he'd heard the stories from her handyman, Felix, and from Beth and Kent. She hadn't been afraid to grieve or mourn, they'd said, but within months of each loss, she had packed up her black dresses and hats and the sadness that went with them and moved forward. Acting and directing, they believed, had saved her, but Hunter knew better. Deidre's strength ran deep, and *that* was what saved her from a life lived in a grieving past.

She'd changed, though, in the days since Brooke's accident, from a woman to be reckoned with to a frail old woman who no longer commanded attention when she entered a room. As she stood beside him now, slump shouldered and trembling, staring at the foot of Brooke's bed, Hunter wondered just how much more misery her poor little body could handle.

"Have you eaten anything today?" he asked, slipping an arm around her narrow shoulders.

"Yes. At least, I think so," she said without taking her eyes from her granddaughter.

"I wonder if you'd do me a favor...."

Her eyes seemed twice as green when she looked up at him through shimmering tears.

"Would you run down to the cafeteria and get me a sandwich? I'm starving." His stomach growled as if on cue. He couldn't have planned that better if he'd tried.

"While you're down there," he continued, sliding a twenty from his wallet, "get something for yourself. We'll eat together, right here." He pressed the bill into her hand and stooped to kiss her cheek. "You're the closest thing to a grandmother I have. Gotta take good care of you, y'know?"

Deidre snorted. But she took the money and grabbed her beaded purse.

He walked with her as far as the elevators, just across the hall, and as the doors opened, she shook the fist that held the twenty and looked up at him. "I love you, too, you...*man,* you," she said, and stepped inside.

He sensed a hidden message in the words, but the steady sound of Brooke's ventilator called him back to her side. Hunter scooted the uncomfortable pink recliner closer to the bed. Taking care not to jostle the needle taped to the back of her hand, he slid his palm beneath it. "If anyone had told me you had a lazy side, I would have called them crazy. But look at you, still lounging around on that air mattress."

Silence, except for the ventilator and the beeping of the heart monitor. The doctors told him that with each passing day, her battered body was healing just a little bit more, and that the drug-induced coma had been necessary because pain could hinder her recovery. He got that…but he didn't like it. Hunter needed to hear her voice and see those too-big-for-her-face eyes light up when she talked about Connor.

"Connor has been asking for you," he said, absentmindedly stroking her cheek. "Looking under beds and behind furniture, saying, 'Brooke, Brooke, Brooke.' He's okay, though, so no worries. My sisters-in-law have been taking turns babysitting. Would you believe they're actually fighting over who gets to keep him?"

Not so much as the flutter of an eyelid.

Hunter hung his head. He'd heard that comatose people could hear everything said in their presence. If only he'd thought to ask the doctor if the same was true for this kind of coma.

"Sent your grandmother down to the cafeteria," he said. "She's really worried about you, you know."

Still nothing.

"And so am I."

His imagination, or did the blips of the monitor

speed up for a second or two? Hunter looked at the machine. No, he thought, gaze fused to the thin green lines, it must have been wishful thinking.

Deidre returned with their sandwiches, and they sat, one on either side of Brooke's rolling tray table, sharing a sandwich, barbecue potato chips and chocolate chip cookies. "There oughta be a law," she said after a few bites. "Charging all that money for stale bread and rubbery ham? It's highway robbery, I tell you."

"Well, the chips are okay."

"If you like eating them with a spoon. Can you believe every package was crushed that way?"

He would have told her it didn't matter. That she should calm down. But he hadn't seen her this animated since that day at the theater, when something had riled her enough that he worried she'd destroy the door with that putty knife. Maybe if he got her going that way again, she'd forget to be sad.

"Which one of your sisters-in-law has Connor today?"

"Jill, I think. Why?"

"Is she the one who lives just off Route 40?"

"Mmm-hmm," he said around a mouthful of sandwich.

Deidre stood and gathered what was left of her portion of the meal and, after dumping it unceremoniously into the wastebasket, slung her purse straps over one shoulder. "I'm going straight home to get Felix, so he can drive me over there. He misses that kid almost as much as I do." She stooped to kiss his forehead. "Would you be a dear and give Jill a heads-up that an old biddy is about to invade her space?"

Hunter laughed quietly. "Sure. No problem." He wondered what had happened between now and the time she'd left for the cafeteria to change her mood.

"Ran into an old friend in the elevator," she said, answering his unasked question. "Young fella who had a bit part in the dinner-theater production of *Pirates of Penzance* I directed a few years back. Guess acting put the fear of God into him, 'cause he's a preacher now. A good one, too," she said with a wink. "Snapped me out of my funk."

She stepped up to the bed and kissed her fingertips to her lips, then touched them to Brooke's forehead. "I know you're working hard to come back to us, sweetie. Keep it up, okay, because we miss you."

With that, she strode from the room like a woman on a mission. Hunter's poor sister-in-law didn't have a clue what she was in for. Now he felt doubly obliged to give her a heads-up.

After the call, he sat back, opened the copy of *Baltimore* magazine that he'd bought in the gift shop. "Listen up, lazybones, because I'm about to read this thing from cover to cover. Out loud. Including the ads. Because why should *you* get off scot-free?"

When he finished, Hunter stood and stretched. "Man," he said, rubbing his Adam's apple, "how do politicians do it? I've only talked for an hour, and I'm hoarse."

He bent over the bed's side rail and kissed the corner of her mouth. "Back in a bit," he said, then kissed the other corner. "Promise."

Outside he found an empty bench in the shade of a tree and sat down to call Sam.

"Everything is ticking along like clockwork," his foreman said. "Got the Smiths' house and the Fletcher jobs wrapped up, and this morning when I grabbed the Stone Contracting signs from their front yards, I grabbed their final payments, too."

"Good work," Hunter said. "And what's happening at the Sheridan place?"

"Those kids of Mitch's had me fooled, I'll tell ya. They've been nose-to-the-grindstone all day every day. They tell me they're working for more of your biscuits and bacon, so congrats, Chef Stone, you made some impression on 'em."

Laughing, Hunter said, "Must be comforting to you, knowing you'll have a career to fall back on when I fire your cantankerous butt."

"Fall back on...?"

"Open-mike Friday nights?"

"Ha ha. Very funny, boss. So tell me, how's your fiancée doing? Any improvement at all?"

So news of his phony proposal had made it that far, had it? "Doctors say things are going as expected. Another day or two, they'll revive her, see if she can breathe on her own. Until then, we just keep hoping for the best."

"You know, this whole thing has made me reexamine my own life. Brought my wife flowers the other night just for the heck of it, and you would have thought I gave her tickets to a world cruise."

"Careful. She might think that's next."

"On the pathetic salary you pay me? No way! And she knows it, too, since she's the one who balances our skinny little checkbook."

"You'll invite me to opening night, I hope."

"Opening ni—" Sam got the joke and laughed. "And a parking pass near the comedy club, too. But enough of this yee-hawing. I work for a tyrant. He's mean as a snake and might fire my cantankerous butt."

That would never happen, and Sam knew it as well as Hunter did. Buoyed by the good news that his company wouldn't sink while he was away from the helm, Hunter pocketed the phone and remained seated, enjoying a few more minutes of fresh air, then hurried back inside. The sun would set soon, and he knew from past experience that he could watch it from Brooke's room.

Maybe he'd get lucky, catch a glimpse of the elusive green flash.

The thought spawned an idea, and he went back to the bench, connected his phone to the internet and typed *green flash* into the search bar. Link after link showed up, some with photographs of the phenomenon. He downloaded and saved a few. Normally, cell phone use inspired the stink-eye from hospital personnel, a policy that made little sense when doctors and nurses used them to communicate with one another, even in the ICU. But Hunter's cooperative spirit had put him on a first-name basis with the staff...and earned him updates not given to most family members. Lucky for him, opening saved files on his phone didn't require an internet connection, so he was confident that his "good visitor" status would remain intact.

"Perfect timing," Brooke's nurse said when he returned. "She just had a bath, and I changed her sheets, too. So she's fresh as a daisy."

Could have fooled him, because everything looked the same as when he left.

Well, not exactly the same. The nurse had removed the bandages that held the intraventricular catheter in place, exposing the angry red skin surrounding the burr hole in her skull. She'd need a haircut when she got out of this place, because the surgery to relieve pressure on her brain had left a softball-sized bald spot right at the crown of her head.

"Bet you'll look really cute in short hair," he said, finger-combing soft curls from her forehead. "Well, would you look at that," he said. "Freckles there, too, not just on the bridge of your nose."

Hunter walked to the foot of the bed. "I don't know about you," he said, loosening the tightly tucked sheets, "but I hate not being able to move my feet. I know, I know," he added, "you can't move 'em now anyway. But trust me, I just did you a big favor. Those pink-painted toes of yours were bent over so far, they made my feet ache."

Her pillow was off-kilter by an inch or so. "You know what I've always wondered?" he asked, straightening it. "Do brand-new babies and people in comas get itchy? Must be torture to have an itch and not be able to scratch it." Were the drugs that kept her immobile and protected her from the damaging effects of pain guarding her against that, too?

Since he had no way of knowing the answer—and she couldn't answer—Hunter proceeded to gently stroke her arms. It was the least he could do since it was largely his fault she was in here, helpless as a newborn. He tossed back the covers with the intention of rubbing from her knees to the soles of her feet. But one look at the thick hip-to-ankle cast on her left leg stopped him. Hunter swallowed. "Good thing you're out like a light," he told her. "Tiny as you are, you'd need a luggage cart to haul that thing around."

Making light of things did nothing to ease his guilty conscience. Why did it seem that he was just plain bad luck where the O'Tooles were concerned? If he really cared about her, about Connor and Deidre, he'd walk out that door and not look back, because what terrible thing might he bring into their lives next?

He watched her, long lashes dusting freckled cheeks as she lay still and pale, one machine breathing for her while another drained fluid from around her brain. She'd always been so bright, so bold and brave. Would she still be that way when she came to? After the broken bones and torn muscles and surgical scars healed? The image of the once-spunky Brooke doing everything in slow motion because her poor battered brain couldn't remember another speed flashed in his mind. It was a terrifying sight, but not terrifying enough to scare him away. He'd stay, partly because he should have had the good sense to put a padlock on that front door…and keep the only key.

Hunter rested both forearms on the bed rail. "I'm staying. Forever. Because I care about you. Have since that night in the O.R. waiting room when you called me everything but a human being." Her tirade had been the reason he'd never found happiness with other women, not even the good ones like Stacy.

He traced the third finger of her left hand and, realizing the symbolism, stopped and straightened.

"So I guess you heard your doctor say that day after tomorrow, if you get good grades on all your tests, he'll start weaning you off these confounded drugs." He would not accept the doctor's warning that sometimes patients don't wake up from comas. If she came to, he'd continued, Brooke was facing weeks—months, possibly—of rehab. Physical, speech and occupational therapy. Healing from the inside out *and* the outside in would take time. Lots of it.

She'd survived three major surgeries—the first to remove her damaged spleen and appendix, the second to repair the nick in her liver and punctured lung. Finally, steel pins had been inserted in her thigh. Hunter wasn't sure if wiring her broken jaw shut had required surgery, or he'd have counted that, too.

He forced a note of joviality into his voice. "Soon as you're well enough to sit up to eat green Jell-O and Deidre-style meat loaf, I'm gonna celebrate with a shower and a shave." He tucked a curl behind her ear. "Bet you're relieved to hear that, huh?"

She'd been here five days; five and a half days ago, he'd taken his last shower. How could he leave her side, even long enough to get cleaned up, when Brooke had no one—not a parent or a sibling—to ask questions on her behalf, to demand answers when the staff used ten-syllable terms? Deidre was sharp for a woman her age, but her uncharacteristically quiet, subdued behavior these past few days was proof that she couldn't go to bat for Brooke. So Hunter had stayed close by, listening, asking questions, demanding answers, taking notes. And when the doctors and nurses left the room, he hopped on the internet to look things up and better understand everything they'd said. With each validation, his confidence in her team increased.

"Remember that conversation we had a while back about the green flash?" Hunter sat on the chair beside Brooke's bed and opened the file he'd downloaded earlier and, propping an ankle on his knee, summarized the details of the article.

"Says here that in order to see it, you have to be in the right place, and the conditions have to be perfect, too. Humidity, temperature, time of day...." It sounded too familiar, and he couldn't say whether it was because he'd read so much about it over the years, if he'd told her all of this, or if she'd told him. "When you get out of here, we're going to start making memories. Good ones. Lots of them. You. And Connor. And me." He got up, stood beside her bed again and this time kissed the tip of her nose. "What better way than by taking you to a place where you can see it for yourself?"

Hunter chuckled, wondering what was going on inside that amazing mind of hers. Except for the few hours he'd spent dozing in the ugly pink chair, he'd chattered like a magpie. Held her hand. Stroked her pale, chafed cheeks. Kissed her knuckles and her forehead and now her nose. "Bet you'd slug me if you could, wouldn't you?" he whispered, grinning.

Out of the corner of his eye, he thought he saw the monitor's green line spike upward. It beeped slightly faster, too, telling him it hadn't just been wishful thinking.

"Leave it to you," he said around a grateful sob, "to come out of this thing all on your own just so you can whack me one."

The monitor beeped again, providing all the confirmation he needed.

He remembered comparing her to his niece's porcelain figurine, fragile, delicate, easily broken. He smiled. "Tell you what, little ballerina, as soon as you can make a fist, this ugly whiskered chin is all yours."

CHAPTER TWENTY-SEVEN

THE NURSE PRESSED the new code into Brooke's infusion pump, its high pitch barely audible above the drone of the ventilator and the blips of Brooke's monitor.

"Only three more dose reductions," she said, "and Sleeping Beauty here will be through with this medication. Hopefully for good."

Hopefully. Hunter was beginning to hate that word.

"And then we wait."

"For what?" He needed to know.

"For signs of awareness." She scrawled some notes on Brooke's chart and let it drop against the bed's footboard with a hollow *thump*. "Doesn't happen every time...just often enough that we want to be watchful when she comes off the meds."

Hunter's heart pounded with fear. "What doesn't happen every time?"

She looked around to make sure they were alone, then spoke so quietly that Hunter had to lean forward to hear her.

"Some patients fight the ventilator," she explained. "If we're Johnny-on-the-spot with the medication amount, we can prevent a panic attack. That's important when someone has been on Propofol this long. But if we can't prevent it…"

"You'll need to drug her into a stupor again."

"I wouldn't put it quite that way, but, yeah. Basically."

The whole point of the medically induced coma was to decelerate her vitals in order to reduce swelling—particularly in her brain—and decrease pain levels so that Brooke's body could begin to heal from the inside out. But too much longer on those powerful drugs and her heart might forget how to pump on its own, and her lungs might not remember how to breathe. She'd need someone here, someone who could keep her calm while the drugs wore off.

He crossed both arms over his chest. "I'll be here 24/7."

"Commendable," she said, "but dumb. Go home. Eat something healthy. Take a hot shower. Shave that handsome face of yours. And get a good night's sleep." She glanced at Brooke. "Because when she comes around, you'll need every bit of energy you can spare, and then some."

"But what if—"

"The whole point of the low nurse-patient ratio and these wall-to-wall ceiling-to-floor cubicles is so that we can keep a close eye on things. You've already been here 24/7, so you know it's true."

Hunter nodded. "Yeah, but—"

"No buts. She's in good hands. So go home. Take care of yourself so that when the time comes, you can do the same for her."

He stared at the monitors, at the infusion pumps and the leads and tubes and wires that connected Brooke to each machine. It appeared that nothing had changed since the nurse decreased the dosage. Yet.

"Maybe you're right."

"Maybe?" Grinning, she walked toward the door. "Hunter, you've been here so long you're starting to sound like a doctor, second-guessing nurses' decisions. Get out. Get out now," she said, feigning fury, "before it's too late!"

Then she sat behind the desk and, facing Brooke's room, placed her fingers on the computer's keyboard and started typing as if he'd already left.

He'd grown tired of vending-machine food. And it *would* feel great to shower and shave. It wasn't likely he'd sleep, but stretching out on his own bed sure would be nice.

"I won't be gone long," he said, kissing her forehead. "Promise. Keep fighting, kiddo. Please?"

Standing at the elevator, he thought, I can't wait to get a reaction when I do that.

Laughing to himself, he stepped into the empty car, and when the doors closed, he said, "Hopefully."

HUNTER SHOWERED AND SHAVED, changed into jogging pants and a T-shirt and made himself a snack. After settling into his favorite chair, he grabbed the phone and dialed Deidre's number to find out why she'd left half a dozen "Call me—it's important!" messages on his answering machine.

"Hey there," he said when she answered. "What's up?"

"I'm at my wits' end," she said. "By mistake, I opened a letter addressed to Brooke."

Mistake? Deidre? Not likely, but he concentrated as she read the letter from a Mrs. Damian.

"'I have been more than fair and patient in the matter regarding your nephew, but I would be negligent in my duties if I allowed this situation to continue. Charlotte Matthews, of Child Protective Services, has informed me that you have in your possession documentation that will substantiate your sister's wishes with regard to the above-referenced minor child.'"

Deidre huffed. "Minor child, she called him. She has the power to dictate his future, but doesn't have the decency to refer to Connor by name? What an evil, callous—"

"Go on," he interrupted. Deidre's voice had

gone all shrill and shaky. If she kept up this way, she could end up in the cardiac ICU. "What else does the letter say?"

On the heels of a trembly sigh, she continued. "'I regret to inform you that if you fail to reply to this correspondence, as you have failed to respond to my numerous phone calls and emails, and if I am not in receipt of the aforementioned verification by the end of business this Friday, I will have no recourse but to place said child in a foster home until suitable adoptive parents can be found.'"

He heard paper crinkling as Deidre said, "Hunter, what are we going to do? Brooke could be in the hospital for weeks yet. And then she's facing months of physical therapy. If this power-hungry old bat gets wind of all that—and the accident and how badly Brooke was injured—she'll judge Brooke incompetent and incapable of ever being able to take care of Connor. And she seems the type who, just out of spite, would take Connor so far away we might never see him again...."

"Only a judge has the power and authority to do that," he said. And first chance he got he'd call Harry to make sure it was true. "Deidre, put the letter in a safe place and quit worrying." He pictured the unlabeled DVD, hidden in his underwear drawer. "I think I know how to stop Cruella de Vil in her hard-hearted tracks."

He'd planned to take the ICU nurse's advice and

try to catch forty winks before returning to the hospital. Instead, he called his old college buddy-turned-lawyer, who over the years had drafted a couple dozen "Pay up!" notices to Hunter's dead-beat customers. Harry promised to do some research and get right back to him. While waiting for the return call, Hunter made himself a triple-decker sandwich to round out the cheese and crackers he'd already consumed. "Who knew fighting city hall would stimulate a guy's appetite this much," he said around a mouthful.

When the phone rang, he nearly jumped out of his sneakers.

"With Brooke in the hospital—and facing months of physical therapy—you won't have any trouble getting temporary guardianship of the kid," Harry said, "providing his dad really did spill his guts in that DVD."

"You have a copy of it. Didn't you watch it?"

"Haven't had time. But I'll make some before I start the paperwork." Harry paused. "You're sure this is what you want to do? Because once this snowball starts rolling downhill, it'll pick up speed. Child Protective Services will get involved, and if they don't like what they see, they really could put the boy in foster care until his aunt is well enough to take him back. You need to be aware of the risk."

"How big a risk?"

"If I had to guess, I'd say five, maybe ten percent."

Funny how things turned out, Hunter thought. Before Brooke's accident, he was champing at the bit to use the disc against her. Now he was gambling that it would protect her. And Connor, of course.

"So what's our first move?"

"So you're sure, then...you want to go ahead with this."

"One hundred percent."

As Harry outlined their strategy, Hunter made careful notes.

"I'll have my secretary type up the petitions right now," Harry said. "First chance you get, stop over here to sign them, and I'll personally walk 'em over to the clerk of the court and schedule a hearing. Meantime, you know what to do, right?"

The minute he ended the call, Hunter dug out the DVD, slid it into his computer and made two copies of it, then typed a short memo, as dictated by Harry:

To: Mrs. Eloise Damian, Services Specialist
Child Protective Services for Howard County,
Maryland
From: Hunter B. Stone
Re: Connor Kent Sheridan

Dear Mrs. Damian:

I hereby inform you that I have petitioned
the court for temporary guardianship of the
above-referenced minor child of Elizabeth
Ann and Kent Alexander Sheridan. Absent
a last will and testament, the accompanying
DVD (copies available upon request) will
show that I am the person they chose to care
for their son in the event of their death.

Feel free to contact me in the event you require further documentation.

Respectfully,
Hunter B. Stone

He checked and rechecked for spelling and
grammatical errors, because Mrs. Damian seemed
the type who'd use something as trivial as a typo
to keep him from protecting Connor from foster
care, and protecting Brooke from losing the boy
forever. Satisfied that the letter was perfect, he
printed out two copies, folded each in four and
tucked them into the DVDs' clear plastic cases. On
his way to Harry's office, he'd stop by the county
building and hand-deliver the padded manila envelope to the clerk.

He had a good feeling about this. So good that
he believed tonight, as he slouched in the hideous

pink chair beside Brooke's hospital bed, he might actually sleep for a change.

Provided he didn't dwell too long on the fact that to help Brooke, he'd have to hurt her first.

CHAPTER TWENTY-EIGHT

THE DOCTOR HAD told her to expect some serious discomfort, and he hadn't exaggerated.

Her physical therapist had said it would take hard work—lots of it—to regain her strength and rebuild her muscles, and she hadn't been kidding, either.

A few times, the agony had been intense enough that Brooke had considered quitting. Weeks of stretching, lifting weights—more reps and heavier dumbbells every day—walking miles and *miles* on the treadmill....

Brooke understood the point of it all, but hauling the heavy cast around was exhausting, character-testing work that left her feeling frail, fragile and whiny.

About halfway through her program, Hunter took it upon himself to ignore her requests to keep Connor away from the rehab center. "It'll be too scary for him," she'd insisted. As it turned out, hearing Connor's "happy to see you" squeals had been just the medicine she'd needed. And having to say goodbye provided all the incentive she needed to push through the pain so that she could go home and be with him all day every day instead of an hour here, an hour there.

She'd just finished a particularly grueling session when Deidre walked into the room waving a Hershey's bar in the air. "Thanks, Gram," she said, "but you shouldn't have. Can't eat chocolate yet, with these wires holding my jaw together."

"Don't be silly. The candy is mine, sweet cheeks," her grandmother said. And producing a strawberry shake from her cavernous purse, she added, "*This* is for you."

Brooke held one hand to her ribs, the other to her jaw and said, "Please, don't make me laugh."

"So is it true? You're getting out of this place?"

"Day after tomorrow...if all my test results are, to quote Dr. Norris, 'satisfactory.'"

"But that's good news. Why so glum?"

"Not glum. Terrified. How will I ever maneuver stairs in this thing?" She knocked on her cast. "My luck, I'll take a fall and end up right back in here."

"Don't worry—Hunter to the rescue."

"What did he do, build ramps everywhere? Install an elevator in Beth's house?"

Deidre slapped both palms to her thighs. "Well, I like *that*. I finally keep something to myself, and *he* spills the beans."

"What beans? Wait...are you saying... Do you

mean he actually built ramps and installed an elevator?"

"No elevator, but he built a ramp at Beth's house, so you won't have any trouble getting into and out of the front door." She nodded toward the big cast. "And the ramp is removable, so when your leg heals, he can haul it away."

"The house is finished?"

"Oh, dear. He's going to be upset with me," she muttered. "That was supposed to be a surprise, too. It looks like something out of a decorating magazine. You're going to love it. But you have to act surprised. He had his crew over there working double shifts so it could be ready by the time you get out of here."

"I *am* surprised." She frowned, partly because talking made her still-healing jaw ache, partly because she wondered what hues a guy whose kitchen was bright yellow had chosen. But being cooped up in this tiny room, aching from head to toe, worrying that she might limp for the rest of her life, was no excuse to behave like a spoiled brat.

"Don't worry, " she said. "I'll give myself a serious attitude adjustment before he gets here."

"Attitude adjustment?" An enormous vase of flowers and five Mylar balloons floated into the room. Hunter peeked around them and said, "Bad day in physical therapy, huh?"

"I warned her that cramming two days' worth of work into every session could do more harm than good," Deidre said. "But did she listen? No."

He put the flowers on Brooke's bedside table and tied the balloons to the foot of her bed. "She's anxious to get out of this place," he told Deidre. "Four weeks is a long time to be cooped up in a hospital room. And she just finished her second week in rehab."

Hunter met her eyes. "The nurse gave me the good news just now. Bet you can't wait to get home tomorrow."

Out of the corner of her eye, she saw Deidre cringe.

"The flowers are gorgeous," she said, smiling up at him. "And so are the balloons. Thanks."

"I'm just glad that in here you can decorate a little. That room in the ICU was like a..."

"Morgue?" she finished for him.

Hunter winced. "I don't know if I'd go that far, but it was pretty stark."

"Well," Deidre inserted, "you know what they say...."

"No, but I'm sure you'll tell us," Brooke and Hunter said, together.

Deidre faked hurt feelings and indignance. "Just for that, my lips are zipped."

"That'll be the day," Felix said, striding into the

room. "Looking good, Brooke," he said, putting a tiny African violet beside Hunter's flowers.

Deidre took one look at him and shot to her feet. "This room is stifling." She grabbed her purse and kissed Brooke's cheek. "See you tomorrow, honey." And with that, she was gone.

For a moment, all three stared into the hall. When Deidre didn't return, Hunter looked at Felix. "What was that all about?"

Felix snorted. "Oh, don't mind her. She's been like that ever since I popped the question."

Hunter and Brooke exchanged a puzzled glance.

"She's got this crazy notion that three's the charm. Said in so many words that because husbands one and three are pushing up daisies—and for all she knows, so's number two—she'll be the end of me, too." He waved the notion away. "Told her I didn't go in for all that superstitious hogwash, but you know Deidre. She won't hang it up. So I told her she was off her nut." He snickered. "That she ain't no spring chicken, and if she doesn't want to sit all alone in those rockers on her porch, she'd better reconsider."

"Wow," Brooke said, wondering how could she have missed a growing romance between Deidre and Felix.

And Hunter said, "Sorry, pal."

"Don't be sorry," Felix said. "She'll come around." He raised both hands in a gesture of helplessness. "But enough about me." He smiled at Brooke. "How are you doing?"

"Better, especially now that I have all these pretty flowers to keep me company tonight. Thanks, Felix—that was really sweet of you."

"Glad you like 'em. But I'd better go after her. In that kind of mood, there's no telling which ditch she'll drive into on the way home."

Chuckling, the men walked into the hall, speaking in low tones and casting an occasional furtive glance in Brooke's direction. They both had their backs to her when she rolled the wheelchair closer to the wall, mere inches from the door… and out of sight.

"Well," Felix said, "things like that take time."

What things? Her recovery? Or maybe Hunter hadn't completed the ramp after all.

"Yeah," Hunter agreed. "It'll be worth all the aggravation and expense once things are legal."

Legal?

She didn't have to wonder about it for long.

"Will you change Connor's last name to Stone? After the hearing, I mean?"

The men continued talking, but Brooke barely heard them. Her head throbbed and so did her leg, but not nearly as much as the ache in her heart. Because it seemed Hunter had started the adoption process while she'd been completely defenseless? Is that why he'd been so sweet, so accommodating?

"Chin up, pal," he said to Felix. "Deidre's all bark and no bite."

Hunter was grinning when he came back into the room. "A marriage proposal. I didn't see that coming, did you?"

Brooke couldn't bear to look at him. Not yet. She needed time to sort things out. Hopefully, being physically and mentally exhausted, she'd misunderstood the conversation. Deidre's eavesdropping had started Brooke on her race to beat Hunter to the adoption punch, which led to the accident that rendered her helpless...and incapable of taking care of Connor at all.

Irony, Brooke thought as a wave of dizziness overtook her. You've gotta love it.

"Hey, you okay?" Hunter knelt in front of her wheelchair and lifted her chin with the tip of his forefinger. "You look a little green around the gills. I'm calling a nurse."

As he started to get up, she said, "Is there...is there anything you want to tell me, Hunter?"

Guilt colored his cheeks and shame glittered in his eyes. At least, that was the way it looked during the brief moment of eye contact.

"As a matter of fact," he said, tucking a curl behind her ear, "there is something I've been meaning to tell you."

She was tempted to stop him, because she wasn't sure she could handle hearing him admit straight out that hours of reading, chatting, straightening her pillow, making sure her toes weren't constricted by too-tight bedsheets had been part of some grand scheme to take Connor away from her.

"Connor has been asking for you. I thought maybe after supper tonight, I'd bring him by again. Just for a couple of minutes."

Why? So he can say goodbye?

Two faint worry lines formed between his eyebrows as he shook his head. "On second thought, I think Deidre was right. You pushed yourself too hard today."

She had to get her strength back, get back to normal, as soon as possible so that she could fight for Connor.

Hunter walked over to her bed and turned back the covers and, after rolling her closer, gently lifted her from the wheelchair. "Get some rest," he said, easing her onto the mattress.

Brooke settled back onto the pillow as Hunter leaned in close. "I'll see you first thing in the morning," he said, pressing a soft kiss to her forehead.

Nodding, she closed her eyes, felt him pull the sheets up and tidy them under her chin.

"Sweet dreams, little ballerina," he said softly.

Little ballerina. Tomorrow, she'd ask why he kept calling her that.

And maybe you'll wake up and realize this was nothing but a bad, bad dream.

CHAPTER TWENTY-NINE

Now that the big clunky cast had come off, Brooke didn't understand the need for Maureen, the nurse who stopped by once a day to help her shower and dress.

"I'm tired of being waited on hand and foot," Brooke said. "I'll have to do things for myself eventually. Why not start now?"

Maureen cocked an eyebrow and gave her a quick once-over. "Maybe..."

The nurse was tall and blonde, and might have been intimidating...if not for her gentle voice.

Brooke smiled, and because her jaw didn't hurt the way it had when it was wired shut, she smiled wider. The accident had taught her many things about herself, among them, the necessity of being grateful for the little joys in life. "So, I can try?"

"Oh, you're just like my daughter, aren't you? Give her an inch, she takes a football field. I haven't said yes yet, remember."

"I'm a nurse, too, so I know how lucky I am to be home. I'll be careful. You have my word on it."

"It wasn't luck that got you here. It was hard

work." Maureen sighed. "Well, all right, then. Since you've already showered, I guess it won't hurt you to try getting dressed by yourself. But take your time. And don't be afraid to ask for help. I'll be right outside this door."

"You're a bighearted, understanding woman, Maureen Carter."

She chuckled as Brooke closed the door. When she was finished in here, she'd see how the nurse felt about letting her try the stairs next. And if that didn't kill her, maybe she could make the trip every night. If she succeeded, Connor would miss the hospital bed, because he loved having an indoor trampoline.

The bed had certainly served its purpose during her first weeks home from the hospital, allowing her to be near Connor and saving Hunter from carrying her upstairs. But she was anxious to get everything back to normal, and that meant putting the furniture back where it belonged, too.

Brooke sat on the bench beside the tub to pull on her white pants. It hadn't been in the bathroom before the accident, and she knew Hunter must have added it, along with the recliner in the living room and the padded stool beside the kitchen sink, to give her places to stop and rest when she was up and about. Where he'd found the time to think up all these little niceties—let alone put them into place—she didn't know. But Brooke thought she knew *why:* guilt.

Wincing, she stood and tightened the drawstring on her pants. "How can anything so routine be such a struggle!" Before the accident, Brooke hadn't fully appreciated the day-to-day things she accomplished without so much as a second thought, like brushing her teeth or putting on makeup.

"Look on the bright side," she said, easing her arms into a matching white T-shirt. "It's easier today than it was yesterday."

Maureen rapped on the door. "You okay in there?"

"Sure am."

"Okay…just checking."

But Maureen sounded suspicious.

That's what you get for talking to yourself.

When Brooke leaned against the vanity to catch her breath, she caught sight of herself in the mirror. The chin-length bob would take some getting used to, but Deidre's hairdresser had been right. "The hair they shaved will never catch up with the rest of it," he'd said. "Besides, think how much easier this will be to take care of while you're recovering!"

Right now anything that made life easier seemed like a blessing. She opened the medicine cabinet and withdrew her toothbrush. How odd, she thought, looking around the room, that Hunter had chosen the same shade of green that she'd painted her powder room in Richmond. He'd given every room a fresh new coat of paint, and Brooke thought it was downright uncanny that he'd selected all of her favorite colors. But as her grandfather used to say, a man can't pull the wool over your eyes without first gaining your trust. And Hunter had done exactly that, by being her sidekick from the morning she had learned of Beth's death. Now, he'd taken responsibility for cooking, cleaning, doing laundry. Made appointments with the rehab facility, drove her to physical therapy sessions twice a week, helped her get through the grueling at-home exercises. He'd become so good at anticipating Connor's needs the boy rarely had a chance, let alone a reason, to fuss or cry. She heard voices and stopped brushing. The television? Brooke didn't think so. Maureen wasn't big on daytime TV. Inching closer to the door, she strained her ears.

"She's like a different person," Hunter was saying, "moody and grouchy all the time. The only one who can coax a smile out of her these days is Connor."

"That happens sometimes after a serious brain injury," Maureen explained. "Just keep doing what you're doing. Things should get back to normal soon."

"And if they don't?"

"Then we tell Dr. Norris."

Dr. Norris…who would order a flood of misery-inducing tests and procedures. The thought made her shiver. If behaving as though she liked having him hover like a Jedi warrior would keep her out of the claustrophobic MRI machine, she'd imitate the Cheshire cat from dawn till dusk.

Brooke hobbled out of the bathroom, eased into the recliner and exhaled a satisfied sigh. "Nothing like a little mascara to make a girl feel all shiny and new."

Hunter and Maureen traded confused looks.

"Hungry?" he asked.

"I'm still full from that big country breakfast Maureen made."

The nurse tapped something into her laptop, shut its lid and gathered her things. "Well, time for me to go," she said. "Heads up—I could be a little late tomorrow. We're short-staffed thanks to summer vacations, so I have to start my rounds in northern Baltimore County tomorrow."

Hunter walked her to the door. "How many patients are you seeing now?"

"Twenty-two, six more than usual." She aimed a finger at Brooke. "You're done for the day, missy. No more exercise."

"Don't worry," Brooke said, working the kinks out of her neck.

Now the finger pointed in Hunter's direction. "And you…remember what we talked about."

"I'll try."

"Do or do not," she said on her way out the door. "There *is* no try."

"What was that all about?" Brooke asked once she was gone.

"Oh, just routine 'how to care for Brooke' stuff, is all."

Yeah, right. And my real name is Brooke Shields. She grabbed the remote and turned on the TV. "In between Deidre's soap operas," she told him, "I saw a commercial for the Dr. Phil show. It's about liars today."

But Hunter was in the kitchen, emptying the dishwasher, and couldn't possibly have heard her over all the racket. "Just as well," she whispered around a yawn. She had no proof that he was working toward taking Connor, and felt like a first-class ingrate talking to him that way after all he'd done—and was still doing—for her.

She was dreaming about work when the doorbell woke her three hours later.

"That'll be the family," he said on his way to the foyer.

"Good thing I put mascara on this morning, then."

He grinned. "You're just as beautiful without it."

"Hunter, before you let them in…"

One hand on the doorknob, he looked at her.

"Later, tomorrow morning, maybe, will you do me a favor?"

"Anything."

If she hadn't overheard part of his conversation with Felix, Brooke would have bet the farm that he meant it. *Get a grip, girl. Remember...he's the wolf, and you're wearing white.*

"Remind me to call my boss? I want to make sure I'll still have a job when Norris finally gives me the go-ahead to get off my lazy behind."

In place of a response, Hunter opened the door. Within minutes the living room was full of Stone men, women and children. How they'd managed to arrive at the same time boggled her mind.

"Happy Fourth of July," Gabe said, bending to kiss Brooke's cheek.

Laughing, she looked over his shoulder at his wife. "Fourth of July? Has he been working the graveyard shift so long that he doesn't know what month it is?"

Now Jesse stepped up to greet her. "He's crazy, but not that crazy. Deidre told us she was planning a big July Fourth shindig and that you were really looking forward to it...before the house fell on you."

"And our baby brother here," Rafe put in, looking at Hunter, "thought better late than never."

As they helped her outside, Brooke wondered

why Deidre had said such a thing, when her lack of enthusiasm about the party had annoyed her grandmother.

The matter was quickly forgotten as she settled into a webbed lounge chair and had a look around. It must have taken Hunter hours to turn the yard into a red, white and blue extravaganza. No wonder he'd been adamant about keeping her in the front half of the house these past few days.

As the brothers fired up the grill, their wives disappeared into the kitchen. "I feel like a sloth," Brooke told Deidre, "sitting here doing nothing while everyone else has a job to do."

"Your job is to get better," Constance said through the open kitchen window.

Half a dozen voices called, "That's right!"

Deidre snickered. "You might as well go with the flow and enjoy your life of leisure while it lasts...you helpless cripple."

"Good thing these guys aren't politically correct cops," she said, laughing.

The kids captured Brooke's attention. Half of them were playing T-ball and badminton, while the other half chased a giggling Connor, who'd gathered up birdies and Wiffle balls. Beth, the O'Toole family's party girl, would have loved this. Maybe Brooke would continue the tradition her sister had started and fill in the rest of the journal with the description of this day.

After a hearty meal of burgers and dogs, potato salad and coleslaw, Hunter rounded up his nieces and nephews and led them to the side yard.

"There's an awful lot of whispering and giggling going on over there," she called to them.

When they reappeared the kids were single file, wearing colorful hats and carrying toy instruments. Jesse put marching music on the stereo—the kids' cue to parade around the yard tooting plastic horns and clanging tiny cymbals as Connor, the grand marshal, pounded a red drum.

When dusk cloaked the little yard, Gabe brought out sparklers that glowed golden on every youthful face. The kids squealed happily, drawing circles and curlicues into the darkening sky as Brooke leaned closer to her grandmother. "This day has been perfect. One of the best in my memory," she admitted. "How did you keep it a secret?"

"Don't look at me," Deidre said as Hunter approached. "I only found out last night, when Hunter called to tell me what time to be here!"

Brooke looked up into his face. "You did all this? For me?"

"Guilty as charged."

Strange choice of words. But she shrugged off the suspicious thought.

Constance joined them on the porch and linked arms with Hunter. "So tell me, when are you leaving on vacation? Ocean City will be beautiful this time of year."

He quirked a brow and stared at his feet. "Bright and early tomorrow," he said, impatience lacing his voice.

A dizzying array of emotions tumbled in Brooke's head. If anyone deserved a break, it was Hunter. She'd miss her shadow, who'd anticipated and filled her every need. And it would break her heart if she learned that the phone call Deidre overheard and what she'd gleaned from his whispered conversation with Felix held even a glimmer of truth.

But knowing that he was leaving frightened her. She'd come to rely on him, and felt like a hypocrite for taking all that he had to give without offering the one thing he wanted: forgiveness.

"Well, Brooke," Jill said, breaking into her thoughts, "are you all packed and ready to go?"

Packed? Brooke sighed. She should have known he'd find a way to include her in the trip.

"No," she said, feeling more ungrateful than ever. "Not yet."

One hand on her hip, Constance faced Hunter. "Oh, dear. We've let the cat out of the bag, haven't we?"

He looked sheepish and annoyed and flustered, all at the same time. "The plan was, break the good news right after you guys cleared out."

Jill gave his biceps a playful slap. "Are you out of your mind? A girl needs more than a few hours to plan her vacation wardrobe." Facing Brooke, she added, "Fortunately, you'll only need light-weight, summery stuff for your fun-filled week at our bayside condo."

"You sound like a real-estate commercial," Gabe said. Chuckling, he hugged her. "Way to sell it, hon!"

Brooke smiled, but it wasn't easy. What if Hunter was planning to spring the adoption news on her at the beach?

One by one, his brothers and their wives joined those already on the deck as Hunter explained, "Don't worry, I've cleared it with Dr. Norris."

Brooke looked at Jill. At Constance and Deidre. At everyone but Hunter. If he'd done this to impress his family, he had succeeded, and the proof was written all over their admiring faces. She considered saying she wasn't ready for a four-hour drive, for two weeks at the beach. But why spoil everyone's enjoyment when they'd gone to such trouble to give her a proper July Fourth celebration?

"How large is your condo?" she asked Jill.

"It sleeps four comfortably. Why?"

Brooke did a quick scan of the Stone family. "Will we all fit?"

A moment of silence before the tinyback yard erupted with laughter.

"We aren't going," Jill said.

Jesse elbowed Hunter. "Because *we* weren't invited."

Hunter sat in the chair beside hers. "It's just you and me, pretty ballerina" he said, pulling Connor into his lap, "and baby makes three."

CHAPTER THIRTY

WHEN THE SPARKLER boxes were empty, Hunter's family cleaned up the yard and kitchen. By nine o'clock the Stones were gone, leaving no evidence that twenty-plus people had frolicked in the yard. How peculiar it seemed that Hunter's family had so eagerly pitched in to help him give her back the holiday she'd missed.

With Connor asleep upstairs and Hunter driving Deidre and Felix home, the house was eerily quiet. Her grandmother had worked up a good head of steam when the motor of her ancient sedan failed to turn over. Something told Brooke that the interior of his pickup was anything *but* quiet.

The thought prompted a slight grin, which was quickly supplanted by the angst roused by the going-to-Ocean-City dialogue. "If you know what's good for you," she mumbled, gathering her pajamas and robe, "you'll follow doctor's orders to the letter." Because until she could stand on her own again—literally and figuratively—Hunter would feel duty-bound to take care of her.

Not long ago she'd bristled when other men tried

to protect or make decisions for her. So why had she allowed Hunter—the guy who'd been the target of her ire for years—to coddle her?

If only the social worker, Charlotte Matthews, hadn't been transferred. Dealing with Mrs. Damian had made Brooke feel a little like a lion tamer. Compliments, cooperation, cajoling—nothing bridged the communication gap between her and the always-angry woman who, in her opinion, was the reason she hadn't received notice of the guardianship hearing before now. And with her only ally in the court system out of reach...

Those weepy, whiny women she'd looked down on before the plane crash, before her accident, didn't seem quite so mawkish as she struggled to slip out of her T-shirt and slacks and into pj's and a robe. *Stop thinking about how much you hurt and how tired you are,* she thought, *and be thankful that you survived.*

Brooke looked into the mirror above the vanity. "Barely."

She heard the front door open and close.

Hunter was back.

Faced with carrying out her half-baked decision to get the beach house nonsense out of the way and find out what he knew about her missing paperwork, her resolve fizzled with the last of her energy.

Brooke hobbled into the living room and found

Hunter stretched out on the sofa. Beside him on the end table, two big slabs of cheesecake.

"I didn't think there was any left," she said, helping herself to a slice.

He sat up and took the other one. "I squirreled this away even before the kids' parade ended. Hid it behind a package of liverwurst." Wincing, he said, "I can't believe you eat that stuff."

"Ever tried it?" she asked around a bite of cheesecake.

"No."

"Then how do you know you don't like it?"

He shrugged. "I've read the ingredients."

"My dad was a huge Dale Carnegie fan," she began, "and one of his favorite quotes was 'The person who goes farthest is generally the one who is willing to do and dare.'"

"Which goes hand in hand with 'The sure boat never gets far from shore.'"

It didn't surprise her that Hunter was well-read, but that he knew Carnegie surprised her. And wasn't it odd that this shift in the conversation had relaxed her? Or maybe it's the cheesecake, she thought, grinning.

"What's so funny?"

Brooke waved the question away. "So this Ocean City trip... When did you get that bright idea?"

"Yesterday." He shrugged. "Gabe and I were

talking, and he suggested the beach, I called Dr. Norris to make sure it was okay." He took another bite of cake. "How long since you've been there?"

"I've never been there."

He sat up straighter. "What? A Maryland native who's never been to the OC? I don't believe it."

"Mom and Dad said they didn't believe in beach vacations…a nice way of saying they couldn't afford it."

"I don't think Beth ever mentioned what they did for a living."

"Mom stayed home. Dad was in construction."

He stopped chewing. "You're kidding."

"Commercial construction. A senior project manager for high-rise buildings all over the country."

He nodded. "I spent a summer between my junior and senior high school years working for Harbor Construction. I'm embarrassed to say I couldn't handle the heights."

"But you're on ladders every day!"

"Two, three stories up, at most. Those buildings were hundreds of feet tall. And when I was involved, they were just skeletons. I-beams that felt like they were just floating up there in the sky." He shuddered. "I prefer to keep my feet on the ground."

"Funny. But I've always seen you as fearless."

"Why?"

Because as a younger man, he'd wanted to be a cop, knowing full well that every time he put on his uniform might be his last. That took courage. But she couldn't admit it without opening old wounds.

Surprise number three: it never occurred to her that the day would come when she felt protective of *him*.

"I have no idea where my luggage is," she said. "Do you have a duffel bag or backpack I can borrow?"

Brooke had heard it said that people could smile with their whole bodies, but until this minute, she'd never witnessed it herself.

Brooke smiled back. "Go home, Hunter."

His smile dimmed, and so did the happy light in his eyes.

"You said you wanted to get an early start." She pointed at the clock. "It's nearly midnight, and I hear it's a four-hour drive to the ocean."

One side of his mouth lifted in a grin. "Three and a half, if traffic isn't too nuts."

"I'll get my things together. Connor's, too. So that when you get here in the morning with the bag, all we'll need to do is—"

"Stuff it," he said with her.

He added their plates and forks to the dishwasher and filled it with soap. "Will this keep you awake?" he asked, closing the door.

"I'll be fine. What time will you be here?"

Hunter glanced at the clock. "Is six too early? I'll grab some breakfast, and we can eat on the road."

"I'll be ready," she said as he stepped onto the porch.

She heard his key in the lock, the jiggle of the knob as he made sure the bolt was set, heard his merry whistle growing fainter as he walked toward his house. Heard her heart beating double time and hoped she wasn't making the biggest mistake of her life by trusting him with her life... and Connor's.

CHAPTER THIRTY-ONE

HE PARKED A sleek red convertible in the driveway, exactly like the one she'd told him about months ago. Brooke didn't know which touched her more—that he'd remembered, or that he'd rented it because the truck's shocks might jostle her still-healing body.

As they crossed the Chesapeake Bay Bridge, it began to rain. "Good thing I didn't let you talk me into putting the top down," he said, turning on the windshield wipers.

Brooke grinned. "Nobody can be wrong *all* the time."

They shared a moment of companionable laughter as Connor squealed at the sight of every sailboat that skimmed the water's surface.

"I brought some basic groceries," he said as they left the bridge behind them. "Once we're settled, you can make me a list and I'll get the rest."

"I can help."

He shot a warning glance in her direction, which softened when she added, "I won't have a very good time if you do everything for me."

"Brooke, one of the main reasons for this trip is to give you a chance to rest and relax."

"You'll have your hands full with Connor, chasing him up and down the beach. If you don't let me help, *you* won't get any rest. Then I'll feel guilty. And get grumpy."

He chuckled. "Let's play it by ear, okay?"

They continued chatting like old friends as the rain pecked the rag roof. As Assawoman Bay came into view alongside Coastal Highway, the skies cleared and the sun came out of hiding.

"Connor, look," she said, pointing, "a rainbow!"

But the baby slept on, and she exhaled a sigh of disappointment.

Hunter reached across the console and took her hand. "He's not even two yet," he said, giving it a gentle squeeze. "He'll have lots of chances to see another one."

She knew he was right. And yet…how lovely would it have been if the baby had seen his first rainbow during this trip?

Within minutes, he was steering onto Captains Quarters Road.

"Well," he said, parking in the open garage beneath the condo, "here we are."

She stifled a groan as he helped her from the car.

"I feel about a hundred years old after sitting that long."

"Your body has been through a lot, so that's to be expected."

Brooke watched as Connor kicked at the wet sand, then sat down and grabbed handfuls of it, giggling as it clumped and stuck to his fingers.

"I'd love to drive that car," she admitted.

"Sorry. It's a stick shift, and your leg hasn't healed well enough to hold down the clutch."

She sighed. "I know, but a girl can dream."

"If you don't overdo it, you might be able to take it for a short spin before we leave."

Brooke didn't know what to make of the look on his face—something akin to fondness—and the affectionate tone of his voice. There were still too many questions unanswered, too many problems unsolved to put all of her faith in this man. Hunter he hoisted the baby's backpack, then picked Connor up, and after unlocking the door he helped Brooke inside.

"I'll put Connor's porta-crib in my room—first door on the right there—and you can have the master. You'll rest better that way, and so will I."

Brooke thought of Sun Tzu's famous quote, "Choose your battles wisely, and do not fight battles you cannot win."

He dumped the contents of the backpack on the living room floor. "He'll be okay while I bring in the crib."

She nodded.

"I'll get him set up first thing, and once he's down for the count, you can do the same. Deal?"

The drive must have tired her out more than she'd realized, because a nap sounded wonderful.

"Okay, but only if you'll promise to let me help with supper."

"We'll see," he said.

Four hours later she walked into the kitchen feeling almost normal. Hunter was chopping vegetables at the bar counter.

"How can I help?"

"Everything's done," he said, using his salad knife as a pointer. "I figured we could eat on the deck."

A light breeze fluttered the canvas awning, startling a gull that had perched on the railing. The sky glowed like a canvas of Texas bluebonnets, and the sun hung low in the sky. Soon it would slip behind the horizon like a big gold coin dropping into a slot. Bay water slapped gently against the boat dock mere feet from the deck, and in the distance, sailboats and pontoons crisscrossed the gray-blue surface of the water.

"Since you're cooking everything, I'll set the table."

Hunter gave it a moment's thought. "Okay, I'll carry the stuff out there after I fire up the grill." He used the tip of his knife to poke the marinating steaks. "Oh, yeah. They're ready." He slid open the door, then locked the gate at the top of the stairs. "C'mon, buddy," he said, gathering Connor in his arms. "Get ready for the biggest playpen you've ever seen!"

Brooke followed and leaned against the railing, drinking in the view. "Beautiful," she whispered. "Like a postcard."

An hour later, the threesome sat around the bistro table in the corner of the deck. Since the condo didn't come with a high chair, Hunter held Connor on one knee. It amazed her that he managed to eat while feeding the baby and prying flatware, salt and pepper shakers, and napkins from quick little hands. Watching the two of them was like sitting front-row center as a comedy team performed slapstick.

After the meal, Hunter spread a quilt on the deck and covered it with Connor's toys. Brooke began stacking plates.

"That can wait until we get Short Stuff over there to bed," Hunter said. "Besides, we haven't had dessert yet, and there's no point cleaning up twice."

"Cake?" Connor said, toddling over to Hunter.

"Aw, why not," he said, carrying the baby inside.

When they returned, Connor led the way, smiling proudly as he carried a fat white envelope that said Brooke. Behind him, Hunter wore a lop-sided grin.

"Sorry," he said, leaning left as he put the cake in front of her. "It's kinda…tilted."

"Sorry," Connor echoed, slapping the card down beside it.

Hunter picked him up, and Brooke said, "It looks delicious." And to prove it, she swiped a fingerful of frosting from the tall side.

He put a dozen or so toothpicks on the table and proceeded to poke them into the cake one by one. "Forgot to buy candles," he explained. "Sorry."

"Hoppy birthday!" Connor hollered. "Hoppy *birthday!*"

"You guys are just as silly as silly can be," she said, grinning. "My birthday isn't until—"

"Don't be a party pooper," Hunter whispered. "Can't you see the kid's really into this?" He deposited Connor on the nearest chair. "I hope this isn't a sign that he's gonna be one of those kids who'll worry us to death, partying his way through high school and college."

Brooke's heart beat harder at the mention of *us*. It made no sense to feel this way, because they'd spent half a lifetime trying to avoid one another.

He fished a book of matches from his shirt pocket. "Now, let's not drag out the birthday song," he said to Connor, "because I have no idea how fast toothpicks burn."

As they sang, loud and off-key, Brooke laughed and cried at the same time. She'd never been happier...or more afraid. Her life seemed even more lopsided than the cake.

"You guys are great," she said, accepting their hugs and kisses as Barry White crooned "You're the First, the Last, My Everything" from the radio Hunter had leaned on the kitchen sill. Quirky fate? Brooke didn't think so. If this rough, tough cake-baking carpenter didn't have feelings for her, he sure had a funny way of showing it.

Everything he'd said and done, from that morning on Beth's porch to this amazing, heart-stopping moment, was proof that he cared about her. Who said love had to be hearts and flowers, bells and whistles? Couldn't it be sticky chocolate frosting topped with charred toothpicks, instead?

Brooke realized in that moment that she'd just admitted she loved him. It made no sense. But who said love had to make sense?

HUNTER HELD UP the baby monitor's receiver and held out one hand. "Are you up for a short walk?"

Brooke joined him on the deck and put her hand in his. What better time to ask him about the adoption than under the round, glowing moon?

They'd only gone a few steps when he said, "I have a confession to make."

Maybe she wouldn't have to pull the adoption information out of him after all.

"Remember when we were moving you into Deidre's apartment, and that big ugly spider blocked the door?"

"I still cringe every time I think about spider goo covering the entire palm of my hand." If he needed to lead into the confession in dribs and drabs, it was okay with her.

"You saved me that day."

She laughed. "Yeah. I guess I kinda did, didn't I?"

"But before you mashed that monster—" he lifted her hand and pressed a kiss to her palm "—I was in the back of the truck looking for something to whack it with. And I remember looking at you cowering up there on the landing and thinking, 'I've never seen a more beautiful sight.'"

He stopped walking and stood in front of her, put both hands on her shoulders. "I was wrong," he said, sounding a little frightened, a little shy. "You knocked that vision out of the ballpark looking the way you do tonight."

This was what he wanted to confess?

"I wanted to bring you out here earlier," he continued. "Thought maybe I could show you the green flash at sunset. But Connor got hungry and, well, you were there, so you know how that went."

"He won't be as tired tomorrow after supper. Maybe we'll catch it then."

A crafty gleam twinkled in his eyes. "Yeah, maybe." He took her hand again. "Let's get back to the condo so you can open your birthday card from *me*."

"But you signed the one Connor made."

"Only because he forced me to." Hunter chuckled. "That's some kid we've got there."

First *us,* now *we*...

While he went inside to get the card, she used the matches that had lit her birthday toothpicks to fire up the tiki torches at each corner of the deck. There was a fat candle on the railing, and after putting in on the table between two lounge chairs, she lit that, too.

The window of his bedroom was open, and she could hear him, humming as he dug through his suitcase in search of her card. Brooke sat in one of the chairs as an old classic wafted from the stereo, "We've Only Just Begun."

Seconds later, he sat down beside her. "Here you go," he said, holding out a 6 x 9-inch manila envelope.

Too large to hold an ordinary birthday card. Would she find adoption papers inside?

She lifted the flap and found a smaller white envelope inside, as well as a packet of blue-sheathed papers. Tempting as it was to look at the papers first, Brooke read the message he'd written inside the card: "From the bottom of my heart, happy birthday." And it was signed "Love, Hunter."

She closed the card and traced the glittery pink ballerina decorating its front. "This seems as good a time as any," she said, "to ask what all the ballerina references are about."

He told her about his niece's figurine, how after reassembling it with construction adhesive, it was even stronger than before.

He reached across the table and, taking her hand, added, "You remind me of that ballerina. Delicate and beautiful, but sturdy. You're a fighter, too. I love that about you."

He cleared his throat, then traded the card for the document.

A tiny nervous giggle escaped her lips as she realized they weren't adoption papers after all. "Is this…" She pointed at the top page. "It's a deed?"

"I didn't know what else to get you."

"So you bought Beth and Kent's house."

Grinning, he said, "Well, technically, it was Connor's."

How had he arranged all this without her knowledge?

"I…I don't know what to say." He looked hurt by her reaction. Disappointed, too.

She'd held her tongue far too long. It was time to clear the air once and for all.

"I owe you an apology, for holding you solely accountable for what happened to my mom. I've never admitted this to anyone, but if I hadn't whimpered and whined when we ran out of ice cream that night, Mom wouldn't have been in the store when the gunman came in.

"I had a lot of time to think about it, lying there in the hospital. And I finally figured out that blaming you made it easier for me to cope with my part in her death.

"So you need to know, I'm sorry for the way I've treated you all these years. Sorry that I behaved like an ungrateful brat when you offered to help with Beth's house. And for thinking you were working behind my back, trying to take Connor from me.

"I'm sorry about all of it, Hunter. You deserved better then. You deserve better now. And I hope you'll forgive me."

To his credit, Hunter didn't interrupt, not even once, and when at last she finished, Brooke stuffed the papers back into the envelope. "Well?" she said, tossing it onto the table. "Did you buy the house for me?"

One side of his mouth lifted in a grin as he studied her face. How dare he sit there looking all handsome and innocent, making her want to be in his arms instead of in this stiff-backed chair, waiting for forgiveness.

"Please say something!"

He broke into a full-blown smile. "You're gorgeous when you're flustered and confused."

Flustered? *Confused?* She pointed at the envelope. "You bought my sister's house right out from under me. How am I supposed to feel?"

"Whoa. Wait. I didn't buy the house. It's a transfer of deed. Which you'd know if you had read the papers. And here's why…."

He explained that while she'd been unconscious and completely vulnerable, her boss had called and asked him to tell Brooke that she felt awful about having to replace her. And within days of that, Mrs. Damian had threatened to put Connor into foster care.

"She'd read about your accident in the newspaper. Somehow found out you'd lost your job, too, and felt she had no choice but to start hunting for a foster family.

"I couldn't let that happen, so I did what I had to do. To protect you. To protect him. I never intended to keep it a secret forever. Only until you were…better."

He drove a hand through his hair. "If that makes you mad, well, I'd rather live with that than stand by while that old bat stuck our boy in some foster home with strangers, and you had nowhere to live."

"I could have stayed Beth's."

"No, you couldn't. You had eight, maybe ten months' savings left. And don't look at me like that. Yes, I went through your stuff. Had to so I could keep the lights on and the water running and make sure that stuffed shirt at the bank didn't have any excuse to start foreclosure proceedings."

"So let me get this straight. You paid my bills while overseeing the renovations at Beth's house and making sure Connor was safe. Spent countless hours at my side in the hospital, and worked to open a school for troubled teens. And did it all without me knowing about it."

"Yeah. So? I didn't sneak around because I wanted to. You weren't healthy enough to deal with any of it. Dr. Norris spelled it out in plain English. Stress could have killed you. Literally."

He was on his feet now, one hand pressed to the back of his neck, the other waving in the air as he paced the length of the deck. "If you're gonna get your nose all outta joint over this…if you're willing to let it end us over it, well, maybe I misjudged you."

He stopped in front of her chair, gripped her biceps and brought her to her feet. "I know that head injury was serious, but for the love of Pete, surely you can figure out that I didn't have a choice."

She stared into his beautiful grief-stricken face and felt ashamed, from the soles of her feet to the itchy almost-bald spot on her head.

He gave her a little shake. "Don't you get it, Brooke?"

Where should she begin? By admitting that yes, she got it. With another apology for letting stubbornness and resentment blind her to everything good in him?

"I get it," she began. "I get that you figured out how I've always felt like a misfit, traipsing along one road, then another, never feeling that any place was home. I get that you took me off that lonely road, made me feel like finally, I belong. I get that you've provided me with a home that's made of far more than bricks and boards and mortar. I get that I don't deserve any of it after treating you like I have all these years…"

Brooke stood on tiptoe—not an easy feat in her condition—and kissed him long and hard. Then she stepped back just far enough to look into his eyes. "I'm sorry, Hunter."

"Sorry? For that?" He chuckled. "Don't be. I'm not. "

"No…I'm sorry for not telling you what I've

known in my heart all these years. *You* could have died that night, too."

Brooke looked up, straight into his eyes. "And where would that leave Connor?" She leaned her head on his shoulder. "Where would that leave *me?*"

She heard him sigh as his arms wrapped around her.

"Deidre told me what she overheard," Hunter said.

This habit he had of jumping from one subject to another was maddening.

He sat her down. Told her about the DVD, how he'd used it to gain temporary guardianship of Connor.

She felt like a fool for having doubted him. An idea sparked, and as it grew, Brooke smiled.

"Go ahead," she said. "Adopt Connor. I won't stop you—"

Her announcement stunned him, and he took a half step back.

"—if you marry me."

Hunter looked up into the inky, star-strewn sky. He didn't move. Didn't speak. And she was afraid maybe she'd just made the biggest mistake of her life.

He drew her close and kissed her. Then he smiled and said, "I thought you'd never ask."

* * * * *

REQUEST YOUR FREE BOOKS!
2 FREE WHOLESOME ROMANCE NOVELS IN LARGER PRINT
PLUS 2 FREE MYSTERY GIFTS

━━━━━━━━━━━━━━━━━━━━━━━━━━━━━

HEARTWARMING™

Wholesome, tender romances

YES! Please send me 2 FREE Harlequin® Heartwarming Larger-Print novels and my 2 FREE mystery gifts (gifts worth about $10). After receiving them, if I don't wish to receive any more books, I can return the shipping statement marked "cancel." If I don't cancel, I will receive 4 brand-new larger-print novels every month and be billed just $4.99 per book in the U.S. or $5.74 per book in Canada. That's a savings of at least 23% off the cover price. It's quite a bargain! Shipping and handling is just 50¢ per book in the U.S. and 75¢ per book in Canada.* I understand that accepting the 2 free books and gifts places me under no obligation to buy anything. I can always return a shipment and cancel at any time. Even if I never buy another book, the two free books and gifts are mine to keep forever.

161/361 IDN F47N

Name	(PLEASE PRINT)

Address		Apt. #

City	State/Prov.	Zip/Postal Code

Signature (if under 18, a parent or guardian must sign)

Mail to the **Harlequin® Reader Service:**
IN U.S.A.: P.O. Box 1867, Buffalo, NY 14240-1867
IN CANADA: P.O. Box 609, Fort Erie, Ontario L2A 5X3

* Terms and prices subject to change without notice. Prices do not include applicable taxes. Sales tax applicable in N.Y. Canadian residents will be charged applicable taxes. Offer not valid in Quebec. This offer is limited to one order per household. Not valid for current subscribers to Harlequin Heartwarming larger-print books. All orders subject to credit approval. Credit or debit balances in a customer's account(s) may be offset by any other outstanding balance owed by or to the customer. Please allow 4 to 6 weeks for delivery. Offer available while quantities last.

Your Privacy—The Harlequin® Reader Service is committed to protecting your privacy. Our Privacy Policy is available online at www.ReaderService.com or upon request from the Harlequin Reader Service.

We make a portion of our mailing list available to reputable third parties that offer products we believe may interest you. If you prefer that we not exchange your name with third parties, or if you wish to clarify or modify your communication preferences, please visit us at www.ReaderService.com/consumerschoice or write to us at Harlequin Reader Service Preference Service, P.O. Box 9062, Buffalo, NY 14269. Include your complete name and address.

Reader Service.com

Manage your account online!

- Review your order history
- Manage your payments
- Update your address

*We've designed
the Harlequin® Reader Service
website just for you.*

Enjoy all the features!

- Reader excerpts from any series
- Respond to mailings and special monthly offers
- Discover new series available to you
- Browse the Bonus Bucks catalog
- Share your feedback

Visit us at:
ReaderService.com